The Seal King Murders

An Inspector Faro Mystery

ALANNA KNIGHT

Allison & Busby Limited
13 Charlotte Mews
London W1T 4EJ
www.allisonandbusby.com

First published in Great Britain by Allison & Busby in 2011.
This paperback edition published by Allison & Busby in 2012.

A CIP catalogue record for this book is available from
the British Library.

10 9 8 7 6 5 4 3 2 1

ISBN 978-0-7490-4027-7

Typeset in 10.5/14.2 pt Sabon by
Allison & Busby Ltd.

Paper used in this publication is from sustainably managed sources.
All of the wood used is procured from legal sources and is fully traceable.
The producing mill uses schemes such as ISO 14001
to monitor environmental impact.

Printed and bound by
CPI Group (UK) Ltd, Croydon, CR0 4YY

To my granddaughters
Chloe and Julia Knight, with love

FOREWORD

There are fourteen published novels and casebooks covering the years 1872 to 1887 of Jeremy Faro's distinguished career as Chief Inspector in the Edinburgh City Police and personal detective to Her Majesty Queen Victoria at Balmoral.

At the request of his many readers worldwide, eager to know how his illustrious lifetime achievement began, this is the second casebook of Constable Faro, dated 1861. The first is *Murder in Paradise*.

CHAPTER ONE

Human-eyed, beseeching, curious.

The seals, staring at the ship as it approached the quayside, took newly appointed Detective Constable Jeremy Faro back, dissolving the mist of ten years when, as a boy of seventeen, he had left the island to join the Edinburgh City Police.

The seals' expressions resembled his mother's, pleading and reproachful when he had returned for brief visits, reminding him that he had deserted her for that city of sin and murder.

Yes, murder. Casting in his lot with the people who had murdered her beloved husband, Jeremy's father. A tragic fatal accident involving a runaway cab on the Mound was the verdict but Mary Faro was stubborn. She 'knew what she knew' and all the lack of evidence to the contrary in this world would never convince her. Someone – notably the Edinburgh City Police – had deliberately killed Constable Magnus Faro.

The ship moved slowly, carefully negotiating the harbour entrance where Stromness lay in wait. Smaller, less ancient than his native Kirkwall, with no magnificent cathedral or ruined Earl's Palace, a scatter of grey roofs and walls spilling down the slope of a granite hill where each house seemed to stand on the edge of the roof below, tight-packed with its neighbours and the houses terraced above. A scene eternally crowned by the swooping shapes of white wings and the shrill cries of seabirds.

Faro narrowed his eyes against the sun, searching the figures gathered on the quayside awaiting the ship's arrival for a familiar face among head-shawled women, and men heavily bearded beneath their bonnets. He touched his smooth chin; bare-faced it might make him stand out in a crowd, but this fashion for facial hair inspired by royalty had no appeal for him.

Was his mother there? He could almost hear her first words. How long was he staying this time? His reply, as always, received with a sigh of resignation, while he contemplated that a week of forced inactivity, a mite overlong for himself, was never long enough for her daily recapitulation of the finer details of his father's last hours and the sidelong glances that implied that their only son had signed up with the enemy instead of scratching a living from an unforgiving soil or sacrificing his short life dragging fish from a reluctant sea. Such was the traditional fisherman-crofter's existence since the Vikings beached their dragon-headed ships along the shore.

This time he must make up some convincing story as the real reason for his visit. The very hint of danger to her offspring would set his mother off on a tangent of recriminations.

This special mission had come from his old friend, Brandon Macfie, detective superintendent of Edinburgh City Police, retired. At their weekly supper in his house in Nicolson Square, he had leant over in a conspiratorial manner, 'I have a small assignment for you, lad. Dave Claydon, my late wife's cousin, was an excise officer in Orkney. A lot younger than Meg, they had naught in common; met him only once when he was taking part in a swimming competition here. Fine swimmer too – he won the cup. But he drowned up there boarding a ship for Edinburgh a couple of weeks ago.'

Pausing, he regarded Faro as if for comment. When Faro managed to look only mildly interested, Macfie sighed. 'Don't you see it, lad? Strange, isn't it, that a champion swimmer should drown?'

Faro shook his head. Macfie obviously knew nothing about the wild, fierce seas around Orkney that could seize quite large ships and break them up like matchsticks.

Macfie frowned. 'His body has never been recovered.'

'Frequently happens, sir. Those wild seas scatter bodies like spindrift. Often end up in far away Shetland.'

'That so?' Macfie's eyes widened, he looked amazed, obviously unconvinced, and stretching out his hand to the sideboard for the port decanter, he dragged over a file of papers which he pushed in Faro's direction.

'It's all there. Reports from the Orkney Constabulary and the newspaper. No, no, not now. Read them at your leisure.' Biting his lip, he went on, 'Somehow, I'm not satisfied with the results, always had an instinct for this sort of thing. You have it too, lad, and I'd like you to use your observation and deduction to see what you can find out for me. Look into it, discreetly and quite unofficially, of course. Don't want to upset our lads up there.'

But Faro knew from his experience that there never was a police investigation, nor ever would be, that did not upset a great many people, the innocent as well as the guilty.

Macfie was saying, 'They naturally accepted what seemed obvious to everyone – to everyone except me, that is. Family, you know. A week in Orkney should give you plenty of time to ferret things out that their constabulary might have missed.'

A fond hope indeed, thought Faro, but perhaps fortuitous, as his last brief communication from his mother was a postcard saying, 'I have taken a situation for the summer with a family here at Scarthbreck.'

Faro had smiled wryly. The little cottage in Kirkwall where he had grown up and into which she had moved as a bride seemed no longer adequate to contain the vibrant, active and restless spirit of Mary Faro.

'Capital, lad!' Macfie beamed at him. 'Your little holiday couldn't be better timed.'

Faro sighed. He was dreading this visit and he wondered why in God's name he had allowed Macfie to convince Chief Inspector Jackson to give him paid leave? True, it was all for his own good: Macfie was anxious for his protégé's further chances of promotion, especially as he wasn't doing too well recovering from his first case, a successful chase and final encounter with the arch-criminal who had plagued Scotland's police forces for years and had almost cost Constable Faro his life.

The bullet that had pierced his chest had weakened his lungs and a winter fever had resulted in pneumonia. Macfie watched over him anxious as a mother hen – even Mary Faro would have been impressed. He was all for summoning her from Orkney to nurse her lad, but Faro, even in his fraught condition, would have none of that.

Macfie, however, was determined; wily too. He had heard rumours aplenty of artefacts going missing from archaeological digs. It was claimed that priceless items of gold and jewels, a treasure trove en route for Edinburgh, had mysteriously vanished, lost when their carrier (none other than Macfie's cousin by marriage) had met with an accident and had, apparently, drowned.

The Orkney Constabulary remained silent on the nature of the artefacts, and vague regarding their proceedings for recovering the drowned man, and this failed to satisfy grieving relatives or the authorities in Edinburgh who, according to Macfie's theory, were not deeply concerned about the fate of the excise officer, suspecting that it was all part of a sinister plot to cheat the Treasury and retain the artefacts, which had never left Orkney.

'You're just the man to look into all this,

Faro,' said Macfie. 'You know your island and your islanders. Make a few enquiries just to set my mind at rest, lad, see your folks and add a decent holiday into the bargain. Do you a world of good – come back a new man,' he added with an encouraging smile.

And pointing again to the papers, 'Dave left a widow, you could start with her.' With a sorrowful shake of his head, he added mournfully that twenty years younger he would have rushed up to Orkney to investigate the case himself. But alas, years of hard living in the police force and a heavy addiction to rich food and wines had ruined his health. Too old now, he was also crippled with rheumatism.

Whatever bees Macfie had got in a well-worn bonnet, he appeared even in retirement to still possess a thumb that extended into the affairs of the Edinburgh City Police, and Faro suspected that Chief Inspector Jackson, a mild-mannered man quite unlike his predecessor, Detective Inspector Noble, was a little in awe of the ex-superintendent. And so Macfie continued behind the scenes to manipulate young Constable Faro, pressing the point of his excellent qualities, certain that he had promotion potential and would go far.

'If he doesn't get himself killed in his enthusiasm, that is,' was how Jackson put it to colleagues over a pint of ale in the local public house. The guffaws that followed said plainly that they thought this extremely likely. Mrs Jackson, however, was a Shetlander, and instead of rivalry between the islands had a fellow feeling for the constable who she decided must have Shetland blood, his appearance so uncannily akin to her romantic notion of what a handsome young Viking would have looked like.

As for Jackson, his mild-mannered exterior hid a shrewd mind and even a tendency, regrettable as it was, to see far-reaching suspicions in even the mildest of offences. This weakness had produced a splendid vision of Dave Claydon's death being more than an accident, perhaps involving drugs, smugglers and other double-dealings. Intrigued by the possibilities, and instead of sending Constable Faro, he fancied going himself, taking the missus and making it a bit of a holiday. There was just one drawback. He was a rotten sailor, sick as a dog even on the village pond to say nothing of a notoriously unpredictable sea crossing.

To Faro he grinned, repeating Macfie's words, 'You're just the man for the job.'

As for those missing artefacts, Claydon, a man of few words, had not left any enlightenment regarding their origins. Speculation remained of a treasure far too sophisticated for the Neolithic settlement discovered in 1850 and under recent excavation. Much more likely they were from the Spanish galleon, *El Rosario*, shipwrecked off the coast way back in 1588, though still the subject of many an islander's daydreams. Black-haired youths with white skins and fine dark eyes claimed that, if they were not descended from the Viking invaders, then their remote ancestor was some nobleman from that very vessel on the run from the defeat of the Spanish Armada.

None, however, wished to claim lowly descent from an ordinary, nondescript sailor, a foreign mercenary, or even a lowly galley slave, and as if to breathe a whisper of truth into the Armada legend and keep it alive, the occasional coin did still appear and encouraged experienced divers as well as local boys to try their luck, always in search of that pot of gold.

When this revived Armada gold fever occasionally erupted in his schooldays, Faro always shook his head. He had no desire to join the divers. An unfortunate episode when cut off by the rising tide – he almost drowned in the underground caves – had put an end to any dalliance with the eager swimmers. Besides which, he did not have a sailor's constitution.

'Couldn't swim – an island lad who can't swim!' It was ludicrous, a constant source of amusement among his fellow schoolmates. Only the fact that Faro was tall and strong and could use his fists to good effect kept the teasing from slipping into bullying.

This state of affairs also gave rise to more sinister hints to account for his fear of water. The rumour that his grandmother was or had been a selkie, a seal woman. He would have loved to meet her, disappointed that she had been dead for years, according to what little Faro could glean from his mother.

He soon learnt that she was not to be discussed. Selkie blood was the island equivalent of a black sheep in a respectable family and Mary Faro clammed up, her lips together in a tight line of disapproval whenever little Jeremy said, 'Tell me about Granny. Where is she? Is she in heaven?'

His childish curiosity had met with an angry response. 'That I doubt. I cannot believe that the Good Lord has taken her to himself.' And violently shaking off the thought, 'I don't know or wish to know anything more about her and even if I did, it would not be for your tender young ears. Decent God-fearing people the Scarths and Faros are – what would we be doing with creatures like that? Sitting down with selkies at our Sunday dinner – the idea of it! What would the neighbours think? We'd never lift our heads again.'

Curious still, as he grew older, Faro was sensible enough to turn his face away and not waste time on such legends. Like fairy stories, he didn't believe a word of them, all this nonsense about the seal king rising from the waves at Lammastide and carrying off a human girl to his kingdom beneath the waves, to be his bride for a year and a day before returning her to mortal life again. Such illogical nonsense.

He'd never heard the like of it, although, as his mother insisted, a decent young girl on the island would never walk on that beach at Lammastide. True, the seals were always busy, restless and barking like angry dogs – no doubt that was how the story had arisen. Their heads bobbing out of the water did have an oddly human appearance.

Oblivious to argument, stubbornly Faro shook his head. From an early age he had to find an answer to everything, stoutly insisting that every question was bound to have one somewhere. Observation and deduction were already his watchwords.

And that was what turned him into a detective in the making, according to Macfie. When the old man almost adopted him, Faro, for once wrongly, assumed it was on account of his potential. Instead, it was because Faro reminded the lonely old widower of his only son, who would have been a similar age to the young constable, had he not died tragically some years before.

Faro had his own theories about the seal king and that once-yearly abduction, and for his grandmother's legendary arrival on the island, a tiny girl caught in the fishing nets of his grandfather, Hakon Scarth. A likely tale just because it was Lammastide when the seals were particularly active – and noisy.

Most likely, putting an answer to everything, Faro believed she had been a survivor of the Norwegian ship that had sunk a mile out from the shore in a violent storm. There were only two other survivors, a couple of Norwegian sailors with little or no English, but enough furious head-shaking and protests to convince the authorities that they had never seen that little girl before. Unlucky they were, children on board a ship. And so it had proved.

Faro had decided, cynically no doubt, that they had their own reasons for denial, especially when considering the fact that the strictly illegal practice of smuggling their women aboard ships was ignored by the authorities. Men needed women for carnal reasons: to look after their bodily needs and to darn their socks on long sea voyages.

Still, he never ceased to regret not having

met his grandmother, selkie or no, a legend that his mother wasn't in the least proud to accept. A decent religious woman couldn't lay claim to such a heathen creature.

As he grew older, questions about his grandmother's whereabouts became more remote, and any hopeful reminders were fielded sharply aside by his sensible, less excitable father with the brief comment, 'Don't you be listening to such things, lad.' Magnus had a short list of answers: 'drowned while out fishing', 'died giving birth', 'ran away with a sailor', 'took consumption'.

All very glib and plausible, seeing as these were the most common causes of sudden death or disappearance from the island. Only the more reliable citizens achieved respectable immortality on the kirkyard's tombstones.

Returning to his bleak police lodging that evening, Faro had a quick scan of the reports. What was the Claydon man doing anyway, by getting a boatman to row him out to meet the Leith ship and being picked up beyond the bar?

The boatman who was interviewed gave vague answers, admitting that passengers and crew who missed ship did this quite frequently, and more often than not were seriously drunk and desperately hiring assistance in the form of a willing boatman for what was an illegal

21

procedure. The conclusion was that Claydon, jumping across, had missed his footing on the ship's ladder and, falling into rough sea, drowned.

It was a night of fog and mist, the boatman explained, but he had remained circling the area, shouting and calling, to no avail. Regardless, the ship headed out to sea, the captain firmly ignoring the incident which, had it been reported, might have cost him his command.

Now, as the ship's anchor attached the vessel firmly to the quay, its arrival heralded by the flashing wings and shrieking calls of seabirds, Faro set aside his list of questions and composed his expression to meet his mother who would have her apron strings ready starched. Bracing himself for a greeting, he had the words and the smile all ready.

'Just come to see you, Ma.'

CHAPTER TWO

As his foot touched dry land, Faro realised that the only other person he had the slightest wish to see again at that moment was Inga St Ola, his first love. During a night on the moonlit beach, she had given him his first initiation into the mysteries of the female body, always so well hidden underneath layers of clothes and consequently a never-waning magnet for boyish curiosity.

Searching the faces of those on shore, heads raised, eagerly awaiting passengers, of course Inga would not possibly be there. She had been absent, he knew not where (on another part of the island perhaps?) on his previous brief visits, so why expect her to appear now? She might be any one of the head-shawled women – would he even recognise her after ten years? She was older than himself, past thirty and no doubt much changed from the captivating girl he remembered. Married, her lovely face lined, her luxuriant tresses grey-threaded, all ruined by the harsh island life and years of childbearing.

He had seen it so often, the natural result of time's ruthless progress, and he could hardly bear to imagine Inga's transformation. And he had changed too. But a man of twenty-seven in Orkney terms was in his prime, and Edinburgh had had a hand in changing the tall, coltish boy into a tall, strong man. His thick, flaxen hair tamed, the cheekbones beneath the soft contours of his face hardened, his gentle expression matured into deep-set blue eyes, straight nose and wide, sensual mouth. Still the ultimate legendary Viking, enthusiastically acclaimed by artist acquaintances who had never met one.

A stir from the midst of the head-shawled women, but it was not Inga St Ola who ran towards him. The diminutive figure that pushed her way forward was attired in a neat grey cape and straw bonnet, the modest attire of an upper-class servant.

Laughing, his mother almost tearful, clasped him in her arms, kissed him, but could not resist saying, 'So you've come back home at last!'

This hint of reproach, all his sins of omission remembered. It wasn't his fault, either: he felt, often indignantly, that he was the one abandoned and not the other way round. Distraught by memories of the death of his policeman father in Edinburgh, she had returned to Orkney and left him alone and uncertain among strangers in desolate police lodgings, when he would have most welcomed her presence.

Feeling misunderstood, he groaned as she added, 'And what brings you here, lad, so unexpected? Not much warning to prepare for you. Here, let me take that,' she said stretching out a hand for his luggage as if he was a small boy again.

'No, Ma, please,' he said, snatching it from her, ashamed that she was making him look a fool, a great big man resisting this small determined woman. He looked around for where the carriages and carters waited to take passengers to their destinations.

She smiled. 'You won't need your legs to carry you all the way to Kirkwall this time. Andy the carter, over there, has things to deliver to the big house at Scarthbreck. He'll take us. Hold on while I check the goods.'

Faro found a seat alongside a mountain of packages, watching her tick items off a list.

As she joined him, he said, 'I'll need a place to stay.'

She laughed. 'A place to stay. And so you shall. That's all been taken care of. There's plenty of room in the servants' lodge. I'm housekeeper there, didn't I tell you?' she said, adding proudly, 'I have my own quarters, much grander than our place at home.'

The journey spoke to his senses as always, calling him back to the world he had lost, winding past the Loch of Stenness and the standing stones of the Ring of Brodgar, older than recorded time, looming against the horizon through the margins of the dark peat fields, where a solitary kestrel hovered in a bleak grey sky, sweeping out of sight for its prey.

Then sudden habitation, a group of houses, knitted tightly together, and a grey, straight street with contours more akin to a city than an island, set down temporarily by an architect who, defeated by its ugliness, had abandoned an uneasy struggle with an unwilling landscape.

'That's Spanish Cove,' said Mary.

'What an extraordinary place and where did it get that fanciful name?'

She laughed. 'It is supposed to be the exact spot where that galleon went down, so they say, all that long time ago.'

Faro knew the story well. So this was the

actual birthplace of one of Orkney's popular legends, *El Rosario*, in flight after the defeat of the Armada, pursued by Queen Elizabeth's superior fleet aided by storm and 'the wind of God'.

Spanish Cove's one long street perched uneasily close to the cliff edge undeterred by sudden storms and wild seas, with a small landing stage far below.

'In the kind of wild weather we get, the cove has provided a refuge for foreign fishing boats. I'm told,' said Mary, 'that the herring catches are very good in these waters. Probably accounts for the houses in the first place.'

Its forbidding aspect suggested smugglers arriving at the dead of night rather than fishermen with their daily catch and Faro said, 'I'm glad it's not our destination.'

'Awful, isn't it?' Mary Faro agreed. 'But the folk who live there don't seem to notice, all crowded together like that. Not like our houses in Kirkwall, with their bits of land. Although these ones do have peedie gardens to grow a few vegetables.'

As he glanced back over his shoulder, she added, 'There's a shop and stables for folk wanting to hire a horse or a gig for Stromness and Kirkwall. The Scarthbreck servants find having such amenities very handy.'

Bewildered, Faro asked, 'I wonder whose idea it was – and when?'

She shook her head. 'Goodness knows. Been there a long time. Look, we'll be seeing Scarthbreck soon.'

And suddenly the horizon was dominated by a distant glimpse of sea, and on the hilltop a fine new house.

Overlooking the vast expanse of Scapa Flow, on closer contact Scarthbreck also seemed to perch in an alien landscape as if aware of its transience, settling uncomfortably above evidence of earlier habitations. The builders had uncovered several skeletons, which confirmed the archaeologists' theories that the original house had been built over a Norse burial ground.

For Faro, the area awoke echoes he had encountered in ancient buildings like St Magnus Cathedral. An awareness of a past unwilling to be obliterated by an aggressive present and completely hidden by this determinedly modern house with building operations still evident in a three-sided courtyard to house stables and the servants' quarters.

Mary Faro said, 'Not only skeletons outside either. The house is haunted,' she added with a shudder.

Faro laughed. 'Surely not, Ma. Can't be more than fifteen years old.'

'That's as maybe,' she said grimly, 'but as the flagstones were being replaced by wooden floors, for extra comfort and warmth – they do like nice things, like a lovely Turkish carpet – well, they found another skeleton just inside the front door.'

That got Faro's attention. An unsolved murder always had immediate drawing power.

'An elderly man, they thought, but they've never found out anything more about who it was or how long it had lain there.'

Faro gathered that the original Scarthbreck had passed through many different hands in the course of its centuries-long existence, so there was no possibility of tracking down the identity of that particular dead man.

'No one knows anything about him, but they couldn't get a servant lass to live in again, after the first one said she'd seen his ghost. You know what it's like, gossip of that kind spreads like wildfire. That's the main reason for the lodges outside. They need servants. Of course, I don't believe in such things,' she added, but her anxious glance revealed otherwise.

'Who are "they"?'

'The Prentiss-Grants, you'll have heard of them even in Edinburgh. Shipbuilders on the Clyde, made an absolute fortune. He got a knighthood for it. Sir Arnold he is now, has a wife and one lass. Right bonny she is.'

A few scattered stones was the only evidence of the original Scarthbreck, once the house of a Viking wolf lord, built when habitations were not intended for comfort, but for the grimmer business of defence and survival.

The servants' lodge, a long, low building with one long corridor, had rooms linked by a succession of doors. The human equivalent of a horse stables, he thought and laughed. In this cheerless, box-like structure, with its no-nonsense courtyard, there was no place for ghosts and skeletons of ancient dwellers.

When he said so, his mother looked grave. 'Folk are so superstitious, I can't be doing with it, talk of a lot of heathen savages, going on about that seal king legend they're all so scared of.'

He laughed. 'I dare say you'll be glad to be back in your safe little cottage again, come the short days, the long, dark nights.'

'I will that. It's all so smart, neat and clean but it doesn't feel like my peedie home. I'm only here for the summer, I made that quite clear. Lots of posh folk coming, from the mainland and from England, for the shooting and fishing. I told them I wasna' interested in staying all year. At least not at the moment. I might change my mind later, but I'd dread the winter up here. It's too isolated for me.'

Far below them, away to the west in a great horseshoe of sand dunes set against a bleak sea, in the outcrops of rock the archaeologists had unearthed a Neolithic settlement.

What had conditions been like for those early dwellers, he wondered. Had they decided to settle there because the dunes offered hollows scooped out on the landward side, shelter from the wind and rain sweeping in from cruel winter storms? Built unwisely upon the sand, despite stone from the outcrops which took shape as walls, roofs and connected cells, they were doomed. No match for a succession of storms, obliterated by blown sand. The occupants gave up the struggle and moved elsewhere, all evidence lost until a decade ago when another violent storm stripped off the top sand, soil and turf to reveal a four-thousand-year-old housing estate.

Archaeologists had moved in immediately but made little progress in a site exposed to all weathers. Of interest to them were the stone furnishings, shelves for beds and storing, and an occasional bead, Stone Age implement or arrowhead, causing a furore of excitement and bringing to the wearied team renewed enthusiasm, brief satisfaction that frozen feet and hands and aching backs were well worthwhile in the cause of the island's story.

Mary Faro was proud of the housekeeper's quarters in the newly appointed servants' lodge. A parlour-cum-kitchen, two rooms with beds, all very spartan accommodation, somehow a continuity of that transience Faro was beginning to associate with Scarthbreck, as if a sudden strong puff of wind might blow the whole place away and leave nothing behind but a few strands of coarse grass and heathland, lost for ever like the Neolithic dwellings.

Suddenly he longed for his old room in Kirkwall and, briefly, in St Margaret's Hope, with their comforting associations of a happy secure childhood. This was all so new, so impersonal, as if the painted walls were not yet dry. There was no feeling of warmth, the welcome of returning home had been denied him – furnishings shabby but with precious associations in rooms full of memories.

Perhaps aware of his thoughts, his mother said, 'At least you won't have to sleep on the couch. I'm fortunate. My position entitles me to a spare room.'

She insisted on unpacking his case. He could not deny her that, and as he watched his meagre possessions vanishing into a cupboard and chest of drawers, he fielded a succession of questions. He considered the situation and wondered how he was to keep at bay his mother's curiosity regarding the true reason for his visit.

He was only mildly interested in the fate of the vanished treasure trove of artefacts. 'Priceless' was not a word in his vocabulary. Gold, silver and jewels were, after all, mere material objects, waiting to be tagged by the museum authorities and set in glass cases. In Faro's opinion, their acquisition could not be compared with what was truly beyond price in his estimation, one man's life or needless death.

Before being interrupted by his mother appearing to tell him that a meal was ready on the table, and lured by the delicious smell of frying bacon, he was already compiling a list.

First, an interview with the boatman and the divers sent to the scene who had found neither treasure, nor Dave Claydon. In the absence of a body there was conveniently no indication whether he had drowned by accident or design.

It was a start, and already Faro had a sense of doom that this was fated to remain one of those unsolved cases which would go down in the annals of Orkney.

Consoled by the fact that it should not take long, he could salve his conscience by enjoying – or should it be enduring? – a bit of home life, the indulgent kind an only son expected, and one he had almost forgotten. As his mother hovered over him, always urging him to eat a little more of that, try some of this I made, or some of that, he put an arm around her, kissed her.

Perhaps the gesture alarmed her for, teapot in hand, she looked momentarily taken aback. The kiss was everything. How could he find the right words to tell her that suddenly he realised that, although she drove him mad sometimes, he loved her? She was all the close kin he had in the world, much as he deplored her treating him as a small boy. Often he wondered, did only sons ever become grown men in the eyes of doting mothers?

It would be different if he had a wife, and as the conversation slanted slyly but inevitably towards that subject, of whether he had a young lady back in Edinburgh, he smiled.

This was one good reason for marrying his faithful Lizzie. He was very fond of Lizzie, told himself regularly that this was the love he had waited for. He was certain that she loved him. He had no doubts about that.

But there was an old saying that in every relationship 'there is one who kisses and one who is kissed'. He had to confess that he fell into the latter category. He had never experienced, perhaps never would, the kind of love poets like Burns wrote about or lovers like Romeo and Juliet died for.

He had known infatuation for what it was, a kind of bewitchment or temporary madness, but what was this mysterious, all-consuming emotion? The nearest he had ever known was with Inga St Ola, who had scorned his solemn suggestion after their brief loving ten years ago that they should get married.

Inga had laughed, dismissing him as far too young and saying that she was a free spirit and had no desire to spend the rest of her life with him, the wife of an Edinburgh policeman. She couldn't imagine such a future. That had hurt then, the memory still did.

His thoughts drifted back to the safer ground of Lizzie. Dear Lizzie. He knew she would be the perfect wife for a busy police detective: amiable, undemanding and kind. A good cook and housewife who would provide for his bodily needs and in due course present him with children – sons and daughters.

He groaned as memory popped up the one fly in the ointment, so to speak, to marriage with Lizzie. Her sullen, scowling eleven-year-old son, Vince, who hated him. What was more to the point, Lizzie wasn't just a respectable young woman, tragically widowed, who he could present to his mother. She had borne Vince as a result of rape by an aristocratic guest in a Highland mansion one summer when she was a fifteen-year-old parlourmaid.

This unfortunate experience entitled her to be spurned as an outcast from any decent Edinburgh society. All Faro's sympathy was with her, but did he think there was any possible way that his mother wouldn't be shocked and horrified at the prospect of a daughter-in-law who was no longer a virgin and had an illegitimate child? Unthinkable! Faro could see her lips tighten, narrow in disapproval.

He knew what Mary Faro wanted. She hoped he would marry some nice, respectable local lass, and he reeled back in horror, remembering those brief earlier visits when she managed to thrust in his path, by accident or design, a shortlist of girls for him to consider as suitable candidates for the role of Mrs Jeremy Faro.

He soon learnt that Scarthbreck was to be no exception, as a very pretty housemaid presented herself at the door, was invited in and introduced by a somewhat hopeful and gleaming-eyed Mary Faro as 'My dear little friend, Jenny. She comes from Kirkwall too.'

Somewhat dazed, he was trying not to listen

to a glowing biography, a story full of virtuous good points. Groaning inwardly, he knew it was all happening again. He had hardly set foot on the island and Mary Faro was on the march again.

To find him a wife.

CHAPTER THREE

If Faro must desert his mother and return to Edinburgh, then it was her fondest dream that he should return with a wife of her choosing, a lass she liked and approved of, a lass she felt comfortable with who would never challenge a mother's role in his life, to whom she could pass on all his likes and dislikes, as well as her own domestic and social skills.

Although the latter enjoyed in Orkney should be of little use in Edinburgh, she swept aside such considerations as unimportant. Her ideal as her son's wife was a lass she could understand, who spoke the same language and would keep closely in touch with her mother-in-law, while keeping a stern eye on Jeremy.

Faro, knowing how her mind worked, hated the matchmaking circuit. It was all too much for him. He remembered again, with acute embarrassment, her previous matchmaking attempts, where tea was provided for by his mother, both parties knowing perfectly well what Mrs Faro was up to.

They were on show, on their best behaviour, careful in their speech, trying to remember not to lapse into broad Orkney with its Nordic vowels, wearing their best gowns and best smiles. And he was on show too.

Then into their midst – almost – stormed Inga St Ola. And she was not on Mary's list. Her lips tightened in disapproval at the mention of her name, while she anxiously regarded Jeremy's face for indication that he wished to renew this undesirable old acquaintance. In the passing years, still unmarried at past thirty, Inga St Ola, by scorning conventions, had gained quite a reputation within the annals of island respectability.

And respectability was Mary Faro's yardstick; proud of her bloodline, she never forgot that the Scarths belonged to the Sinclair Stuart clan, the elite of the island, a family who claimed descent from wicked Robert, Earl of Orkney, bastard son of King James V and half-brother to Mary Queen of Scots. It made her cross that her son preferred to ignore any connection with the tyrannical rule of the earl, who had in his spare time repopulated Orkney through a small legion of illegitimate sons.

As for Inga St Ola, Faro's imagination had painted a different picture of this once lovely girl changed beyond recognition by the hardships of island life, marriage and childbearing. He was in for a shock. A pleasant one for a change.

When, on the morning after his arrival, the Scarthbreck gig set him down with Mary to shop in Stromness, it had been raining and the woman calling his name from across the street wore a black shawl over her head.

He stopped and looked round politely.

A trilling and once familiar laugh. 'Is it yourself, Jeremy Faro? Well now, don't you know me anymore?' she said, plucking off the shawl and shaking free the abundant tresses he remembered. Luxurious, shining dark hair. Head on one side, her smile provocative, a look he remembered and which often haunted his dreams. Her teeth were still excellent, her complexion radiant and Faro almost staggered back, overwhelmed by her nearness, this unexpected meeting.

'Have I changed so much?' she pouted, that expression, too, he remembered.

Recovering his manners, he took her hand,

kissed it. 'No, no, Inga,' he said softly. 'That's the trouble, you haven't changed at all.'

Again the trilling laugh. 'No trouble at all, I assure you.' And suddenly serious, looking him up and down with an intensity that stripped him naked, she said slowly, 'But you have, Jeremy. And for the better. Why, you've grown up at last.'

That was too much. 'What do you expect after ten years away in Edinburgh?' He heard a note of pride in his voice, and wishing for the first time that he was in uniform to impress her, he added softly, 'Of course I'm different to the lad you knew. In years, that is. But you – you're still the same. How on earth, living here . . . ?' and he left the rest unsaid in a gesture to the grey streets.

It was her turn to be amused. 'Luck, I suppose, although most of the folks here about, dead jealous, will blame it all on Baubie Finn.'

'Baubie Finn?'

'Aye, the island witch woman. You must have heard of her, works miracles; or should I say witchcraft? Nothing's past her.'

Inga was teasing him as of yore but Jeremy had heard of Baubie Finn: old beyond time, there had always been a Baubie Finn, her name spoken in awe even by so-called God-fearing, respectable Orcadians who went to the kirk each

Sunday and said their prayers each night.

Baubie Finn was dangerous. A seal woman, not to tangle with.

He shook his head, looked at Inga, longing to touch her. 'You're even lovelier than I remember.'

She liked that. Standing on tiptoe she kissed his cheek. 'Dear Jeremy, you always knew the right words to say.' And regarding him quizzically, 'What are you doing here? Your ma isn't ill, is she? At least the last time I saw her, she was flourishing as usual, larger than life.' There was a certain grimness in that statement, a hint that Inga and Mary Faro didn't see eye to eye, never did and never would.

Faro sighed. 'She's fine, I just decided it was time I visited my native heath.'

Inga continued to look up at him, and letting her believe that was his sole intention, he gave her a crooked smile. 'And now, I'm glad I came.'

He wanted to know about her. Surely time hadn't stayed still. Nothing stayed still in Inga St Ola's life. He heard the urgency in his voice as he asked, 'Are you married?' Perhaps an affluent marriage to some local worthy was the answer to her unchanged appearance, although such a lady would never wear a black shawl and would dress in the height of fashion.

She laughed, throwing back her head and pirouetted, showing shapely, long, slim legs, and ankles she was proud of. 'Do I look married, Jeremy, I ask you? Me, a fisherman's wife? Could you ever believe that I would be any man's chattel? Remember my free spirit? Well, it's still untrammelled, still the same.'

Out of the corner of his eye, Faro saw a familiar figure, his mother bustling along the street, carrying a basket and heading relentlessly in their direction.

Inga saw her too. 'I must away. Be seeing you, Jeremy. At the Kirkwall market, maybe,' she added casually. And again on tiptoe, she kissed his cheek quite brazenly this time, obviously hoping his mother would see it.

And Mary Faro did. He knew that by her tight-lipped expression. 'So you've met that woman again.'

'An old friend, Ma, an old friend.'

Mary searched his face anxiously but in vain for what she most feared, some indication that his feelings for Inga St Ola had been renewed. She had been aware of his infatuation with this older woman before he left the island to join the Edinburgh City Police and could never decide which worried her most. Especially as, soon after his departure, she learnt through island gossip that Inga had also gone away to the mainland. No, she hadn't said why – not a word to anyone. So Mary was haunted by the possibility that she might have followed Jeremy to Edinburgh.

Every letter filled her with anxiety – would there be some mention that she dreaded? 'Inga is here', or worse, that they were married? There was nothing to justify her fears, however, and when Inga returned a year later saying that she preferred life on the island after all, Mary drew a sigh of relief. This was reinforced when on his brief visits Jeremy had made no mention of that woman.

Mary was not the only one to be haunted by dreams of Inga. Jeremy, too, was haunted by dreams of a very different nature that night, of Inga and love fulfilled. He awoke to sterner reality. The main reason for his presence – Macfie's drowned cousin allegedly bearing priceless artefacts to Edinburgh.

What were they? An essential was to establish what the vague description implied.

A casual question about the ferry and Mary told him that although the boatman Amos Flett worked from Stromness, he lived just streets away from their old home. A good man, devoted to caring for his invalid brother. 'Dying of consumption, poor soul.'

And Kirkwall was the excuse Faro needed to see Inga again. She would be at the market.

All that was necessary, the invention of an imaginative selection of reasons for going there alone.

'Could you not wait until my half-day and we'd go together?' pleaded Mary.

'Time is short, Ma, there's things I want to do right away. I'd like to see South Ronaldsay again. And we can go to Kirkwall on your half-day, if you like. I'd like that fine.'

With that plausible excuse for an early morning start, she had to be satisfied. So off he went with the carters heading for the Friday market, accompanied by the usual noisy cattle and livestock.

His presence was readily accepted and he found an uncomfortable, cramped seat where no one questioned him or showed the slightest curiosity in a man's private business. Farmers did not question those they considered their betters, and with a natural politeness later on they would describe him thus, 'He kept himself to himself. He came from yon Scarthbreck – a gentleman, aye, you could tell that by his boots.'

In Spanish Cove a few more passengers were waiting to scramble for seats, mostly women armed with baskets and produce to sell, others with empty baskets to fill from the Kirkwall market. This brief stop confirmed once more Faro's first impression that the inappropriately named Spanish Cove resembled an ugly terrace of grey-faced houses lifted bodily from some poor city district and dumped down to perch uneasily above savage rocks and wild seas on a cliff top in Orkney, its inhabitants strangers in an alien environment.

He gave a hand to an elderly man hampered by a box, its contents obviously fragile. Taking a seat beside him the new passenger thanked him and said, 'Rare specimens. I gather tiny orchids that grow on the cliffs back there. Taking them to be labelled and identified by a government botanist.'

Faro learnt that Mr West was a retired schoolteacher. Disposed to be friendly, he said, 'I am a widower, for many long years. But I am not entirely alone. I have my homing pigeons – I know all their names. They are more than a hobby – very precious companions and I am quite devoted to them.' He smiled. 'My pigeons and my plants. Indeed, the very reasons I have no wish to ever leave Spanish Cove. It has some of the best botanical specimens on the island. Such an interesting area, the tiny harbour too. I spend hours watching the ships and the local lads practising their diving.'

'Are they looking for the Armada galleon?' Faro asked.

'If it still exists somewhere down there. They

obviously keep hoping for buried treasure. But I hear there are underground caves and that's the sort of thing lads like to explore.' He laughed. 'I expect you were the same when you were a lad.'

Faro smiled wryly and made no comment, remembering that he had once almost drowned and that Dave Claydon's body may have drifted into one of the dangerous caves to remain undiscovered until some sea fiercer than usual swept it on to the shore.

Leaving West and the carters near the market stalls in front of St Magnus Cathedral, he breathed deeply, joyfully. This was always for him a moment to look forward to, a moment of nostalgia fulfilled, back in Kirkwall, where he had grown up. Seeing his childhood home again, the cottage near the rose-red cathedral. His earliest memories were waking to bells on a Sunday morning, listening to the choir practise on still evenings, being one of the Christmas carol singers.

And there up the hill was his old school. Everything looked the same, the children shouting in the playground, leaping about, could have been himself again, the clock turned back, shedding the passing years, leaving no scars.

He was glad Ma intended keeping the cottage, having providently let it to a visiting artist for the summer.

'He's from Paris, very elegant and foreign in his ways. But he speaks good English,' she added, proud to boast of an illustrious tenant.

Faro decided that whatever she had said to the contrary, although so impressed by Scarthbreck, she had made up her mind already not to remain as permanent housekeeper if asked, and that once the summer was over, the 'Big House' emptied of guests, she would return home.

He had no difficulty in spotting the ferry boat, the sole occupant a young man staring out to sea. He turned round, wishing Faro a polite good day.

'Is the ferryman around?' asked Faro.

The man grinned. 'That's me, sir.'

Faro was taken aback: the name Amos suggested an old salt, rich in experience of all the seasons and the vagaries of tides, but the ferryman was possibly younger than himself, with a mop of dark-red curls, a roguish smile and, quite alarmingly, although the surname was as common as Scarth or Faro in Orkney, or Smith and Brown elsewhere, Amos bore a strong resemblance to Erland, a friend from his schooldays. Fletts were all distantly related and in a small community could trace their origins back to a distant or not-so-distant common ancestor.

'What can I do for you, sir?' Amos asked. 'We leave in twenty minutes, sir. Bound for the Hope?'

Amos was not what Faro had expected but seemed eager to be friendly. He had none of the guarded manner of the island folk in the presence of a stranger. Perhaps it was only the thought of business at last, and Faro had to disappoint him.

Shaking his head, he said, 'Not today, I'm up here seeing my ma, but I'd like to have a word with you, seeing as you are not too busy.'

The lack of a promising customer cast a moment's gloom over Amos's face, but he rallied quickly and grinned. 'Go ahead, sir.'

So Faro began to explain. 'It's about a man who drowned recently. He was cousin to a mate of mine in Edinburgh.'

If Amos thought this was a peculiar request, he gave no indication. 'It's a long way to come for a funeral, sir, all the way from Edinburgh, especially as you've just missed it. We laid him to rest three days ago.'

So his mission was all in vain. Faro didn't have time to sort out feelings of relief or disappointment as Amos pointed towards the horizon. 'Washed away out to sea after he drowned. Then, a week ago, his poor body was recovered up the coast.' He shrugged. 'No one had expected to see him again. Reckoned he was gone for good. That's the way of things,' he added with a melancholy shake of his head.

'Does that happen often?'

'Aye, more than you think. The tides here, they can wash bodies into these caves along the shoreline, to other islands. Never seen again. Sometimes as far as Shetland, or we've even been told one turned up in Scandinavia. Not much left to identify after the mountainous seas and the fishes are done with them.'

Faro never did like fish very much, even from childhood. Perhaps someone had told him that story or it was the legacy of his selkie grandmother.

'You'll need to tell your mate about it. That you missed the funeral and all.'

Faro nodded vaguely. He wasn't sure how to phrase the matter delicately. 'When he drowned . . . you were there. How did it happen? His cousin, my mate, you know . . . could you tell me about it?'

Amos nodded, gazed away from Faro out to the sea. 'A terrible night it was. Fog thick as pea soup.'

'Were there other passengers beside Dave Claydon?'

Amos shook his head and Faro continued, 'Surely that was odd. Was it because of the weather?'

51

'No. Wasn't the ferry like you see here, just my own boat. It was like this. We had finished our trips for the night, the ferry was docked and my mate Rob had cleared off home when this gentleman dashed over, said he'd just missed the Leith boat, would I oblige him – for a small payment that was – to row him out in my boat and catch the ship at the bar. He'd hail them and they'd drop a ladder for him.'

'Sounds a bit illegal,' said Faro, for whom smugglers came readily to mind.

Amos laughed. 'Of course it does, but we all do it. It happens all the time. We get well paid for our trouble, sir. Besides, this gentleman had booked a berth, so they were expecting him.'

But hardly off a ship's ladder in the middle of the sea, Faro thought as Amos went on.

'Anyway, off we went. I'm used to obliging in this way, so he had got my name from somewhere, gave me two pounds for my trouble.'

And that was a lot of easy money, Faro thought, small wonder boatmen were tempted.

'We raced the boat, got to the harbour bar first, then he shouted and someone heard him. Although I couldn't see the ship, I heard its engines. The fog was so thick, but we heard the ladder clatter down. Got as close as I could, held his luggage till he got a foothold—'

'What was this luggage?' Faro interrupted.

Amos shrugged. 'A stout leather bag he was carrying. Then I handed it back to him.'

'Was it heavy?'

Amos considered for a moment. 'Yes.'

'Had you any idea what it contained?'

Amos gave him a thoughtful look. 'He didn't mention the contents, but it might have been books, something like that. Anyway, he must have been halfway up the ladder, out of sight, as I had already turned the boat so I wouldn't be in the way when the ship started again. Suddenly I heard a cry, a mighty splash and I guessed he had fallen off the ladder.'

He paused, remembering. 'Then shouts came from the ship, "Man overboard", and I could hear voices, devil of a fuss, but one of the crew told me later that the captain said this passenger's name wasn't listed. He had no rights to be climbing up a ladder and the member of the crew responsible for putting it down would be prosecuted, as this was totally illegal. Anyway, after a quick scan of the surrounding sea, nigh impossible in that weather, the captain said he had a schedule to keep, tides and so forth, so off they went.

'I only heard about this later. All I saw was the ship above me, sailing away, and there I was circling about, shouting, but after a while I knew my passenger must have drowned. I went back, notified the coastguard. They did what was necessary, a lifeboat was launched, but never a sign nor trace of him. Nothing.'

'The bag he was carrying?'

'Nothing,' he repeated. 'As I told you, I handed it up to him, so it must have gone down with him.'

'Did you know who this passenger was?'

'Dave Claydon, the excise officer who would normally board the ship at Kirkwall.'

Footsteps announced the first of the passengers were heading towards the gangway. Suddenly busy with tickets, there were no further questions Amos could answer.

Thanking him, Faro went ashore. He had a lot to think about, as none of this story fitted the account he had been given. The accident with the ladder for instance. There were sinister gaps in the boatman's account too. The ship's captain would have no wish to be involved and possibly lose his command by the shipping company for being party to an illegal, although fairly regular, practice of boarding.

As they had talked Faro felt a rapport with the young ferryman, and hearing of his devotion to a much older, invalid brother, this struck a chord of guilt as he remembered Erland Flett, the friend he had never understood and for

54

whose tragic early death he still mourned.

Later he was to realise that was the reason for the rapport, his need for a friend of his own age and background. Edinburgh was a lonely place. His fellow constables regarded him as a stranger, and being befriended by Macfie had not helped to increase his popularity with the rank and file. Apart from the old superintendent to whom he owed so much, there was no one with whom to share a pot of ale and a good chat in the local howff. The constables had their own cliques and were not eager for his company in their leisure hours. The only true friend he had made was Lizzie.

Being a policeman had its drawbacks, and although Amos was sure to find out his true identity, he was not anxious to reveal that he was investigating the matter of the drowned excise officer and the missing artefacts bound for Edinburgh. He already knew from his own experience that mention of the police made even the most innocent become guarded and suspicious.

Now that Dave Claydon had been buried, how could he hope to satisfy Macfie's anxiety about whether his drowning was an accident? The sinister question remained – did he fall or was he pushed? As for that leather bag he was carrying, had he handed it to the man at the top of the ladder or had it gone down with him, as Amos surmised?

He decided to write to Macfie, conveying all the information he had gained so far, although most was in the uncertain realm of theory only. Considering all Macfie's connections, perhaps he could find out from the Edinburgh Museum what they were expecting to receive, since some correspondence must have been exchanged.

For the immediate moment, however, he was happy to thrust aside all else but the delightful prospect of seeing Inga again.

CHAPTER FOUR

As Faro walked towards the market stalls keeping a lookout for Inga, he realised his talk with Amos had raised some questions that urgently needed answers. Time was not on his side, so where did his enquiries begin?

There seemed little point in talking to his mate Rob, who had left the scene before the incident. As for the ship in question, even equipped to interview the entire crew, he knew the impossibility of discovering the identity of the man at the top of the ladder. Aware of the captain's wrath falling upon their heads – each and all would deny anything to do with the illegal boarding incident.

Macfie's copy of the police report had been

brief and to the point. Hopefully, *The Orcadian* might give a more personal slant, a mention of Claydon's body recovered and the funeral, in the absence of sensational news of which there was little in Kirkwall: troop movements in war-torn India or crimes in the far-off mainland alike did not merit more than an occasional sentence, unless there happened to be a local link.

The print run was limited and newspapers were a precious commodity, passed down from hand to hand, eagerly awaited reading matter in a place where the only essential was to be able to count, and reading for pleasure was not considered one of life's necessities. Books were scarce even for those who could read and afford to buy them. Unlike big cities such as Edinburgh and Glasgow, lending libraries for avid readers were rare, and most folks' interest was confined to events in their surrounding area. Certainly the drowning of a local man was guaranteed sensational headlines.

Faro's road to the newspaper office lay in the general direction of the police station and on an impulse he decided to acquaint himself with the Orkney Constabulary, with some faint idea based on a conversation with Macfie that it might prove useful.

He was in luck. Introducing himself at the counter, a mid-fortyish uniformed officer appeared from the inner office. Tall, well-muscled, with a healthy-looking complexion, a flourishing moustache and wiry dark hair, he introduced himself.

'Sergeant Bill Stavely. Young Jeremy Faro! Knew your father, Magnus. Come on in,' he said, and to the counter clerk, 'Organise some refreshment, will you?'

Invited to take a seat, Stavely sat opposite, and subjecting Faro to a careful scrutiny said, with an air of approval, 'Well now, small world. So you took after Magnus, in more than looks.' He shook his head. 'I was right sorry to hear about his accident – we were on the Leith beat together. I'm a Yorkshireman by birth, came to Edinburgh when I was a lad, and after joining the police I would happily have stayed there, but the wife was from Stromness. Eight years ago, her ma took seriously ill. They were close and Lily wanted to come home again, especially as there was a much younger brother, Halcro, to take care of. We didn't take to being parted, travelling up and down here wasn't easy, so I decided to follow her.'

He smiled ruefully. 'Although I might have got higher on the ladder had I stayed in the big city, I've never regretted that decision. Bairns grew up here, three lasses and one lad – sixteen he is.' A sudden pause suggested pride mixed with perplexity. Faro asked the obvious. 'Does he want to follow you into the police?'

'I'd like that fine, but he has to make up his own mind.' Stavely's face darkened remembering the frequent disruption of domestic bliss and Lily's tears at Ed's rebellious behaviour, particularly his fondness for drink and what his father decided were undesirable associates, the lowest elements of young males in Kirkwall. That was bad enough, but lasses had also loomed on the scene and both parents decided he was far too young, which he considered unfair since they had married before they were twenty.

These thoughts remained unspoken and after a few general remarks Faro mentioned Macfie. Stavely beamed. 'Knew the old fellow well. How is he?'

And that led right to Faro's mission regarding Dave Claydon.

Stavely shook his head. 'Poor Claydon. That was bad luck. Buried only a few days ago,' he added grimly. 'Enough to give a widow nightmares; Thora was in a state of collapse, completely distraught.'

He sighed. 'The ferryman, Amos Flett, last person to see him before he drowned, identified the body and spared her that final ordeal.'

The counter clerk came in with a written message and Stavely sighed, 'Have to go. Business calls.' He stood up, shook hands. 'Enjoyed meeting you. Anytime you're hereabouts, look in for a chat.'

Faro left heading for the newspaper office and wishing there had been more time to find out Stavely's thoughts on Dave's bad luck and any speculation on what that leather bag might have contained.

Hopefully *The Orcadian* would have something vital to his enquiry on offer, with the chance that there would still be a back copy with more information on the accident than he had received from Macfie and that someone could give him the widow Claydon's whereabouts.

At the desk he announced that he was on holiday and had promised that he would look in on Mrs Claydon and offer condolences from her Edinburgh relatives. The clerk regarded him bleakly, but perhaps consoled by the Orkney dialect into which Faro had lapsed, he said, 'Aye, sad case it was. Jimmy wrote it up – he was at the funeral and, right enough, he'll know her address. I'll see if I can find him.'

At that moment the door was flung open and a large, untidy man dashed in. He had a mop of wild, greying hair, a bewildered look of frantic purpose and his general appearance suggested that all his clothes had been flung on in a great hurry.

'Jimmy!' shouted the clerk. 'A mannie tae see ye.'

Jimmy slithered to a halt and regarded Faro breathlessly. 'What is it? A fire somewhere – any casualties?' he added hopefully, already conjuring up the next edition's headline.

'Yes . . . I mean, no.' And to the man's ill-concealed disappointment Faro retold the Edinburgh family connection with the drowned man.

'Aye, aye – Dave Claydon, body washed up; he's been buried already. One of my best features,' said Jimmy puffing out his chest with evident pride since it was, in fact, his only important feature since his arrival on the newspaper five years earlier. Reluctant to relinquish his moment of importance, he obtained the best possible mileage by frequent reports, keeping readers in mind that the search for the drowned man continued without success.

'Such a scoop,' said Jimmy. 'Body washed up on the shore. Sensational. Especially as the only other item of any interest to the locals was that Josh, Amos Flett's invalid brother, was dying.' He shook his head. 'However, as everyone had been expecting that for years, it wasn't exactly headline news.'

Meeting Faro had brought a momentary cheer to Jimmy's dismal expression. In a dire lack of news apart from the market day scenes in Kirkwall and the farming prices for various animals, an Edinburgh relative's distress would stretch into another reasonably sensational headline, and rubbing his unshaven chin thoughtfully he said, 'The widow Claydon bides up the road yonder.'

At Faro's request Jimmy was delighted to produce copies of the last two editions. The first, containing the story of a Belfast man on holiday walking along the shore near Spanish Cove and his dismay at finding Dave Claydon's mortal remains, and the second, an account of the funeral.

Thanking him with several pressing questions unanswered, Faro hurried back along the street to the address he had been given – a neat stone house about a hundred years old with a pretty garden, but Mrs Claydon was clearly not at home. About to leave, a curtain twitched on the house next door and an elderly woman emerged and looked Faro up and down suspiciously as if assessing his respectability.

Obviously, gentleman callers were of great interest to Mrs Claydon's neighbours, Faro decided as he explained the reason for his visit once again. He wasn't sure by her expression if she believed a word of it or not, but with a shrug of dismissal, she said, 'Helps out in the bakery in Main Street, they're like to have a market stall today.'

The idea of approaching Mrs Claydon at such a scene with the sort of questions he had in mind had little appeal and, walking towards Kirk Green, he was considering a visit to the local minister who had conducted the funeral service and whether it would be advantageous to introduce himself, explaining Macfie's connection.

'What are you doing here, Jeremy Faro, looking so grumpy?'

The voice and the laugh belonged to Inga.

He grinned. 'Not grumpy, just thoughtful – and delighted to see you. Such an unexpected treat.'

'Not quite so unexpected. I did mention market day with the hope that you would take the hint. And so you did.'

'And what brings you here?'

She shrugged. 'Material, odds and ends. I'm a seamstress; I sew fine petticoats and underwear for the gentry ladies, and in my spare time I knit jerseys and stockings for the fishermen.'

Faro smiled. 'I didn't realise you were so domestic.'

'Are you being sarcastic, Jeremy?' she asked indignantly. 'I can cook too, you know. Anyway, I'm finished for the moment,' she added, indicating the basket over her arm. 'A few more items to collect and a customer to see this afternoon.' She paused. 'However, if you would like my company for a while . . .' She added with an arch glance, 'I'm good at company too, if you can remember.'

He laughed. 'A long time ago, that was.'

'Very well. Let's walk for a while, down to the shore. There's less folk about and we can throw stones at the seals.'

'Do we have to be so drastic?'

'Only if you cannot think of interesting chat to keep me from dying of boredom.' And with a complete change of subject, the question he dreaded. 'What brings you here, anyway? I saw you lingering outside the police station a while back, I was in a shop.' Pausing she smiled. 'Thought you were having a holiday from being a policeman and chasing criminals.'

'And so I am. Seeing Mamma again.'

And clinging to his arm, with another disconcerting change of subject she demanded, 'Found yourself a wife yet?'

'Of course not.' Instantly regretting that emphasis, he added cautiously, 'I do have a young lady.'

'A young lady, eh?' Inga repeated. 'How nice. Any thoughts about a wedding emerging?' She stopped and pointed to a bench. 'Do let's sit down. I'm exhausted. Your legs are far too long,

I can't keep up with you.' Sitting close to his side, she looked up at him, chin on hand. 'All right, Jeremy. Tell me all about her.'

And so he told her about Lizzie and Vince.

'What a horrible small boy. Can't she have him adopted or something?'

Faro explained that Lizzie loved Vince and was determined to keep him with her. She had made great sacrifices, was prepared to work hard on menial tasks, and accepted her role as an outcast in decent Edinburgh society.

'As for me, I am certainly not going to part them, that has never been my intention.' At Inga's rather cynical laugh, he went on, 'As a matter of fact I have hopes of winning over that obnoxious brat some day. He's a clever little lad, right enough. Wants to be a doctor.'

'A doctor,' Inga repeated. 'Eleven years old – what a weird ambition.' She added seriously, 'It's a long time for you to wait for your Lizzie and if you want my opinion, you're wasting your time there, Jeremy.'

Despite Inga's negative advice, Faro found it a great comfort talking to her, sitting there in the sunshine, with a chorus of seabirds and seals barking like excited dogs from the rocks.

'What else do you do, besides sewing?'

'I work in the bakery over yonder, occasionally – feast days and so forth.'

'Doesn't look as if you eat much of the profits,' he chuckled with an admiring glance at her trim figure. But mention of the bakery reminded him of his quest.

'Do you by any chance know a Mrs Claydon?'

'Thora Claydon. Certainly do. Comes in part-time as well. What's your business with her?' Inga demanded suspiciously.

'Just a promise to an Edinburgh colleague. Her late husband was a relative. Said I'd call in and give her greetings and their condolences.'

'Make sure that's all you give her,' Inga murmured and added, 'I doubt you'll make much progress there. She'll be quite resistant to your charms. Keeps herself very much to herself since Dave died. Nobody gets to know anything about her. Never were what you'd call a sociable couple. Dave was popular, though – there was a large turnout for his funeral.'

Faro remembered the newspaper's long list of mourners as, pausing, Inga looked across at the seals with a faint shudder. 'Just listen to them barking! It's that time of year!'

Her remark recalled for them both that August was also Lammastide.

'Remember the seal king legend?' she said. 'Being a girl it used to terrify me. However, he never came and snatched me up. Thora,

67

however, had a very interesting experience, a past that everyone, including herself, hopes to forget. Never talks about it, but it was quite a sensation that will go down in history as one of our island myths.'

And Faro found himself hearing again of the seal king's annual rising from the sea and carrying off a girl walking on the shore to be his bride in his kingdom under the waves. But in this case the girl was Thora Harbister, Dave's fiancée.

'She returned, just like the legend said, found walking along the shore, lost and bewildered, at the very spot where she had disappeared, a year and a day later. Claimed she couldn't remember a thing about the experience, no matter how everyone tried to get the truth of what had happened.'

'What about her parents?'

'Didn't have any. She and her sister Elsa were orphaned when they were peedie bairns.'

'No aunts or uncles?'

'No one. Anyway, although Dave must have been upset, loyally he stood by her, married her, just as they had planned. That is what most folks called being exceptionally faithful; some were deeply shocked, and to this day it's still a talking point.'

'Her memory never came back?'

'Not a whisper.'

It was an intriguing story, a tale of unswerving devotion and now its sad link with the present.

Faro asked, 'Did you know Dave?'

Inga shook her head. 'Not really. Maybe met him a couple of times, but we never had much to say to each other. I thought him rather a dull sort of fellow, intense but dull.' She laughed.

'What about Thora's sister?'

Inga shook her head. 'No one knows. She never discussed it either. Truth is, they didn't get on together. But when Thora went missing, she took her place at the bakery, kept her own counsel, and when Thora came back, Elsa left the island, took off to the mainland. Haven't seen her for years. Don't think Thora cared. But when Elsa didn't even come to Dave's funeral to support her sister, her only relative, there were raised eyebrows in plenty. A real talking point, I can tell you.'

'What was the trouble between them?'

Inga shrugged. 'Dave Claydon. Rumour was that Elsa, the older sister, saw him first and Thora stole him. Maybe Elsa couldn't bear the thought of her marrying Dave.' She shrugged. 'No one could blame her for hoping that her little sister had gone for ever and that would give her another chance of hearing wedding bells with Dave.'

'Were there any children?'

Inga shook her head. 'No, perhaps just as well. Pity though,' she added with a laugh. 'Maybe they would have been mermaids.'

'Have any other girls had the same experience and come back?'

'Not that anyone's heard lately.' Inga gave him a pitying look and laughed. 'Surely you don't believe all that nonsense, Jeremy?'

And Jeremy Faro didn't. Not then, anyway.

CHAPTER FIVE

Thora Claydon's disappearance as the seal king's bride and the forgiving nature of her fiancé, Dave, increased Faro's determination to meet her. The whole episode was so completely unreal, completely alien to his theory that for everything there had to be a logical explanation.

He decided to try again and reluctantly remove himself from Inga's congenial company. Even as he toyed with plausible excuses, Inga announced that she must make the most of the rest of her day, as living at Spanish Cove there was little in the way of transport to Kirkwall, apart from the carters on market days. The alternative was horseback, which she didn't enjoy, or, from the same stable, a gig, a luxury which she couldn't afford.

'I hope you will come and visit me in my little house by the sea. It's on your way to Scarthbreck – you can't miss it.'

Although Faro received the invitation eagerly, he found it difficult to imagine Inga living in such a dreary place, its exotic name in reality belying any images of sunny Spain.

'Have you lived there long?'

'Long enough. I never stay in any place – there's a lot of world outside to explore.'

And with that enigmatic statement she was gone, and suddenly the prospect of having her near at hand had him deciding that this holiday offered more excitement than a week at Scarthbreck gathering information for Macfie about Dave Claydon's drowning and his subsequent funeral, although the mystery of his enigmatic wife was an added attraction.

Considering Claydon, the facts gathered so far and the account from the ferryman, Amos, indicated a straightforward accident. Making an illegal attempt to board the Edinburgh-bound ship in a wild sea, he had slipped on the ladder, and although he was an excellent swimmer by all accounts, perhaps he had been injured by the fall between ship and boat, concussed and drowned.

That Dave's body had not been immediately recovered was no mystery to Faro or to anyone who knew the islands. From his earliest years, Faro had an almost daily knowledge of the huge, wild seas around the coast and the wretched misery they brought as they claimed members from almost every crofting and fishing family.

In terms of human suffering, the precious artefacts that had also disappeared meant little to Faro, who guessed that, instead of remaining sealed in a glass case in Edinburgh's museum, they were resting at the bottom of the sea alongside the legendary wreck of the Spanish galleon and the remains of many humbler fishing boats lost through the ages.

Deciding that he had all the information he was ever likely to obtain to satisfy Macfie's curiosity, Faro concluded that there were no sinister implications and never had been, merely facts blown up in newspaper reports for Jimmy Traill's readers, who were eager for sensational stories.

What was much more intriguing for Faro was an earlier mystery, Thora Claydon's interlude as the seal king's bride that Lammastide, just after he had left the island ten years ago.

Where had she been for a year and a day, living out the seal king legend? Certainly common sense told him she could not have survived as a human in his kingdom under the waves. That was illogical nonsense.

So what was the truth? That was what he determined to find out and put an end for all time to this legend which made girls afraid to walk along the shore at Lammastide. This was the nineteenth century after all, the age of enlightenment, of scientific progress, although regretfully such matters were doomed to move at a very slow pace on his native island.

As he walked briskly towards the house for the second time that day, he thought about Thora's disappearance. She'd gone missing near Scarthbreck and the recently excavated Neolithic settlement, the location of which was revealed when a sudden storm removed centuries of sand under which it had lain buried. In an area already notorious for fierce seas, treacherous undercurrents and dangerous caves, the archaeological discovery of this prehistoric dwelling lent it an added reality as they tried to make sense out of the pieces of stone furniture and the occasional cooking pot and hand tools.

Scant material indeed to build up a picture of what life had once been like for a forgotten people whose history had gone unrecorded and was followed by a settlement of Norse invaders. It was at this same place where, many centuries later, Scarthbreck had arisen, built on a long-lost burial ground. And in more recent history, the unidentified body of a man was found lying near the entrance.

And Faro wondered if all his answers lay not with Thora Claydon, but within the scene of his mother's temporary summer employment.

His second visit to Thora Claydon promised success, but the woman who opened the door was a surprise. Small and pretty still, rather than the older, more harassed woman he had envisaged. Nor was there any evidence of widow's weeds, although this was not strictly Orcadian tradition, where everyday dress was black – a practical matter, since in large families the infant and elderly mortality rate were both high.

However, he had to admit that, fragile and bird-boned, her appearance fitted the legend attached to her. It would not have been difficult for a strong puff of Orkney wind to blow her away, much less a lusty seal king to carry her off.

At the mention of Macfie, she politely invited him in. The house, too, was a surprise. He did not expect luxury from Dave's income as an excise officer. But there it was all around him, a house whose contents on a miniature scale lacked only the exterior of a well-appointed Edinburgh town house.

Ceilings were low and windows small but the furnishings were lavish. Handsome paintings adorned the walls, there was silver in plenty and a table set with candelabra and fine china.

She observed his look of surprise and said, 'No, I am not expecting visitors. I keep it like this for Dave, in his memory. It was what he liked most, a well-set table in a well-kept home,' she added smiling sadly.

And Faro was relieved she had been spared the last gruesome ordeal of his recovery from the sea as she shivered and added, 'Until last week I still believed that one day he would walk in and explain what happened that dreadful night.' A sudden change of subject, a wistful, 'Will you take tea, Mr Faro? Visitors are rare and I have no servants.'

Nor did this luxury fit in with her work in the bakery, Faro thought, although the scones and bannocks were perhaps evidence that she needed a hobby to take her mind away from a doleful future. Had Dave left her reasonably well off from some independent source? The luxurious home failed to justify earnings as an excise officer and a courier of valuable artefacts.

As he delivered Macfie's message, such were his innermost thoughts. She smiled sadly in acknowledgement. 'I never met any of Dave's family after we married and I came to live in Kirkwall.'

None of their conversation fitted Inga's description of Thora either. There was nothing of the recluse in her attitude, she seemed happy to have a visitor, eager to hear about Edinburgh, full of praise for the wonderful city Dave had always promised they would visit.

She shook her head and sighed. 'It never happened and, alas, never will now.'

'I am sure Mr Macfie would make you most welcome,' Faro said enthusiastically.

'It is so far away,' she said making it sound like China, her vague nod confirming that this was one invitation she was unlikely to accept. 'Are you staying long, Mr Faro?'

Explaining about his mother and Scarthbreck, he sensed a change in her friendly attitude. 'I know the place, I lived nearby once and I know it well,' she repeated and then stopped speaking, staring towards the window, seeing scenes long lost.

'That was my girlhood home before I married Dave,' she added a moment later, almost as if she had no life before Dave. Faro remembered the seal king episode and that her husband's drowned corpse had been found in the same area.

'Did your family come from there?' he asked, knowing the answer.

Her face clouded over for an instant, then she said, 'We had no family. They died when my sister and I were children. We had distant relatives, cousins on the mainland, but we had never met. So we decided to look after ourselves, decided to stay together, a tiny croft in South Ronaldsay where we managed to survive working for the neighbouring crofts, gutting fish, mending nets, looking after hens and cows.'

She held out white, long-fingered hands, a deep sigh, seeing them chafed red in winter. Then she smiled, 'But folk were kind to the poor orphan lasses. They hadn't much either, and our lives were built on their discards, for which we were always grateful.'

Faro ventured, 'Your sister – where is she now?'

'She moved away.' Without any change in expression, a swift movement indicated that particular subject was closed. 'Will you take more tea, Mr Faro?'

Her distress was so visible, he no longer had any wish to bring the subject round to Dave's last fatal journey. He said, 'Thank you, but I must go now. I am travelling back with the farmers.'

'A not very comfortable journey.' Smiling she held out her hand. 'It has been a pleasure meeting you; my warmest regards to Mr Macfie and please, if you are in Kirkwall again, do come and visit me.'

He felt that she meant it.

On the way out, he noticed packing cases which had been concealed from view when the door was opened by her.

Following his gaze she said, 'A short trip to the mainland – I need a change of air.'

He nodded and said daringly, 'I am sure your sister will be delighted to see you again.'

Her smile was replaced by a vague nod as she closed the door.

As her sister had not come to Dave's funeral, it was confirmation of what Inga had said, that the breach between them after so many years apart must be very deep indeed.

More cheerfully, he hoped to see Inga on the farmers' carts and there she was, but with no chance of sitting together, seated between two young lads who were obviously very taken with her charms, looking constantly into her face, laughing and obviously flirting, which she seemed to be enjoying.

At Spanish Cove, they lifted her down to the road and Faro leapt off his cart, but apart from calling out that he hoped to see her soon, he had to leap back as the cart prepared to move on without him.

He looked back at her standing in the road,

longing to tell her that he had found Thora Claydon friendly and far removed from the cold, reserved woman she had implied.

Climbing the hill to Scarthbreck he went over that meeting. Thora had disappeared somewhere near the recent excavations, a shoreline notorious for wild seas and underground caves, where the Neolithic settlement added a sinister touch of reality to ancient legends associated with the area.

He looked up at the house brooding on the skyline. Thora's reaction to the mention of Scarthbreck – he was certain it had its place in the scheme of things and that the answers lay not in Kirkwall, but perhaps here just beneath its walls.

Mary Faro was waiting, an appetising supper laid out on the table. Her reaction to his market-day travels jolted him back to reality.

'Now that you have kept your promise to Mr Macfie, you'll be able to enjoy your holiday properly.'

He tried to look pleased, as was expected of him, meanwhile wondering how, with so little time and so much still unknown, he was ever going to manage to fit in another meeting with Inga.

CHAPTER SIX

Mary Faro was eager to show him around Scarthbreck. The family were absent and with obvious pride in the importance of her role as housekeeper she led him from room to room. Clear skies and spectacular views from the windows, taking in the excavations and distant islands like humpbacked whales basking in sunlit seas, calculated to add perfection to a magnificent interior, but Faro was not overly impressed.

In a hushed voice, Mary Faro showed off all the new marvels, but her anxious glances towards her son indicated clearly enough that his reactions were a bitter disappointment. There was no way of explaining, of making her understand, that for him the house also presented a hidden feeling of melancholy and depression. Again he was conscious that although newly built, the house was already haunted. Haunted by the past on which it had been built, by shadows of the Viking war lords, by torture and terror. Shadows seeped through the barely dried paint, and penetrated every corner of those determinedly luxurious indications of wealth.

It was as if ghosts of that earlier house had been incarcerated in the very walls and moved restlessly behind the velvet curtains. You could imagine them lying in wait, peering from inside elaborate gold-framed portraits, the formidably life-sized images of past generations gazing down from every wall.

It was not a good feeling and was one Faro knew that he could not convey in words for his mother to understand. Her air of bewilderment indicated that she was clearly disturbed by this lack of enthusiasm, as she added reproachfully, 'I suppose all this is nothing compared with all those grand Edinburgh houses you're acquainted with.'

He shook his head. Nor could he find words of explanation beyond saying that he did not have access as a humble policeman to these mansions of her imagination. Sadly he realised, not for the first time, that it was as if they spoke across a vast precipice, and although the same words were uttered, both interpreted them in a different way.

'No matter,' she sighed. 'This will be something to remember when you're back in yon lodgings.' She had never seen them but they were always dismissed as gloomy and shabby, which he could not deny. 'This will be something to tell your friends, how rich folk live in Orkney,' she added with pride.

What friends? he wondered. He had so few.

His mother continued, 'I expect they think we all live in caves.'

He laughed. That at least was almost true. But he was glad to return to the servants' lodge, those impersonal barrack-like rooms, no longer stalked by Scarthbreck's uneasy wraiths of the past.

Determined to see Inga again after their brief meeting in Kirkwall, still drawn to her, he sensed that the attraction was mutual. But it was not until he met Baubie Finn that he realised this was the one person with whom he could have walked around Scarthbreck and shared his feelings.

Perhaps this extra sense, so alien to Mary Faro, was something he had inherited from his long-dead selkie grandmother; an awareness of the thin veil separating past from present, an awareness that city living obliterated – even a city with Edinburgh's bloody past. It was also a sense that would serve him well in years to come as his career advanced.

Certain that he had learnt all that was to be found out regarding the drowning of Dave Claydon, satisfied that he had kept his promise to Macfie, he decided he might as well enjoy the rest of his holiday, especially as he firmly decided that it should include Inga St Ola's fair presence as much as possible.

He would respond to her invitation and call on her that Sunday afternoon, a time he calculated that she was most likely to be at home. Sunday was a day of rest regardless of one's religious inclinations, and began for most working folk with church in the morning.

So Faro followed the general pattern, dutifully accompanying his mother, hoping that Inga might be there. Looking round the congregation, there was no sign of her. Only a little disappointed but not completely surprised, he suspected that Inga worshipped the older pagan gods of Orkney, more akin to those ancient Neolithic dwellers than nineteenth-century Christianity.

The Scarthbreck servants all walked together the mile to the local church. An uninspiring, gaunt, box-like modern building, the only indication that this was a place of worship a kirkyard, whose slanting tombstones, inscriptions long lost, hinted at earlier occupants of this area within sight of Spanish Cove.

Mary Faro as housekeeper was in charge of the maids; paying no heed to a more-than-usual amount of giggling and nudging, she was delighted to observe that this was a reaction to the strange young man in their midst, her handsome son. There was one girl in particular that Mary had her eye on: pretty but less flighty than the others, intelligent too, Jenny liked books and was a skilled seamstress.

Yes, Mary decided, this lass would do very nicely. She had already marked her down on top of a list of those whose qualifications would guarantee a place in her quest for a suitable daughter-in-law.

Faro found the sermon too long, with a minister who droned on at great length regarding the sins of the flesh to a congregation who huddled like lost sheep in their pews and stared up at him wide-eyed, as if 'lust' was a rare word in their vocabulary and they'd like to hear more about its implications.

On his rare appearances at the kirk in Edinburgh, Faro was prepared to accept such admonitions from the pulpit in the grandeur of St Giles' Cathedral, surrounded by superb architecture, elegant churchgoers in their Sunday best, splendid hymns and an excellent choir, but lacking such distractions in a chilly, bleak building, he found his mind drifting to more agreeable subjects than original sin.

He had no doubts, however, that the lady in question who consumed his dreams, namely Inga St Ola, was well versed in that particular topic. As time was short, he hoped that this Sunday afternoon would present an admirable opportunity to see her again and examine her thoughts on that subject, among others.

Released at last, as he and Mary walked arm in arm through the kirkyard, Faro was aware that the remains of Dave Claydon lay buried in Kirkwall. His observations produced no comment from Mary Faro, whose thoughts were firmly engaged on the more pressing and urgent matter of producing a suitable future daughter-in-law from among her limited candidates.

When Faro mentioned casually that he would take a stroll towards Stromness, she pointed out that, being several miles distant, it was more in the nature of a day's excursion. And with Jenny at the forefront of her mind, said that she usually provided the maids' tea in the afternoon and had hoped he would be present.

Stubbornly, Faro shook his head. 'A splendid

idea, Ma. But tea parties are not for me. I want to walk, explore – it's a fine day and I have so little time.' A lie, he thought, but a forgivable one if his mother suspected his real intentions.

'What about your Sunday dinner?' Mary asked. 'We all eat together in the lodge.'

Faro laughed. 'After that huge breakfast? Please spare me, I'm not used to being fed like this.'

'Well, you should be. You are far too thin.'

Faro shook aside her protests, promised to eat something later and, kissing her briefly outside the church, hurried off down the road, conscious of her anxious frown, but quite unrepentant.

Inga was at home. She opened the door, her face registering surprise and delight as she greeted him with a kiss of welcome.

As he responded with hopeful warmth, she said, 'So good to see you again, Jeremy.' Taking his arm, she led him inside.

Low-ceilinged, humbly but comfortably furnished in the traditional way of crofters' houses on the island, there was an indefinable but unmistakeable ring of home about Inga's tiny parlour, which was sadly lacking in the newly built servants' lodge. It brought a sudden nostalgia for his childhood home, with the additional welcome from the peat fire glowing in the hearth.

The fire was so much a part of island life – its flame tended day and night, even in summer, and only extinguished and relit once a year at Beltane. Its cheerful glow touched a large sideboard, an oak dresser with china gleaming from its shelves, and a sturdy kitchen table. Stools well worn by the passing generations completed the furnishing.

And his first disappointment. They were not to be alone.

'I have a visitor, Jeremy. Someone I want you to meet.'

A visitor was the last thing he wanted. Not a suitor, he hoped, gazing round the room that was dominated by the Orkney chair, its high back and wings woven to keep chill draughts at bay.

Inga smiled. 'This is Baubie Finn – my friend, Jeremy Faro.'

The woman, who sat concealed by the chair, turned to greet him.

She was a further surprise. Expecting an old crone, a wise woman bent by the years, this Baubie Finn at first glance in the faint light appeared just a little older than Inga. Small, slim and, far from the shawls and crude rags, an eccentricity imagination readily painted in a selkie, she was exceptionally neat, so conventionally dressed that she would not have raised a single eyebrow in the congregation at the kirk that morning.

In fact she was so ordinary, with black hair sleekly pulled back, a pleasant, round face with fresh colouring, he felt almost cross, cheated even, when she stretched out a mittened hand. He had expected Baubie Finn to be interesting, vaguely intimidating, himself in awe since childhood of a supernatural being, from what he had heard of selkies. He had never met one – until now.

And as they talked, her conversation was quite normal and ordinary, only the round, luminous grey-blue eyes in that pleasant but oddly contourless face conjured up memories of the seals gathering around the ship as it docked.

He suppressed a faint shudder, pushing that irreverent likeness aside. She had a lovely voice: gentle, hardly much above a whisper. For the imaginative, the inevitable hint was of mermaids' siren songs. That almost convinced him, and he had a strange feeling that there was some magic about her after all.

Then a new idea: if she was as old as Inga had told him, then perhaps she had known his grandmother who, had she lived, would have been roughly sixty now. But then he changed his mind; perhaps the business of age might offend a lady – one mentioned age at one's peril in Edinburgh fine society, where all ladies tried to be at least a decade younger than nature and nurture intended.

'You'll have tea with us?' Inga said. He accepted, and as she brought down from the oak dresser another fine flowered china cup and saucer, he took in his surroundings. Cosy and warm, comfortable armchairs. Nothing spoke of wealth or ostentation. It was all – he fought for a word – just *homely*, the kind of room a man could stretch out his legs on that home-made rag mat by the fire after a long day's work and feel that good food and love would soon be on the menu.

'Jeremy,' Inga was laughing. 'What a daydreamer you are. Come back, I've had to ask you twice already – had you any success with Thora Claydon?'

Embarrassed, for Inga had been the subject of those dreams, he said he had delivered Macfie's message. 'I found her very friendly, not at all what I had been led to expect,' he added reproachfully.

Inga put her hands on her hips, stood back regarding him and laughed again. 'Dear Jeremy, you are so naive. Look at him, Baubie – he hasn't the least idea that all women find a good-looking young man irresistible. They all long to be your friend,' she added sarcastically.

Baubie was watching him, a slight smile playing about her lips making him feel foolish and self-conscious.

'Well, she didn't seem odd or strange at all,' he said defensively.

Inga turned to Baubie, who was listening intently. 'You remember Thora, the seal king's bride.'

Baubie smiled. 'That old story, of course, everyone knew about it. Best bit of gossip in years. One of the island's great unsolved mysteries.'

Inga, busy refilling teacups, turned to Faro who asked eagerly, 'You were there . . . er . . . Mrs Finn. You knew her as a girl?'

'I did, indeed, and I was here on the island the very night she walked into the sea and the day she reappeared a year and a day later – almost to the minute – on the very same spot.'

'What did you think?' Faro asked.

Bauble shook her head. 'I didn't believe a word of it, then or now, never will. No mortal girl could live under the sea, or in an undersea cave – the seal king's alleged "kingdom beneath the waves" – and survive the tides, the fierce seas hereabouts, for one day, much less a year.'

'Then where had she been?'

Bauble gave a wry smile. 'That's what everyone is curious to know, even to this day.'

And subjecting him to an intense scrutiny she said, 'Inga tells me that you are a policeman.'

Faro darted Inga a sharp look of reproach, as Baubie turned to him again, 'A detective – isn't that the kind of mystery your kind sort out?'

'Not really, Mrs Finn.'

She held out a hand, smiled. 'Baubie please, I am not a "Mrs".'

Faro felt his face redden. 'I beg pardon. As I was saying, detectives only sort out mysteries where there is a crime or some illegal activity involved.'

'Deception does not count then?'

'Afraid not.' But even as he said the words, he knew this was one mystery that would intrigue him and never let him go until he had found an acceptable answer that did not lie in the supernatural.

As they shook hands and as Baubie showed no signs of taking her leave, he politely took his. As he returned along the brisk walk to Scarthbreck, his disappointment at not having a romantic dalliance with Inga was somewhat abated by thoughts about Baubie Finn.

A strange encounter indeed, with a woman quite different from what tradition and superstition had led him to expect. A wise woman she might be by repute, although nothing in her bearing or her conversation had hinted at anything more than a conventional, pleasant, well-preserved woman of mature years who would not have been out of place in the salons of Edinburgh society.

Quite ordinary and in a strange way disappointing, he thought. Not quite what he had expected from meeting a selkie. Indeed, he had felt so much at ease in her company that it was difficult to realise that this was their first meeting and that, until this afternoon, they had been strangers.

Normally so observant, it was not until later that Inga whispered the reason for those mittened hands.

CHAPTER SEVEN

On his return to Scarthbreck, Faro was met by his mother. Hoping he would not have to evade her curiosity regarding where he had spent the afternoon, he found instead an air of excitement about her and a bustle of servants rushing about far more than he would have expected on a Sunday.

Had the owners returned unexpectedly from their holiday abroad? In reply to his question Mary said, 'No. But you'll never guess what has happened. The daughter of the house walked in an hour ago. What a to-do, the house in turmoil. Nothing prepared, no beds aired.'

She shook her head in bewilderment at such a flurry, such an indulgence in unwarranted activity, having to organise things properly instead of her usual peaceful Sunday afternoon rest before tea with the maids.

'Miss Celia was full of apologies at arriving ahead of her parents and insisted that she would take tea with the staff, if that would be alright, as she was well acquainted with their Sunday routine and did not want to spoil it. She hinted that they had so few things to look forward to.'

Pausing, Mary shook her head. 'There are rumours among the maids that she's one of those ladies who have strong feelings about women's rights, modern things her parents would never approve of or understand.'

A little bemused by the outrage such behaviour suggested in a young lady, she went on, 'She's like that, Miss Celia, quite at home with the servants. Her nanny could have told you some stories, and her last governess went off in a huff shouting that no one spoke to her like that. All the servants heard her as well.'

Mary strongly disapproved. The upper class should know their place too, or she believed the whole world would crumble away and fall to pieces. The word 'equality' made her tremble if she awoke in the middle of the night and considered its implications.

'I hope you'll have a chance to meet her,' she added hopefully, although she could not quite envisage this encounter leading to a romance which would end in matrimony. Her handsome son was only a policeman after all, with few expectations, while Miss Celia was an heiress and a real lady. A romantic ending quite beyond even her aspirations, although Miss Celia's advent had put all thoughts of those pretty maids out of her mind, for the moment.

Jeremy regarded her sternly as she added while setting the table, 'You just missed Miss Celia. What a shame. I'm sure she would have loved to hear all about Edinburgh.'

They were to meet, however, and Mary was to learn soon enough the dire consequences that encounter was to bring about. After a supper of steak pie and apple pudding, Jeremy knew that he must walk some of it off with a little brisk exercise, or he would never sleep that night. A lovely evening glowed beyond the windows, with the promise of a sunset and a wine-red sea.

His mother declined the invitation to accompany him. Her feet were sore and she was quite worn out with all this extra activity of overseeing the maids and the hasty preparations for Miss Celia.

'I'll take an early night as I have to be up at six,' he was reminded.

Walking along the shore in the mysterious twilight, the lace frill of waves at his feet, even the seabirds were mute. The silence was broken only by the whisper of his footsteps on the sand and nature's evening benediction, the susurrus of a gentle sea. The only occasional disturbance as a seal's head broke the calm water, looked around and promptly disappeared again.

He breathed deeply, at harmony with the world. For the first time since he got off the ship, he was enjoying the moment. Wanting the peace of it all to last, he sat on a large rock nearby and took out the pocket telescope Lizzie had given him – as a joke she had said, 'You would be better off with a magnifying glass, but it might come in handy on your travels. Searching the horizon for clues.'

Dear Lizzie. He felt sudden guilt. That promised letter on arrival had not yet been written beyond the first line. He must finish it immediately. But what to say beyond the conventional holiday phrases and wishing he had a poet's ability to convey this moment of magic?

There was the inquisitive seal again, closer now, staring up at him. He laughed out loud. Was the seal a vanguard ready to tell his majestic master that the coast was clear? An absurd thought, but one could imagine anything on this, a perfect night for Lammastide, where a sinister legend might come alive before the sun, sinking slowly, vanished beyond the horizon.

Suddenly he realised he was not alone. A prickling sensation at the back of his neck warned that he was under observation.

Turning his head swiftly, he saw a girl watching him from the sand dunes. Tall and pretty, even at a distance, beautifully dressed in a voluminous, fur-hooded blue velvet cloak that even Faro realised, from his beat along past Edinburgh shop windows, was the finest city fashion.

Curious wear for a warm August evening, he thought, but doubtless a visitor who did not trust the vagaries of Orkney weather.

As she smiled and waved a greeting, he did not require much imagination to guess as she called, 'Hello there!' that this was Miss Celia Prentiss-Grant also enjoying an evening stroll.

She ran lightly down to his side. 'You're Faro's son,' she said. 'She talks about you all the time.' Faro felt a blush of shame and embarrassment. Laying aside the telescope, he bowed and took her outstretched hand. 'Your name's Jeremy, isn't it?' she added softly. 'I'm Celia.'

He bowed again and she said, 'When I saw you sitting on that rock I wondered if you were the seal king waiting to gather up an unsuspecting bride.'

He smiled. 'Sorry to disappoint you.'

'Not in the least.' And looking him over candidly, her expression said that she was pleased by what she saw.

'Obviously that legend doesn't worry you, walking alone on such a night of local drama.'

She laughed. 'I can't imagine how awful it must be – the bride of such a creature. But it is a lovely haunting legend and this is the right time of year. At least the last seal king's bride – I expect you know the story, everyone still talks about it, I heard it when I was a little girl – didn't have to submit to a long and painful examination by her parents. Every hour has to be accounted for, so what would it be like – a whole year and a day to explain away?'

She obviously found no humour in the thought, and a shadow crossed her face. Silent for a moment biting her lip, frowning and deep in thought, then she laughed. 'I wonder why her distraught parents never ran to the police about their missing daughter.'

'I gather that they were too terrified.'

'Terrified?'

'Afraid all their family would be cursed. According to legend, defying the seal king's rule meant death. Their men out fishing would have their boats wrecked. They'd be snatched up by him and drowned in revenge.'

'How horrible. But one can't honestly imagine

parents being taken in by such superstitious nonsense these days.'

Faro could have told her lots of even sillier superstitions that bound the lives of ordinary folk in Orkney. 'Are you staying at home for a while?'

'Not if I can help it. Just a few matters to attend to and then I'm off again.' He waited but was not to be enlightened. 'Shall we walk?' she asked.

She talked about London, their other home and how she loved the theatre and the museums and art galleries. Small wonder, thought he, that she was soon bored in Orkney, this rich eighteen-year-old whose only role in life was to be shown off to various suitors and make the best possible marriage arranged by her parents. He guessed she would be extremely fortunate if love was ever considered a necessary ingredient.

As they progressed slowly along the water's edge, he realised there were others on the beach that night, drawn out by the mild sunshine and the possibility of seeing the Northern Lights, that strange phenomenon of these islands.

Ahead of them Sergeant Stavely, his wife and a tall youth were enjoying an evening stroll, while three young girls were throwing sticks to a large yellow dog, occasionally diverting their attentions to a competition of skimming stones across the water with shrieks of delight.

'Hello there!' Greetings were exchanged, the boy introduced as the Stavelys' son, Edward, while Faro received a rather arch glance from Stavely as he bowed to the girl.

'Good evening, Miss Celia.' A curtsey from Mrs Stavely. The sergeant knew his place, but his son, painfully shy, did not even glance in the girl's direction.

'You're a long way from home,' said Faro, surprised at meeting the Stavelys so far from Kirkwall.

Stavely laughed. 'Enjoying a change of scene. Having a couple of days off, visiting Lily's brother, Hal – he lives a couple of miles up the road.'

With no desire to linger, polite goodnights, an awkward bow from Edward and the three, gathering the younger children and calling the dog to order, walked swiftly ahead.

A sudden turbulence in the sea, a head popped up nearby, regarded them with an old man's face of suspicion and indignation, then disappeared again.

At Faro's side, Celia giggled. 'I do hope that none of those children's stones hit His Majesty. Do you think that was him out having a look around for a prospective bride?'

Faro said, 'Doubtful, very doubtful.' When

she glanced at him frowning, he added, 'Did you not think him a little elderly for a bridegroom?'

She shook her head, gave him a wry look. 'You should see some of the hopefuls I've encountered in London salons and you would soon change your mind. Age is no barrier where men – and money – are concerned.' Then with a laugh, pointing at the sea, 'I do wish he would appear – I'd love to see him. I wonder, does he wear a crown?'

It was Mary Faro who appeared, bustling breathless along the sands but remembering a curtsey.

'Well, Faro, anything important? What is it?' demanded Celia somewhat impatiently.

Faro looked at her sharply and frowning, having to remember that this was not intended for him, the surname was how servants were addressed by their masters.

'Nothing, Miss Celia.' Another curtsey. 'The maids have prepared your room, put a fire on to air it. All is ready for you.' Her hesitant manner hinted that the curiosity of seeing her walking with Jeremy, rather than a real interest in the girl's well-being, had driven her down to the shore, aching feet disregarded, with a message that could have been carried by one of the maids.

The girl looked at her smiling gently, and

exchanged a knowing look with Faro, as if she too had guessed the real reason for this intrusion.

'Splendid, splendid.' And with that she turned her back on them both and continued her walk. Over her shoulder she called, 'Good evening, Mr Faro, enjoy the rest of your holiday.'

Faro watched her go regretfully. He had been enjoying her company. Suddenly impatient with his mother's interruption, he was silent, not listening to her chatter, deprived of an attractive girl's light conversation.

Once indoors, the evening changed. The magic vanished with the sudden ferocity of island weather. A faint haze on the horizon heralded not a sunset, but grew into a monstrous white shroud covering what had been a dazzling sunlit sea an hour earlier.

Faro watched it from the window as Mary Faro said, 'Good you had your walk earlier, you wouldn't get far in this. It could last an hour. Let's hope it doesn't last a couple of days, though. Makes the place so cold too.'

Being trapped behind this forlorn blanket worried Faro. It was something people living on the east coast of Scotland also knew only too well. A sudden cold flow of air and the warm sunny day vanished, a scene which Edinburgh's extinct volcano, Arthur's Seat, its head in the clouds, saw with unwelcome frequency.

Restless, he decided that he had better finish his letter to Lizzie. He then discovered that the telescope was not in his pocket, and remembered that he had laid it aside to shake hands with Celia.

He swore. Expensive, he knew this was a gift Lizzie had saved up for and could ill afford. He couldn't just leave it there to be swept out to sea on the next tide. Pulling on his boots again, he had reached the door when his mother called, 'Where are you off to now, Jeremy – in this fog?'

'I dropped something – I must go and look for it.'

Making his way to the shore was an eerie experience, the mist seemed to clamp down on him and he realised how easy it would be to get lost as he stopped and listened, guided by the sound of the waves lapping the shore. Oddly enough, his solitary footsteps were there in the wet sand and led him to the rock – and most thankfully, the telescope.

With a sigh of relief he picked it up, and heading back in what he knew was the right general direction, he returned to the lodge. His mother was nowhere to be seen. He tapped on her bedroom door, there was no response. Tiptoeing in he saw that she was fast asleep, snoring gently.

'Goodnight, Ma. Sweet dreams,' he whispered and, leaning over, kissed her forehead.

In his room he finished the letter to Lizzie and, feeling just a little guilty, wondered if he would meet Celia again. She was certainly a stimulating presence at Scarthbreck and, recalling their conversation, a very pleasant Lammastide surprise.

It was not to be the end of surprises. Faro was awakened early next morning by his mother.

'There's someone to see you, Jeremy.' She looked close to tears. 'Quick as you can.'

'What's the matter?' But she merely shook her head.

As he dressed he knew the only person he wanted to see was Inga St Ola, the subject of his dreams, preferably alone. But standing squarely in Mary Faro's parlour twisting his helmet was Sergeant Stavely.

'What do I owe the—?' Faro got no further.

The look on Stavely's normally smiling, friendly face froze him into silence.

CHAPTER EIGHT

'There's been . . . an incident – down at the shore,' said Stavely. 'I'd like you to accompany me, Faro. Have a look at it.'

A stifled sob from Mary Faro. Stavely was regarding him intently.

'Of course.' Faro was puzzled, but without another word the sergeant turned on his heel and led the way out of the lodge, walking quickly down to the shore, ignoring Faro's attempts at conversation as if he had suddenly turned stone deaf.

The fog shroud had lifted, leaving a solid-looking, heavy, iron-grey sea, a chilling wind. A scene so melancholy that it seemed the island was in mourning. The shore was deserted apart from what appeared to be a bundle of clothes lying near the water's edge.

Closer, the bundle suggested the fur of a drowned animal but, as they walked rapidly towards it, became a bundle of clothes which took ominous shape.

Faro's sigh of relief was short-lived as he recognised, neatly folded on top, the elegant blue velvet cloak with its beautiful fur-lined hood that Celia Prentiss-Grant was wearing as she walked away from him on the beach less than twelve hours ago.

Speaking for the first time, Stavely turned to face him, asked sharply, 'Recognise these, Faro?' pulling the cloak aside respectfully to reveal a loose-fitting blue gown and a frilled petticoat. 'Well?' he demanded.

'Presumably these are what Miss Celia was wearing last night. But I don't understand—?'

'Exactly that,' Stavely interrupted with a heavy sigh. 'But you do recognise them?'

Faro shook his head. 'Only the cloak.' He looked at Stavely's expressionless face, bewildered by the implications of such an unusual find on the beach that morning. 'What's going on, Sergeant?.'

'That's what I'd like to know and I rather hoped you might be able to enlighten me.'

'How do you expect me to do that? I haven't

the slightest idea how they got here. What about the girl – where is she?'

'The young lady, you mean.' It was a reproach for Faro's informality. 'We would like to know that.' And staring out across the sea, 'When I took the dog for his walk at seven this morning,' he stretched out his foot delicately in the direction of the clothes, 'I found these. Recognised the outer garment that Miss Celia was wearing when I saw her on our evening stroll. I knew I was not mistaken, for this is not the kind of wear a local lass could ever afford, and being of a naturally enquiring nature, I wondered what she was up to. I went to the big house, where Mrs Faro told me the maids had discovered that the young lady's bed was never slept in last night.'

He paused, for breath this time, letting that information sink in before adding, 'Then I recalled that you were accompanying the young lady on her walk along this very shore last night.'

His speech sounded so exactly like an official police statement that its awful significance was not hard for Faro to interpret.

'Did it not suggest to you that she decided to take a swim?' But even as he said the words, Faro realised how bizarre they sounded.

'In such weather?' demanded Stavely. 'Here

we have a delicately reared young lady stripping off naked in a public place – on a beach? And apparently to swim on an evening not one of our hardiest diving lads would ever contemplate,' he added scornfully. 'And wearing her boots too.'

Faro had already noted their omission from the bundle of clothes and said, 'In our short conversation, I gathered she was of a very independent mind, Sergeant, very modern, and in my experience, the kind who might do unconventional things.' He did not point out that presumably she was wearing underclothes, and was therefore, strictly speaking, not completely naked.

'Unconventional things, eh?' Stavely repeated. 'That is, in your own experience.' He almost smiled. 'You had met the young lady before?'

'How could I? She arrived alone last night, before her parents were due to arrive later this week. We met quite by accident when I was, like yourselves, Sergeant, enjoying an evening stroll.'

Stavely was silent for a moment, regarding him doubtfully. 'One would have gained the impression that you were well acquainted. Laughing and talking like that.' He added, 'Hardly the behaviour of strangers.'

Faro gave an exasperated sigh. How could he explain to this very conventional policeman that it was not unknown for confidences to be exchanged between strangers without the formality of an introduction. How to tell him that ordinary folk who travel long journeys on ships and railway carriages were not unaware of the experience.

In truth, however, he also found it impossible to believe that, after leaving him, the girl had decided to go swimming and – the implications were horrific – had subsequently drowned. There was something else at the back of his mind, a whisper refusing to be banished.

The seal king legend.

Although every ounce of common sense he possessed knew it to be a myth, the fact remained that this was not only Lammastide, but that Celia Prentiss-Grant had disappeared at the identical place where Thora Claydon had vanished ten years ago.

Was Stavely thinking the same, he wondered? There were ships on the sea now, small fishing craft, patrolling an area not far from the shore. Stavely had been busy and efficient. These were not fishermen out for a day's catch. The only catch they had in mind, and hoped their nets would not encounter, was the body of the only daughter and heiress of Scarthbreck.

Soon the story of her disappearance would be all over the island and in the local newspaper, possibly even making news in the small paragraphs of the national press.

Stavely's expression was dismal indeed as he regarded the little fleet. 'Let us hope that there is some innocent explanation.'

'Although it is hardly the innocent explanation you desire, Sergeant, we must not dismiss the possibility of suicide.'

'Suicide!' Stavely stopped in his tracks, his very mobile eyebrows shot heavenward. 'A young lady like that! With all the world's goods at her command. Impossible!' He would have laughed at the suggestion had it not been so ridiculous. 'It is beyond belief you could even consider such an idea.'

Maybe impossible to reconcile with Sergeant Stavely's reverence for riches and luxurious living, but Faro knew of many reasons why an eighteen-year-old might take her own life. The first that came readily to mind was not unknown even in Edinburgh's high society – a suitor rejected by a daughter's parents as unsuitable, or worse, an unwanted pregnancy resulting from an unhappy love affair, ended with a leap over the railway bridge.

'Before you dismiss the idea, Sergeant, it would be as well for us to learn what brought her back to Orkney in such a hurry, without her parents.'

In answer Stavely made an impatient gesture. He had already leapt to his own conclusions and Faro was clearly aware that in the absence of anyone else on the scene, in Stavely's mind he figured as the prime suspect. Ridiculous as it seemed from his point of view, he felt numbed by the implications and asked warily, 'And what happens next, Sergeant?'

'Her parents are being notified, a telegraph has been sent to London.'

Faro thought of their anguish, the tragic end of a holiday. Again he returned to that important question of what had driven her to return to Scarthbreck last night. Completely alone, when girls in her class never went anywhere unaccompanied by a personal maid – an omission to which only she could supply the reason.

A couple of constables had appeared on the beach and Stavely indicated they gather up the clothes carefully and take them back to the station. He watched them perform this task with the utmost reverence, bewildered by the implications of the missing girl and what lay in store for a local policeman, whose island duties lay in the region of minor thefts, occasional arson and perpetually unresolved smuggling activities.

As they walked back to the road where

a police carriage was waiting in melancholy anticipation of a drowned victim, it became clear that Stavely had not the slightest notion of how to deal with such a situation when he turned and said in a tone of righteous indignation, 'Nothing like this has ever happened here before.'

Heading in the direction of Scarthbreck, Faro's moment of compassion for the sergeant was replaced by irritation. Had he forgotten the Thora incident ten years ago, the notorious matter of the seal king's bride, the mystery of where she spent that year and a day still unresolved?

As they approached the servants' lodge, Faro said encouragingly, 'Perhaps they have some more information.'

Stavely shook his head. He did not seem hopeful and, turning to Faro as he opened the door, he said sternly, 'I'm afraid you will have to remain here. You won't be at liberty to return to Edinburgh until we have all this sorted out.'

And leaving Faro no longer in any doubt of what he was thinking regarding a suitable prime suspect, he added, 'If the worst should happen, you will have been the last person seen with the young lady before . . .' He paused for a moment, then reminded him, 'Witnesses will be sought and you will recall that Mrs Stavely and I saw you both together, as did one of the maids out walking with her young man,' he concluded heavily.

In the housekeeper's parlour Mary Faro sat at a table, sobbing and quite beyond reason, certain that Miss Celia had drowned, and how were they going to tell her parents?

Both men tried to reassure her that there was no evidence of such a dire occurrence and for her benefit insisted on an innocent explanation which, alas, temporarily failed their imaginations.

But Mrs Faro remained beyond comfort or comprehension, and when Stavely asked her how Miss Celia had arrived, she merely stared at him.

'A hired gig, I expect.' And she jumped to her feet, rushing to the window, staring out and stifling sobs, red-eyed with weeping. 'It's terrible, just terrible. I can't believe it – that this should happen. I'm in charge in their absence, you know,' she moaned.

In vain they rallied to impress upon her that, whatever happened, the servants, particularly herself, could in no way be held responsible for their daughter arriving home alone.

At last, Stavely got a word in and produced an official-looking notebook. 'I need a formal statement from you both.' And to Faro, 'After we met you and the young lady, I gather that you returned with your mother and remained here for the rest of the evening. Is that correct, Mrs Faro?'

Mrs Faro darted a sharp, warning glance at Faro. 'Of course, of course, Sergeant. We neither of us left the house – a terrible evening like that . . . the fog . . . Isn't that so, Jeremy? We were here until bedtime and—'

Stavely cut her short. 'Very well – if you will just sign a statement to that effect.'

Faro held up his hand. 'A moment, Ma. My mother had gone to bed, but I went out again.'

He was conscious of a reproachful hiss from his mother. Stavely glanced at her, then turning to Faro, unable to restrain a look of satisfaction, asked slowly, 'And where did you go?'

'Back down to the shore.'

'The shore, eh?' A gleam of triumph in the sergeant's eye.

Another stifled gasp of protest from Mary Faro.

'I had dropped my pocket telescope and went in search of it.'

'And did you find it?'

'I did. It was on a rock where I had been sitting.'

It sounded like a lame excuse and obviously Stavely thought so too, as he nodded vaguely and asked, 'How long did this search take you – how long were you absent?'

'Naturally, I did not pay any attention to the time, but I should imagine no more than twenty minutes, once I'd found what I was looking for.'

'And did you meet anyone by chance?' Stavely demanded sharply.

'No one. Besides, it would have been difficult to see in that fog. Anyone else present could have been unnoticed only an arm's length away—'

'Twenty minutes,' Stavely interrupted, writing the words in his notebook. Pausing, he looked hard at Faro. 'Perhaps you might have been out for an hour or more, since you have no exact idea of the time and no one to testify to how long you were absent.'

'I can only tell you that I came back as swiftly as possible, I had no desire to linger in such weather,' Faro said, trying to restrain his impatience. 'Surely you're not suggesting that I had anything to do with the girl's disappearance?' He paused, angry that it was becoming all too clear that the sergeant's notion that he had done away with Miss Celia was no longer just a possibility.

'Really, Sergeant, that is quite absurd!' But he did not feel like laughing and Stavely did not look amused. And being an Edinburgh policeman did Faro no favours. Policemen could be killers too, and Stavely's imagination was painting a scene of Faro in a frenzy of lust, tearing off Miss

Celia's clothes, raping and then drowning her, with the fog as alibi. 'Be reasonable, Sergeant, I had just met the girl,' Faro appealed, hoping a lightness of touch would render Stavely's suspicions preposterous. 'Why on earth should I wish her any harm?'

Stavely shook his head sadly. 'It can happen, Faro. It can happen. There's the beast in all of us, just lurking there. We're all just like that villainous seal king of yours, under the Queen's uniform.'

CHAPTER NINE

They took Mary Faro with them and walked round to the house, explaining that the first place to look for clues relating to someone missing was their last residence. In this case Miss Celia's bedroom.

The first clue was that her bed had not been slept in. The maid Jenny had taken up her breakfast that morning and was also in a fine state of nervous weeping.

Dismissing her, Stavely's demand that they search the bedroom was countered by an outraged cry from Mary Faro. She blanched at the suggestion, firmly stating that she could not allow anyone such access without Sir Arnold's permission.

Faro realised that he had been especially privileged to have that brief tour. She informed Sergeant Stavely that he must await the owners' return, which would be doubtless as soon as transport allowed, once they heard of their daughter's disappearance.

'I respect your orders, Mrs Faro,' said Stavely, 'but by awaiting her parents' arrival, valuable time in tracing the young lady is being irretrievably lost.' Letting that sink in for a moment, he went on, 'And I do not think her parents will thank you for that. Speed is of the essence in these matters. We, the police, will take full responsibility for any dissension this may cause between you and your employer.'

A shake of the head, a despairing sigh and Mary Faro led the way up the handsome oak staircase to a bedroom, its magnificent view, the best in the house, overlooking the shore where Miss Celia had vanished.

Faro accompanied the sergeant, and as the two men stood in that pretty, very feminine room, Stavely shuffled his feet uncomfortably. Clearing his throat, he glanced around nervously, an intruder in intimate surroundings, as if the young lady might be hiding behind the curtains, ready to rush out and demand to know what they were doing.

But despite an overflow of frilly lace and satin,

the room was clinically tidy. The postered bed pristine, its covers bearing only a faint impression where Miss Celia had sat down, perhaps to change her footwear. Her sole luggage, a small trunk, lay solitary on the rug, waiting to be unpacked.

Perhaps in the hope of some clue, the sergeant bent down, tried in vain to open it, and accompanied by Mrs Faro's shocked sigh of disapproval, discovered it was locked.

Impatient now, frowning, he gestured sternly that she should leave them to get on with their search. She did so, but with every indication that this was seriously out of order, allowing them to remain without supervision in Miss Celia's bedroom.

Faro nodded towards his mother, trying to convey that he would keep an eye on the sergeant, who did not feel that any apology was called for.

Mary Faro stared at him reproachfully and slammed the door with more noise than was necessary as Stavely sighed and returned to the small trunk, rattling the lock to no avail.

Faro said, 'She would carry the key in her reticule.'

Aware that this was the one essential item without which no woman ever travelled, near or far, both men searched, but there was no evidence of a reticule.

Stavely turned to Faro, 'So where is it, then? It wasn't with her clothes when we found them. Hardly an article a lady would wish to carry on a moonlight bathe. But then, nor is she likely to go for a swim without removing her boots.'

There had been no moon, just a bolstering fog and Stavely's attempt at humour took on a grisly significance.

'You were talking to her, Faro – did you not observe anything?'

Faro shook his head. 'I did notice her boots, which looked very delicate and expensive. Her hands were free but the reticule could have been concealed under that voluminous travelling cloak. Perhaps a little old-fashioned now, but some are still provided with secret pockets for ladies to conceal their jewels and money. A precaution dating from the time before railway trains, when carriages were held up by highwaymen.'

Stavely stared. 'We never had anything like that here in Orkney. Smugglers, yes, but highwaymen . . .' he shook his head in disbelief.

Faro was thinking ahead. Under Stavely's watchful gaze, he looked into the wardrobe and, withdrawing a dress, decided that the shapeless one they had found more resembled a nightgown. With no knowledge of ladies' fashions he concluded that it must be the latest Paris mode.

He said, 'It is most unlikely that she drowned, but there is another alternative.'

Stavely regarded him sharply. 'See what you mean. I'm thinking the very same. She could have been abducted and her kidnapper has the reticule in his possession.'

With another attempt at lightening the situation with a mite of nervous humour, he grinned. 'Seal king wouldn't have much use for that in his kingdom under the waves.' Then grimly, 'Kidnapping is something we must keep closely in mind, and if that is the case, then we'll be hearing soon enough. A ransom note delivered to Scarthbreck. After all, she is an heiress, a valuable commodity.'

There was only one drawback to that theory. Why should a kidnapper strip her down to her underclothes and leave her outer garments neatly piled on the shore? Faro felt all indications were meant to suggest to the finders that she had walked into the sea and disappeared.

And the question was there – a legend which no one really believed, but which obstinately refused to be dismissed. It hung in the air unspoken, while the rest of the day passed in great activity, now stretching far beyond Scarthbreck.

The island had been alerted with its own particular method of conveying gossip and news. And this was sensational news. Ten years after Thora Claydon's mysterious disappearance into the seal king's kingdom under the waves, another young girl had disappeared at almost the same spot.

Speculation was rife. Thora had survived, had reappeared walking along the shore, lost and bewildered, in the very clothes she had been wearing, with that missing year and a day blanked out of memory. Soon she would marry her faithful fiancé, Dave Claydon, who had waited so patiently, and the couple would live a perfectly normal, but sadly childless, island life.

The question in everyone's mind now was, would Celia Prentiss-Grant also survive to return and live a perfectly normal life as the heiress of Scarthbreck?

But this time the seal king's bride had left her clothes behind, an awkward matter for the police to explain, especially to her parents.

Stavely said sternly, 'We must keep this to ourselves. It must not be made public, at all costs. Once the newspapers get hold of that abandoned clothes story, can you imagine the whispers among the island's salacious-minded citizens? Calendars will be consulted and a lookout kept for the anniversary of her disappearance.'

He shuddered. 'The curiosity must have been

enough ten years ago. But she wasn't practically naked. This time I can see a great crowd gathering to watch a young woman walk out of the sea in her underwear. Practically an occasion for selling tickets,' he added grimly.

It was an image to toy with in a society where clothes were rarely discarded except in the privacy of the marital bedroom. Even then not always, as most children were conceived under a modest sheltering of bedclothes. As for undergarments, they were a luxury reserved for rich folk.

There was a stir in the newspaper office too. The weekly edition was due to be published on the day following Celia Prentiss-Grant's disappearance and Jimmy Traill was grateful indeed for a truly new and sensational headline.

On his way to the scene of the disappearance, he appeared at the servants' lodge and Faro wasn't entirely surprised to see him. It was difficult to know which was more breathless, Jimmy or his exhausted horse, which had been ridden hard from Kirkwall.

'Glad to find you, Faro. Right on the spot where it all happened. Have you a story for me?'

Endeavouring to calm the newspaperman down by offering him a cup of tea in Mary's kitchen, Faro related the arranged story that the girl had disappeared without trace, omitting any mention of the abandoned clothes.

Jimmy shook his head vigorously. Snapping his notebook shut, he gave Faro a delighted smile. 'Splendid, splendid. This is just what our readers will love. The seal king legend revived once more in full detail. Something to give them the shivers.'

As he departed for the shore to take a closer look at the scene, Faro closed the door on him, realising that in the forthcoming edition of the newspaper the seal king would receive more than his fair share of gratuitous publicity.

Jimmy had excelled himself, and even he was unprepared for the immediate outcry from readers who believed every word written in the press was gospel truth.

They demanded that all seals be killed immediately. Had seals been capable of reading newspapers they would have found this very offensive indeed.

As for Stavely, he had problems of his own concerning the nocturnal activities of his son. Ed had not returned from the evening stroll with his parents, announcing that he had other plans, namely that he wanted to see some action. They heard him come in very late, stumbling about in the dark as he went to the bedroom he was sharing with his uncle Hal.

At breakfast the next morning, he failed to appear and Hal, who Stavely decided was never a good influence on his nephew, made light of it, and said laughingly that he had probably met some of the local farmers' lads and had too much to drink.

'Lads of that age, what can you expect?' he added. 'We all have to sow our wild oats when we get the chance.'

Sowing wild oats was one thing but Ed had not shown the slightest interest in Miss Celia. His boorish behaviour was hardly within the bounds of politeness. A consoling thought, but Lily, gathering Ed's clothes to wash, discovered a bloodstained shirt.

Thinking that he had fallen down, poor lad, she asked anxiously, 'Did you hurt yourself last night?'

He looked at her in amazement and said, 'Of course not, Ma.'

She held out the shirt and he shrugged. 'Bit of a tussle, my nose must have been bleeding.'

And when his father heard that story, he was a very unhappy man indeed.

CHAPTER TEN

In the quiet of his own room, wondering how long he could evade his mother's gloomy and tearful speculations, Faro sat down grimly to consider the events of the last twenty-four hours. Sticking to his usual procedure, he made a careful list containing everything known about victim and suspects, in the hope that by so doing it might also reveal the inescapable fact that for every crime there must be a motive.

First of all, if Celia was the victim, why? He dismissed suicide. She might have removed the cloak, although it could have been useful, as two heavy stones in the pockets would keep her from floating to the surface again. It was doubtful, however, that she would have removed all but her underwear, and the neatly folded clothes did not suggest a sudden unpremeditated impulse by a passing rapist or the actions of a kidnapper intent on ransom.

Without knowledge of any kind regarding the Prentiss-Grants, the facts thus far simply failed to make any sense of the girl's disappearance. With a sigh of exasperation, he laid down the pen and, blessed with an extraordinary retentive memory, he went over every item of Celia's brief conversation with him, in the hope he might remember any remark which might hold some significance.

He could think of none. Only one fact was predominant. Although she was beautiful, young and rich with, as Stavely had indicated, the world at her feet, Faro had sensed flaws, an underlying vague discontent and frustration with her life of luxury, which might in time become rebellion.

Even that short acquaintance had revealed that she was on the threshold of a new womankind, bred by the industrial revolution in the nineteenth century, a growing army rebelling against the tyrannical trappings of male-dominated centuries, where daughters in rich homes were on sale to the highest bidder in the marriage marketplace.

Faro's knowledge of Lizzie's tragic background,

and his recent encounter in England with the bohemian life of artists and models, had given him greater understanding of a situation which seemed to the average man quite out of the bounds of decency.

If this could be related to Celia's disappearance – neither suicide, nor kidnapping – was she merely determined to go against some plan for her future which had set her into violent opposition with her parents? Although this was the most logical reason for her hasty departure from London, alone, the scene of abandoned clothes by the shore hit a more sinister note.

The question remained, why had she chosen to return to Scarthbreck? It held no magic for her, and the fact she had returned hinted at a strong personal attachment to someone who lived here. And as she was but eighteen years old, this had to be kept secret at all cost from her parents.

Again that led to the abandonment of her clothes, which refused to fit any logical theory beyond going for a swim and failing to return, the obvious reason too dreadful to dwell upon.

What about the missing reticule? Why was it not with her clothes? It could, of course, have started off that way but had been removed by some passer-by. However, bearing in mind the appalling weather, a casual evening stroller with dishonest impulses seemed unlikely.

And at the back of his mind, still obstinately refusing to be dismissed, the shadow of a legend.

The coincidence of Thora Claydon and the seal king.

The only difference was that she had returned wearing clothes identical to those she had on the night she disappeared.

Frustrated, he pushed aside the list and stared out of the window to be rewarded by the bleak prospect of sea and sky united in an indivisible grey line, a landscape devoid of all colour, as gloomy and solemn as his own thoughts.

With the instincts of a born detective he loved a mystery, but preferably one in which he was not already marked down and firmly fixed as the prime suspect. Perhaps at this very moment, he thought grimly, the sergeant was also making a list of his own, headed Constable Faro.

In that supposition Faro was wrong. Although he was the only suspect, Stavely was at that moment absorbed by problems relating to his own, and the terrible thought in the back of his mind that refused to be banished was that Ed also had those vital missing hours to account for. Although he had appeared so disinterested in the girl, Stavely realised that he did not know his son in the slightest. Being a young male, had his lusts been aroused at the sight of the pretty girl, whose presence he appeared to ignore?

Had Ed returned to the shore, lain in wait?

That bloodstained shirt refused to be ignored.

Stavely shuddered, but resolved that whatever Ed had done, the world would never know that Sergeant Stavely's wayward son also had hours unaccounted for on that fatal night. And as far as he was concerned, Constable Jeremy Faro would remain the prime suspect.

There was one other. What of Lily's younger brother, Hal, who was not at home when they and the three girls returned? They did not hear him come in, and although Stavely had enquired politely as to whether he had a good night out, this had been met by a sullen silence.

Hal's croft was also accessible from the shore, and dismally he wondered if he had two additional suspects, motives unknown, concerned in Miss Celia's disappearance?

To tell the truth, he had never liked his young brother-in-law, who was sly and vain, with no intentions of getting married and settling down. Occasionally he heard the two young men sniggering together (revealing a lighter side to Ed's character), which was a surprise, as he was normally so dour and surly with his parents. But Stavely feared that it boded ill, and that Hal was a bad influence, urging them to let Ed work on the croft with him instead of joining the police or becoming apprenticed to a lucrative trade.

Faro heard his mother's footsteps. Any moment now she would appear, with the inevitable consequence of having to listen to her frantic recapitulation of the last twenty-four hours.

Determined to avoid the encounter, he thought about Inga St Ola. If there was one solitary blessing in disguise in this whole sorry business, a few extra days confined to Scarthbreck meant that he could see her again.

At that moment it was what he most needed, her practical sensible approach, and he had a sudden longing to listen to her version of the disappearance of Celia Prentiss-Grant.

Making a noiseless exit from his room, with a sigh of relief he managed to slip out of the lodge unnoticed, although fully expecting to hear his mother's voice behind him as he hurried down to Spanish Cove.

As he approached the long dismal street, he was surprised and not best pleased to see a handsome young man emerging from the house where Inga lived. With a sudden pang of jealousy he recognised the ferryman, Amos Flett, who, turning his head in Faro's direction, shouted a cheery greeting as he ambled away down the road towards Stromness.

Inga was home. She was delighted to see him and the Orkney chair was empty.

'Where's Baubie?'

'Just a couple of doors away. Taking care of the old fisherman's wife. She has bronchitis and is receiving some of Baubie's special remedies.' Taking his hand, she smiled. 'Do y'know, I was wondering how I could find an excuse to call on you, without encountering your ma.' With a quizzical look, she added, 'I am not her favourite person. So sit down and tell me anything you know about our missing heiress.'

Pulling up a stool alongside, she regarded him intently. 'Isn't all this perfectly awful? Now the island is swimming with stories, all these hints about the seal king and how Thora Harbister disappeared in exactly the same circumstances ten years ago.'

She paused. 'However, apart from it being Lammastide, the whole thing, in my opinion, is not only sheer coincidence but sheer nonsense. I don't believe a word of this seal king story – never have – but some folk here will believe anything.' A sigh and she added, 'As you are well aware, you have to be away on the mainland for a bit to see things in the right perspective. I've only been away once in my whole life, the year after you left, and although I longed for home, when I came back, I'd had time to recognise the flaws.'

Pausing, she glanced towards the window, as if seeing for a moment that other world, then turning again she smiled at him. 'There has to be a better theory than a superstitious legend. I'm sure you already have come to some sensible conclusions about that. So tell me – what do you think happened?' And, chin on hand in a well-remembered pose, she waited patiently for his response.

'I agree with you about the seal king theory. But what you don't know is that I had met her that evening, just hours before – quite by accident. I was walking along the shore.'

He was rather pleased that Inga's benign expression changed fleetingly to one of jealousy, and for a moment he wanted to divert the conversation to the subject of Amos Flett.

'Go on,' she was saying. 'This should be interesting. You'd just met, so what did you talk about?'

Once again, Faro went over the details of that conversation, and in truth it sounded a little banal as Inga interrupted somewhat impatiently, 'There's nothing new there; everyone here knows all about the Prentiss-Grants and that Miss Celia is nothing more than a rather spoilt only child. But that doesn't tell us why she came back suddenly to what, by all accounts, wasn't her favourite place on earth and then promptly vanished.'

Frowning she added, 'There's nothing she said to you to indicate what she had in mind, was there? Although one would hardly expect such revelations, even to a lad she found so attractive that she had to force her company upon him.'

Faro made a grimace and Inga shrugged. 'I just get the impression, helped on, I must confess, by local gossip, that she was used to getting her own way. Every shop in Stromness and Kirkwall will tell you that from childhood Miss Celia was a little madam. Seems to me most likely that she had come back all the way from London, alone, because of a violent disagreement with her parents.'

As those were Faro's own thoughts, he told her about the clothes Stavely had discovered.

'Now, that is bizarre. What! Abandon a lovely fur cloak – a pretty dress and petticoats.' Inga's shocked expression said that her reverence for elegant clothes which she could never afford was deeply outraged. 'Had she gone into the sea in her boots? No one ever does that. That's awful.'

Boots were a rare luxury almost unknown among crofters. As a schoolboy Faro had gone barefoot in summer and was surprised to see boots being worn by working folks in Edinburgh, while island men and women fortunate enough to own a pair treasured them greatly, their survival watched in eager anticipation of being handed down to less fortunate members of the family.

'She apparently did keep on her undergarments,' Faro muttered.

Inga laughed. 'You should see your face, Jeremy. No need to look so embarrassed about under-drawers, most of us would wear them every day, if we could afford them.' She thought for a moment. 'But it does seem odd, her cloak and all lying there neatly piled together, just as if she had suddenly decided to have a swim. But surely not on a night like that.'

'There's something else,' Faro said. 'The sergeant and I went back to Scarthbreck and searched her bedroom – looking for anything that might give us a clue. Her reticule was missing . . .'

'Now, that *is* odd. I can't imagine any woman . . . specially one like her . . . Wherever she went, we can be sure it went with her,' she said, shaking her head. 'That definitely puts an end to any ideas about an evening swim. Was she carrying it? Maybe a man wouldn't notice.'

'I would,' Faro said indignantly. 'But she could have been carrying anything over her arm under that cloak.'

'And even our weather could hardly justify a fur-lined cloak in August,' Inga said.

Faro frowned. 'Know anything about Paris fashions this year?'

Inga laughed. 'Wish I did. Why?'

'Just the gown we found.'

After he described it, she said, 'That shapeless style is very old-fashioned, belongs to the days of the Prince Regent. Very useful for pregnant ladies.' Her eyes widened. 'Could that have been the reason? Did she look . . . well, large?'

That was another factor at the back of his mind and it accounted for the shapeless gown. Shaking his head he said, 'The cloak concealed her shape rather well. You may be right.' Pausing, he added desperately, 'Do you think she might have been kidnapped?'

'Kidnapped! Here! Where everyone knows everyone's business, even what they had for supper last night?' She laughed. 'I think that theory is very doubtful.'

'That's the sergeant's theory.'

'You don't surprise me. He's not an islander.'

'He thinks the next thing will be a ransom when her parents arrive.'

Inga laughed even more at that. 'If the kidnapper is a local man, then everyone who knows him will want a share in it.' She paused,

139

thoughtful for a moment. 'But I'd be prepared to stake a fortune, if I had one, that there is a man somewhere in all this, and a young woman in the family way.' And nodding triumphantly, 'Yes, now that makes sense, doesn't it? A young man, much more substantial than the seal king. I'll bet her parents have found out, and for once they aren't prepared to let her marry him. As for a baby . . .'

That was a distinct possibility, Faro thought, until Inga added, 'Of course, I can't think of anyone in this area who would have the temerity to court Miss Celia, much less propose marriage. No one here has that kind of money to support such a wife. So who was she running away from – some man in London? In other words, was she seeking refuge here?'

Again he shook his head and Inga said, 'I'll keep you informed of what happens. Such a shame you can't stay and sort it out.'

'That's where you're mistaken. I am instructed by Sergeant Stavely that, as the last person to see her before she vanished, I am to remain, until she turns up. Alive, or . . . please God not dead.'

Inga frowned. 'Is that usual?'

'Yes, quite usual.'

'But you're a policeman.'

'Makes no difference.'

Inga looked at him sharply. 'Are you telling me that he thinks you did away with Miss Celia? That is incredible.'

'He saw us walking together that evening,' Faro explained, 'and so did one of the Scarthbreck maids.'

'But you went back to the house with your ma.'

Faro shook his head, explained about the missing telescope and how he had returned to search for it.

Inga's laugh was somewhat shaky, but she took his hand, held it firmly, 'Honestly, Jeremy, this is just plain daft.' She stood up, smiled and said, 'Sorry, you'll have to go now. Have a client coming any minute now for a fitting.' And kissing him lightly, 'Don't worry, there must be an innocent explanation and I'm sure you will find it.'

Leaving her, Faro was far from sure. He was halfway back along the road when he realised that he had forgotten to remark very tactfully on her acquaintance with Amos Flett, who did not fit into the role of a client coming for a fitting.

The idea amused him and he decided there would doubtless be other occasions as, at that moment, he had to leap aside to let the Scarthbreck carriage pass.

Celia's parents had arrived, and he caught a glimpse of Stavely sitting alongside. Hopefully they would provide the key to the mystery of their daughter's sudden arrival and why she had abruptly vanished.

CHAPTER ELEVEN

Judging by his mother's agitated manner as Faro entered the servants' lodge, the interview with the Prentiss-Grants promised to be painful.

'You're to see them immediately.' As she spoke she looked him over carefully, assessing what sort of an impression her son would make. It took him back to schooldays, restraining herself from brushing his hair back and making sure his clothes were neat and tidy.

Walking over to the house she whispered by way of consolation, 'You've nothing to fear. They've been talking to the sergeant. He'll have put in a good word for you.'

Regarding her anxious expression, he said, 'I hope they didn't attach any blame to you, Ma.'

'Of course not. I could hardly keep Miss Celia in chains. Besides, I was taken aback – we all were – when she arrived home like that without warning. I thought something dreadful must have happened, but the other servants made light of it, the maids said she was always having rows with her parents.'

Outside the dining room, she tapped on the door. Called upon to enter, Faro observed that Stavely was still present, or almost present, lurking in the shadows, doubtless to recover from his share of the interrogation which had begun in Kirkwall and carried on relentlessly during the carriage drive to Scarthbreck.

The Prentiss-Grants were seated together on one side of the dining table and looked up briefly, the only acknowledgement of his presence. No greeting, no attempt to shake hands or put him at his ease. Nor was he invited to take a chair, but was instead made to stand before them like a servant who had misbehaved, or worse, as a prisoner in the dock, or a condemned criminal – a scene with which he was familiar in Edinburgh courts.

He glanced towards Stavely seeking oblivion in the background. At least he had been offered a chair, presumably as a mark of his rank, having superiority over a mere constable.

Sir Arnold leant forward, a formidable

figure, large in girth, red-faced with a bristling moustache and the booming voice of a military disciplinarian.

'We are given to understand from Sergeant Stavely that you were the last person to see our daughter before she chose to disappear.'

Faro decided that the choice of words conveyed that they believed she was still alive and well, as he replied, 'We met while I was walking along the shore earlier that evening.'

'We?' the voice boomed.

'We met,' Faro repeated.

'A prearranged meeting?'

Faro suppressed a sigh of exasperation. This opening gambit told of things to come, and they were not going his way. Nor did he correct Sir Arnold by saying that, in fact, the last person to see her was not himself but some person or persons unknown who had abducted her, considering it was unlikely that she had gone for a swim and drowned. He also refrained from mentioning she must have first removed most of her clothes.

At Sir Arnold's side, his wife cleared her throat, an obvious overture to saying her piece. Millicent Prentiss-Grant was a slighter version of her husband. According to her portrait on the staircase, she had once been a renowned beauty, or else had the advantage of a singularly imaginative artist. Relentless time had done the rest, sharpening soft contours into severe angles, replacing a once-smiling countenance with a formidable air and a toned-down, but extremely harsh and shrill, version of her husband's booming voice.

Leaning forward in an attempt to intimidate Faro from beneath haughtily raised eyebrows, she demanded, 'Are we to understand that you were acquainted with our daughter?'

Faro shook his head. 'No. Not until the time we met on the shore.'

'We take it that you had not been formally introduced.' Her tone was icy, disapproving.

Faro looked her straight in the eye. 'No, madam, I had not had the pleasure. I should point out that, as I live in Edinburgh, a formal introduction was most unlikely as I had only recently arrived on a visit to my mother, your housekeeper.'

This lack of a formal introduction weighed heavily against the constable. The couple's exchanged glances seemed to declare the fellow some sort of a bounder, and a fortune-hunter too. If such an emotion were possible, they regarded him with renewed distaste.

Lady Millicent's lip curled. 'So we are to understand that you were out walking and approached a young lady who was a complete stranger.'

'Not quite, madam. The young lady approached me, and as we were heading in the same direction, we walked along the shore together.'

Sir Arnold's eyes rolled heavenward in disgust and his fist banged down on the table. 'I find it very hard to believe that our daughter would associate with a total stranger in such a fashion.'

The look that accompanied this remark condemned Faro into the lowest ranks of seducers. In his defence he said, 'I am a detective constable, sir, perhaps she felt it was safe to talk to me.'

'So you talked too, did you?'

'We did indeed.'

'And may we enquire what was the nature of this talk?'

'We talked of casual matters of little consequence. She wished to talk to someone. I decided she was lonely.'

'You decided she was lonely.' The words came slowly and heavily in shocked comprehension from Sir Arnold. As his wife tut-tutted, Faro said, 'Yes, sir, that was my impression.'

The fist banged down again. Lady Millicent shrilled, 'Your impression, indeed. The very idea!'

Sir Arnold leant forward and took a better look at Faro. 'May we ask what gives you the right to express such an opinion?' he roared. 'Miss Celia would never confide in a stranger, the idea is beyond decency.'

His wife also leant forward, her manner threatening. 'And what, may we enquire, did she confide in you?' Faro detected a note of anxiety as she added, 'We cannot imagine that she informed you of her intentions.'

Her husband's hand was on her arm, a warning gesture.

'Not at all. Our brief conversation concerned the difference regarding life in London and Orkney.'

'She did not tell you the reason for her return?' Lady Millicent insisted.

'No, madam, but in my official capacity I was about to ask you the same question.'

A moment's silence, a look of bafflement exchanged between the couple. Heads shaken, a hand raised in an abrupt and unmistakeable signal of dismissal.

Resisting the temptation to slam the door behind him, Faro left the dining room aware that he had learnt nothing. Regarding the abandoned clothes at the scene of their daughter's mysterious disappearance, he wondered if the Prentiss-Grants were aware of this bizarre circumstance.

He wondered if Stavely had brushed that

matter aside as too indelicate or embarrassing a subject to mention to the girl's parents.

Outside the house, there was no sign of Stavely, who had seized the opportunity to slip out unnoticed. Instead, he could be found comfortably seated in Mary Faro's kitchen behind a steaming cup of tea and a plate of freshly baked scones.

Stavely looked up and said defensively, 'Before you say a word, it wasn't a pleasant experience for me either. I hadn't met either of them before and I can tell you, the Orkney Constabulary, and myself in particular, were made to feel personally responsible that his daughter had vanished.'

'Any mention of those clothes she was not wearing?'

Still smarting under the discomfort of that first meeting and a carriage drive where the discomfort was not completely due to the reckless speed of the horses, Stavely shook his head vigorously. 'I considered things were bad enough without that.'

He pushed across the table a large photograph that Sir Arnold had removed from its frame. 'We have to find an artist to copy this. They want a copy printed in *The Orcadian*, and on posters displayed everywhere across the island. With a reward offered for information. Immediately.'

The photograph was of Celia, looking even younger than her eighteen years.

Faro said, 'She hasn't been missing for three days yet.'

Stavely shrugged. 'I agree. She might walk in with a perfectly feasible explanation. And what fools the police will look then.' He shook his head. 'His nibs has a theory. He firmly believes that she is being held somewhere and this offer of a reward for information will scare off her kidnappers and put an end to their hopes of a ransom.'

'I don't like it. I have known of such cases where kidnappers have lost their nerve and have killed off their victim to conceal their identity,' Faro said, pushing the photo back towards Stavely, who grimaced.

'Ours is not to reason why. And in this case, it's yours to deal with.'

'And how am I to do that, pray?'

'Take this photo into Kirkwall, find an artist.'

'Who?'

Mary Faro was clearing the table. She laughed. 'You're in luck, dear.'

Stavely grinned. 'Your mother has just informed me that there's one living in her house in Kirkwall.' He stood up. 'No time for delay. Ask him to make a quick sketch and take it into the newspaper office. They'll get posters

150

printed. Time is of the essence. Be brisk.'

While Faro was wondering how he was to get to Kirkwall on the instant, as it were, his mother reappeared from her bedroom, wearing her cloak.

'Her ladyship has some urgent shopping and I have to collect her pearls which have been restrung. A minute, while I collect her list.'

Watching her hurry towards the house, Faro asked, 'Did you get anything useful from your interview, Sergeant?'

'Nary a word, only a strong feeling that I wasn't being told everything and that the main clue was being deliberately withheld.'

'And?'

'They weren't going to confide in me, a mere policeman. But from what they did not say, I would be willing to bet that there had been one unholy row before she flounced out and took ship to Orkney.'

'But why? I got the impression she was rather bored with the island, and for a young girl who had never left home alone, the decision to take ship required organisation. We can only conclude that there was a very strong reason for her flight.'

Stavely seized the suggestion eagerly. 'I've been thinking the very same. A reason to be kept secret at all costs.'

That secret could be an unwanted pregnancy, Faro thought, as Stavely went on excitedly, 'I'd be prepared to bet my last shilling that young love's dream is involved here. That's the obvious answer.'

Outside, the carriage was waiting and Mary had not yet reappeared.

Stavely looked round, a puzzled frown, 'Who on earth would she find, I mean, of her own class, here at Scarthbreck?'

'I don't think we need worry ourselves about that, Sergeant. Young men, handsome but humble, have their appeal to rich young women, and there is the added thrill of crossing the social barrier. It isn't unknown for girls like Celia to enjoy such dangerous liaisons, often with unforeseen and terrible consequences beyond their imagination.'

As he said the words he found himself remembering the *cause célèbre* of Madeleine Smith. Accused of poisoning her lowly lover, she had escaped the gallows with a Scottish 'not proven' verdict.

Stavely was silent as Faro continued, 'So where do we go from here?'

'Heaven only knows,' Stavely said sharply, thinking of his own son, who might well fit into such a category. 'But I firmly believe that we can dismiss suicide. Self-destruction does not fit in with what we are learning about a spoilt, rich, young girl.'

'I agree. Those abandoned clothes were just a cruel joke left to confuse us – and scare her parents. The next thing will doubtless be a very large ransom note.'

'So you believe she was kidnapped?'

'Not necessarily,' said Faro, 'but there will be a ransom note, I am sure of that.' From what he had deduced so far, there were two possibilities. First, that she had a lover in London, was pregnant and had taken refuge in Orkney; second, that her disappearance was part of an audacious plan to foil her parents and get her own way.

Was the poster of the missing girl, with a substantial reward for information, only an attempt by her father to foil kidnappers? Faro was certain the father knew a lot more than he was prepared to admit regarding her precipitous flight from London.

Stavely's sigh was that of a very worried man. 'As far as I'm concerned, we can't get to the bottom of this case soon enough. I am to stay here – official orders from Kirkwall – on the spot where it all happened, to conduct my enquiries.'

Constables were already conducting an inch-by-inch search from the shore to Scarthbreck's extensive gardens. Divers were out in the skerry.

He shook his head. 'We're a law-abiding lot on the whole, and bearing in mind our lads' experience has been limited to dealing with only minor crimes, like poaching, drunken fights and a bit of smuggling, I fear this operation will take some considerable effort, as well as being a complete waste of time.'

He paused and added, 'As for you, Faro, arrangements have been made with your lot in Edinburgh to extend your stay accordingly.' He did not need to add that, as far as the police were concerned, Faro, who had been seen walking with the missing girl, was the prime suspect.

'Very well.' Faro had his own reasons for wishing to extend his visit, and this unexpected trip to Kirkwall opened unexpected possibilities of meetings with Inga.

Stavely gave him a resentful look. 'All right for you to sound so cheerful, you're not a family man. You've no one depending on you,' he grumbled. 'At least you'll have a pleasant environment, well looked after by your mother, who is an excellent cook.' Wistfully remembering the plate of scones he had depleted with considerable enthusiasm, he added with distaste, 'I'll have to stay with my brother-in-law Hal, who lives almost entirely on porridge, cheese and ale.'

Mary Faro appeared, bustling down the front steps. 'Sorry to keep you waiting. Her ladyship seized the opportunity to compile a list of items urgently required,' she added, wearily considering the magnitude of the shopping list involved. Then turning to the sergeant, 'Give me that note for Mrs Stavely. I'll drop it off.'

Relieved at not having to inform Lily of his prolonged stay and suffer her inevitable angry reactions, handing it over, he said, 'Collect a clean shirt, if you please. I hope I'll only need the one.' He sighed deeply. 'Lily won't be pleased by this piece of news.'

Nor was he pleased at the prospect of sleeping in Hal's house as, sparse diet apart, its amenities were not even basic, sorely lacking a woman's touch or any sense of order. Even to the most unobservant male eye, it was an uncomfortable, chilly and dirty hovel and after years of being cared for with all possible devotion by a loving partner, who was also a careful and efficient housewife, Stavely braced himself to endure what he prayed would be only a very temporary separation.

This enforced stay did mean he could keep a sharp eye on Ed's activities, so slothful and boorish at home, but always willing and eager to escape to his young uncle, on the excuse of helping him on the croft.

For his own relief and satisfaction, he hoped to find out exactly where Ed and Hal had been during those missing hours of Celia's disappearance and that they had an alibi.

He was acutely aware that any involvement by members of his own family in such a scandal would have grave personal issues and put an end to his hopes of promotion, disappointing Lily whose heart had been long set upon it. However, that would be minimal compared with her distress as a doting mother, in whose eyes her wayward only son could do no wrong.

CHAPTER TWELVE

In the carriage, Mary Faro's distress over the missing girl had given over to preoccupation on how she was to manage her mistress's shopping list, with items scattered the length and breadth of every shop in Kirkwall.

As they reached the outskirts and prepared to climb the hill to her cottage, she looked at the photograph of Celia.

'Monsieur Latour should manage a copy of that easily. I understand he has exhibitions in Paris and London. Let's hope he's in. He could be miles away on a nice sunny day like this, calm too, no wind to blow the easel away. Just perfect for one of his seascapes.'

Outside the cottage where Faro had grown

up, she gazed up at the windows anxiously. 'I'm comfortable enough in Scarthbreck and I should be grateful enjoying all the little luxuries, but it isn't home and I love my own little place. I was lucky finding someone keen to rent it. The extra money will be so useful, and it's not good for the house to be empty, could get damp. Monsieur Latour has promised to take good care of it for me. Such a nice chap, he is, for a foreigner.'

Faro smiled. 'Tell me about him, Ma.'

'Emil Latour is quite famous, lives in the Latin Quarter in Paris. Always wanted to visit Orkney. Speaks very good English too. Oh, you'll like him.'

Faro, who did not have his mother's capacity for trust and instant rapport with strangers, was not quite so sure about that.

Mary hesitated at the door, her wry glance saying that she was feeling foolish. This was her own home, after all.

A sigh of relief at the sound of footsteps as the artist opened the door.

His eyebrows raised in sharp surprise and perhaps even dismay, Faro thought, at the meaning of this unexpected visit from his landlady. However, he recovered quickly, and gallantly bowed over her hand, enquiring politely after her health and well-being.

Faro decided that Emil Latour was everyone's

idea of a French artist, from the neatly trimmed moustache and beard to the beret and paint-stained smock. He ushered Mary Faro into her parlour with all manner of flattering compliments in flawless English, which pleased her exceedingly, and did at least help with an explanation for this intrusion and the urgency of what was involved.

Introducing her son so proudly as a detective constable, Faro produced the photograph and handed it over to the Frenchman who frowned, considering it silently for a moment.

Although no doubt curious, politeness forbade him enquiring why a policeman should wish for this sketch. He glanced somewhat warily at Faro, nodded and said, 'A little time only. You will wait, perhaps.'

The parlour was now his studio, an easel in one corner, but although his garb brought back memories of the Pre-Raphaelite Brotherhood and Faro's most recent encounter, there were little of the smells of oil paint and linseed he associated with William Morris's Red House and its artist residents.

In fact, Latour's temporary studio was surprisingly orderly, everything neat and tidy, suggesting to Faro that, if he was an example of the Bohemians across the Channel, whose lifestyle was regarded as questionable and highly improper, then they were considerably better organised than their British equivalents.

Latour pinned up the photograph to a sheet of paper on the easel, and drawing rapidly, a life-size sketch of Celia's head emerged. Mary Faro ignored his invitation to take a seat and took the opportunity to wander around the room in a wistful search of her favourite things: a monstrous clock and two oversize florid vases, deplored by Faro but of sentimental value, bequeathed to her by an ancient aunt.

Faro glanced over a stack of paintings and went to her side. She was very still, looking at one now banished into a dark corner. Touching his arm, she whispered almost tearfully, 'Remember that day, Jeremy?'

Silent, he nodded. His father, Magnus, had been a keen amateur watercolourist, a talent, alas, which Faro had not inherited. One glorious summer's day, visiting a fisherman cousin at the north of the island, they had rowed across to Egilsay.

Magnus Faro had always wanted to visit the island where the saint after whom he was named was martyred.

Finding a suitable viewpoint of the twelfth-century remains of the round-towered church, he immediately set up his easel and paints. Mary, young, happy and laughing, had taken eight-year-old Jeremy's hand to explore rock pools and set out the picnic.

Jeremy Faro would never forget that day on Egilsay. The church fascinated him. He was drawn into its shadows, watched the tiny figure of his father painting, engrossed. Then the scene suddenly changed, as if for a brief moment the veil of time was whipped aside.

What he was witnessing terrified him. His cries set his parents rushing to his side, picnic and watercolour forgotten. Had he been climbing again, fallen down, hurt himself? He could only shake his head. He could not tell them, could not explain that for a moment the present had vanished, spilt back seven hundred years.

They wouldn't let it rest. They had to know. Sternly they demanded he tell them the truth. And as lies were something he had been brought up to regard as hell's greatest sin, he gasped out incoherently, sobbing that he had seen, as if it was happening now, the moment of the saint's murder re-enacted before his eyes.

And he was white-faced, shivering despite the warm sunshine. He clung to them, holding their hands. 'I thought I'd lost you both – I was away back there' – he pointed – 'long ago. I wanted to come back – to now, to be with you.' A shudder. 'Safe with you, Pa. You wouldn't let them harm me.'

That night in his temporary cot at the foot of their bed in the cousin's croft, he heard their whispers in the darkness. His mother's tearful, 'I don't like this. It's not right, not Christian.'

His father's soothing murmur. 'He's just a child, Mary. Such things happen.'

A horrified, 'To you?'

'No, no, never to me.'

A pause, then slowly, 'Then it's all Sibella's fault.'

'How could that be, Mary? That's nonsense.'

'Is it? Is that why I've never had another bairn? Just the one, just Jeremy.'

'We tried,' Magnus whispered. 'It just wasn't God's will. At least we weren't childless. We must be grateful. We had Jeremy, a precious son.'

'One bairn, when I've longed for more, waited – for a lass. It just wasn't fair, everyone round us having bairn after bairn, year after year. It was all Sibella's fault,' she repeated.

'No, Mary. You must never believe that. He never knew her.'

'I made sure of that. But the blood, the selkie blood – it's there in him.'

Young as he was, Jeremy knew that Sibella Scarth, his grandmother, was the selkie who died, who his mother refused to talk about.

What he had overheard that night stayed

with him and made him resolve to be very careful in future, for Egilsay was not to be his only experience of such moments.

Once he saw the Viking ships approaching St Margaret's Hope, heard the yelling, the laughter, the drumbeat of the oars. In Edinburgh as well as Orkney, no place was too far for selkie blood to travel. It was as if, for an instant, he stepped off the circle that was time and found himself in a world lost for ever. These instances were less frequent when he left childhood, but they still lurked, sometimes just an eye-blink away.

And although the past no longer recreated itself in tangible scenes, the feeling of danger, of awareness, was all that remained of his lost-time experiences that he was unable to share with anyone. How could he find the right words? People would think he was mad, and he must be forever vigilant: such imaginings did not befit a policeman.

He knew now that he had only ever encountered two people who he was certain would understand. One was the highly improbable earthbound Inga St Ola who, he felt certain, still revered the pagan gods of Orkney. The other, met recently and briefly, a frail thread that renewed for a moment his link to the selkie world, Baubie Finn.

* * *

Such were his thoughts as he squeezed his mother's hand in recognition of that long-ago day in Egilsay. He returned to his contemplation of works which had replaced his mother's homely and sentimental copies of paintings made famous by Millais and Holman Hunt and on view in almost every home. Copies were now banished to a stack in a dark corner of the room. Faro was surprised that the artist had not also seized the opportunity to add the florid vases to the stack, his finer feelings outraged by their tasteless presence.

He was eager to see his paintings of the islands, the reason for this sojourn in Kirkwall. There were a few rough sketches scattered on the sofa and, disappointed, Faro was still wondering how the artist spent his days. Had he found unexpected diversions and new friends? A few moments later, the poster was ready.

Latour handed it over and Faro said, 'This is excellent. Sir Arnold will be in touch,' he added, although the matter of a fee had not been discussed.

'A pleasure, sir.' A bow. 'I hope this rough sketch will be agreeable.'

'I have been admiring your work,' Faro said rather lamely.

Another bow, vague gestures. 'I prepare for my next exhibition in London.'

The visit was not to be prolonged. Although he was certain that his mother, who addressed the artist as Emil, was disappointed not to be offered the inevitable cup of tea required by traditional Orkney hospitality, they both had much to do.

'How will you get back?' Mary demanded anxiously. 'The carriage will be waiting for me.' And consulting the list withdrawn from her basket, she said, 'But this will take me the rest of the day. Do you want to wait, dear?'

'Don't concern yourself, Ma. I'll find a carter heading in that direction.' And before she could protest he kissed her briefly and hurried in the direction of the newspaper office.

With the poster neatly rolled under his arm, he decided that Latour wasn't strictly truthful, or perhaps he was merely forgetful – one of his works which Faro had seen at the cottage was a copy. Faro was quite sure he had seen the original in Red House, a landscape with figures by Burne-Jones.

By a piece of good fortune, the first person Faro met in *The Orcadian* office was Jimmy, looking more rumpled and dishevelled than ever as he sat at a desk, glowering over tomorrow's copy.

Delighted at this unexpected distraction, he greeted Faro warmly. 'Sit down, sit down.'

And sweeping aside the untidy mass of papers and notes from a chair, he shook his head. 'Bad business, this missing girl. You couldn't have timed it better – you're just the man I want to see.' He looked up eagerly. 'I expect this is in your official line of business. Any news of any kind for the press?'

'Nothing. That's why I'm here,' he added, handing him the poster and a brief résumé of Sir Arnold's wishes and instructions.

Jimmy whistled. 'This is great, absolutely great progress. We'll publish it, of course. What a headline and what a story! Our printers will make copies for posting at all the street corners.' Pausing, he added, 'I take it that you have interviewed the girl's parents.' And tapping his teeth with a pencil he asked, 'Anything quotable for the newspaper?'

'Not really.'

Jimmy frowned. 'That's a pity. Readers are always interested in parents' reactions. Mother's tears, only daughter, that sort of thing. Sure there wasn't anything we could use?' he added wistfully.

'I'm sure.'

'How did you feel about it? Last man to see her . . . well, we hope alive?'

Faro didn't care what that 'last man' angle might imply to readers eager for sensation. He smiled. 'No comment – and even if I had, I'm a policeman, remember; expressing my opinion would be going right against the rules.'

Jimmy sighed. 'I suppose you're right – but between us?' he added eagerly. 'Speaking confidentially?'

Faro refused to be drawn. 'No comment, Jimmy. Absolutely none.'

However, meeting the journalist again, Faro decided to prise out what he might know unofficially regarding Thora and Dave Claydon.

'This new mystery has distracted me temporarily from my original thoughts. You will recall? Reporting on Dave Claydon's accidental drowning to his relative in Edinburgh?'

Jimmy's eyes widened delightedly when Faro said, 'I've been studying the facts and I now suspect a possible crime of greater dimension.'

'Another crime, eh?' Jimmy rubbed his hands together with glee when Faro went on, 'No one has ever explained what happened to the artefacts Dave was carrying when he drowned.'

'Presumably they went down with him.'

'Have you any idea what was involved in this vague description "priceless"?'

Jimmy had the grace to look uncomfortable. 'It's what people like – you know?' Faro didn't and he went on, 'The kind of word that sells newspapers. We didn't know exactly. Dave never said. He made frequent trips to Edinburgh for his job, so presumably he was taking things that had been found to the museum there. The archaeology lads frequently find bits and pieces, like yon brooch and some beads from the Neolithic settlement beside Scarthbreck.' He shrugged. 'Some folk got quite excited about that – might have been from there.'

'What about the Armada galleon?'

Jimmy rubbed his unshaven chin. 'Could well be. All the local lads dive there in the hope of finding buried treasure.'

'Ever find anything?'

'If they do, they keep it dark. Dare say if it's jewellery, something of that sort, they hang on to it and look for a possible buyer.'

'Are there many people on the island with that sort of money?'

'Only one I can think of is Sir Arnold, if he was interested in such things.' He thought for a moment. 'Or the lads might try to sell it abroad. There's always foreign ships come into harbour during the summer.'

'Smugglers, eh?'

Jimmy nodded. 'Unofficially, so we hear.' Pausing, he looked eager again. 'Are you thinking there's a crime involved?'

'I have a feeling that there's some connection between the two young women who vanished at virtually the same spot ten years apart, and that Dave Claydon's name fits into it somewhere.'

'What a story that would make,' Jimmy sighed. 'Pity that Claydon's dead and buried in the local kirkyard and can't tell us what he ever found out about that missing year in his wife's early life. Everyone was surprised when he still married her – now that *did* hit the headlines. Especially as he'd been involved with her older sister.'

'Tell me about her,' said Faro.

'Did my best to get a story out of her. Even went down to the Hope to interview her,' he added regretfully.

'The Hope? Oh, St Margaret's you mean.'

'Aye, that's right. She came back from the mainland, gather she didn't like it much.' And rubbing his chin which sorely lacked the attentions of a razor, his eyes gleamed. 'Wonder if it's worth seeing what she thinks about this coincidence with the Prentiss-Grant girl.'

'She still lives there?'

'As far as I know, yes. Isn't exactly forthcoming, mind you – or so I'm told.'

Faro's thoughts were galloping ahead as Jimmy continued. 'Alike as two peas, apart from one being blonde, the other brunette. Perhaps that's how poor old Dave went astray, couldn't tell them apart either.' He chuckled. 'Still, when

Elsa didn't come to his funeral, folks were a bit shocked, I can tell you. Families come first here. Thought the way he died would have healed the breach and that Thora would have been glad to have a sister's comfort, especially when they had both loved the same man.'

Faro said nothing, but thought that suggestion rather naive. It didn't work like that. All through history, from highest to humblest, records would show that the nearer in blood, the nearer in hate, and that rival siblings could create havoc and family feuds lasting for generations, as well as accounting for a fair number of murders.

Jimmy shrugged. 'Maybe Thora tried. My Auntie Bet's from the Hope. She was a distant relative, a cousin's cousin and the closest the two had to any kin. Very upset about the whole business. Told me the newly-weds came down at least once, presumably to see Elsa – and to make up the quarrel, but Elsa wasn't at home. She obviously didn't want to see her sister and Dave and had cleared off elsewhere to avoid a meeting.'

'Have you ever asked Elsa about her experiences away from the island? That would be a story,' Faro added encouragingly.

'Not much point, folk wouldn't be interested if it wasn't island news. Hardly makes headlines and doesn't sell more newspapers or rocket the circulation figures. Besides, I could hardly ask her why she hadn't been to the funeral, could I?'

'What did your auntie make of it?'

Jimmy shifted uncomfortably. 'Haven't been down since they took her into the asylum a couple of years ago. Went off her head apparently – maybe it's something that runs in the family, like Thora's loss of memory. I hope it's not on my side. The local folk said she never got over Thora's disappearance and was never the same again when she came back and got married.'

He shook his head. 'But I do feel badly about poor old Auntie – guilty, you know. Went to see her once but she hardly recognised me. Just wanted to gabble on about Thora and what a good lass she was. I know I should keep in touch, but well, it's a long way to go and see an auntie who doesn't know who you are. She was the only family I ever had: my folks died of TB when I was a bairn, and Auntie Bet never made any secret of caring more about the two Harbister girls than her own flesh and blood,' he added bitterly.

It was a sad tale in many families with old relatives and no one willing to look after them when they became too much for their neighbours.

Faro understood that Jimmy was hurt by his

aunt's rejection and guessed that he was also keen to avoid any return to the bitterness that must have grown with the passing years as he shrugged and said, 'Thora Claydon is old news and I'd need a proper excuse to give my editor for going down to the Hope to go over all that old ground. It's the wrong time for me to be away, right now. Crucial to be on the spot ready for the Celia Prentiss-Grant story to break,' he added cheerfully.

An urgent call from the inner office had Jimmy scurrying away, shouting over his shoulder, 'If you get any news, I'm first, remember.'

CHAPTER THIRTEEN

During their conversation Faro had already made his decision, he would go to the Hope. Tom, the Scarthbreck coachman, was lingering near the cathedral, smoking his pipe. Faro left a message for his mother not to wait as something had turned up.

He covered the distance to the ferry landing as quickly as he could and was just in time to leap aboard as it moved off, his arm grabbed by one of the passengers.

Amos, at the wheel, shouted a greeting. Faro was surprised to be recognised again, seeing the number of people he ferried back and forth twice a day.

When the passengers were settled, Faro drifted

over and watched Amos negotiate his way out of the harbour. Once safely at sea, the ferryman turned and called cheerfully, 'Enjoying your stay?' He grinned. 'Change from Edinburgh, is it?'

His friendly manner gave Faro an idea. The sea between North and South Ronaldsay was dour and grey, but mercifully calm. When they reached the quay at St Margaret's Hope, Faro lingered, hoping to have a word with Amos after the other passengers departed.

Safely anchored, Amos set down the rope and said, 'Trust it wasn't too rough for you?'

Faro laughed. 'I lived here briefly once upon a time. It's good to come back again.'

Amos shrugged and gave the landscape a bleak look. 'Prefer the bright lights of town, myself.' Then regarding Faro curiously, 'Visiting family, are you?'

'Not really. Just old friends.'

A wry look. 'Rumour has it that you're the young Faro who deserted the island for Edinburgh to be a policeman.'

It was Faro's turn to smile. 'News certainly travels fast.'

'You have no idea, sir,' Amos said. 'Try keeping a secret – not a bit of use, they'll just read your mind.'

A pause and Faro made a decision, saying awkwardly, 'I'm just here out of curiosity. Past memories, that sort of thing.'

'Hope you enjoy them. Last trip back is at six, so you have plenty of time.'

Stepping off the ferry, Faro turned, as if he'd had a last-minute thought, and asked, 'Does Elsa, Thora Claydon's sister, still live here?'

Amos was suddenly very still. 'You know her?'

'Not exactly.'

Amos laughed. 'Thought she'd be a bit old for a young lad's fancy.'

Faro ignored that. 'Still lives here, does she?' he repeated.

Amos stared towards the horizon, considered the anchor rope. 'Have no idea, mate. Ask at the post office. See you later.'

And with that, no longer friendly but somehow cool and dismissive, Amos bent his head and went about the business of collecting money from the waiting passengers.

Faro left the harbour and walked past the tiny house in Front Street where he had lived so briefly as a child. There weren't any memories lingering there apart from riding on his father's shoulders and watching the seals. The place seemed smaller than he remembered, deserted and grey, untouched by sunshine. Its shadows, cold and withdrawn, brought an ominous feeling that his journey had been a waste of time.

At the post office, his question about Elsa Harbister's address was regarded with a disinterested shrug.

'Left here years ago.'

That cleared up one mystery, a valid reason why she hadn't been at Dave Claydon's funeral. Perhaps she didn't even know he was dead. 'Any idea of her last address?'

'Used to live up the hill, yonder. First house past the crossroads, beside the church. Her sister lives in Kirkwall, maybe she could help you.'

With little hope of success, Faro climbed the hill, found the house, and stood outside for a moment. It looked empty, and as he expected from the shuttered windows, there was no response from within.

'Can I help you, sir?'

He turned to see a man watching him from the church door opposite. White-haired and elderly, his occupation denoted by his clerical collar, he gave a gleam of hope and Faro said, 'I was looking for the lady who used to live here, Elsa Harbister.'

'She left the Hope some years ago. And the present tenant is in poor health and now lives with his relatives.'

'Were they acquainted?'

The clergyman looked puzzled; he obviously thought this an odd question. 'I'm not quite sure.'

'I beg your pardon, I was hoping some of Elsa's relatives may still be here,' Faro said bleakly.

'She used to visit a sister – in Kirkwall, I believe. She may be able to tell you more about Elsa.'

A sudden flurry of rain and a sharp wind threatened to close the conversation. The clergyman opened the church door, beckoned him inside, a noticeboard revealing his identity as Rev. James Wademan. 'Such weather for summer, sir.'

Cold and dark, with the familiar musty smell Faro associated with old bibles, the sole occupant was an elderly woman busy with duster and mop. Was her industry rewarded each Sunday by a congregation of devout worshippers, he wondered? The line of empty pews stretching down to the altar with its plain cross might accommodate all South Ronaldsay's inhabitants.

'Good afternoon, Mrs Bain.'

'Afternoon, Minister.'

Rev. Wademan turned to Faro. 'Mrs Bain has been with us for many years. She is one of our senior elders and sustains us all with her gallant efforts.'

Mrs Bain straightened her back, smiled gratefully as the minister went on, 'Perhaps you could help this gentleman. He is in search of a lady who once lived here.' And consulting his watch, he frowned. 'I have a meeting.'

'The gentlemen are waiting in the vestry, Minister.'

Rev. Wademan smiled. 'May I leave you in Mrs Bain's capable hands, sir?' He bowed and scuttled past the pews and out of a small door near the altar.

Mrs Bain put down her mop and waited politely. 'What was it you wanted, sir?'

'I'm looking for a Miss Elsa Harbister,' and taking a certain diversion from the truth, 'for a relative from Edinburgh – I'm here visiting my mother.'

Mrs Bain smiled. 'I thought from your accent you were from the island.' And once again he was directed to Thora in Kirkwall. 'Sad about her man being drowned. Read about it in the paper.'

'Did you know her sister?'

Mrs Bain nodded. 'Knew them both when they were bairns. Tragic lives they had, losing both parents, boat sank in a storm. Always close, always together. Just a year between them, more like twins really. Folk were proud of them, made something of their lives. Never parted,

178

until . . .' she hesitated, frowning, 'that business about Thora.'

Feigning ignorance, Faro asked, 'What business would that be?'

'Both wanted the same man. Then, when her sister went away for a year . . . like that.'

Did 'like that' mean she knew about the seal king legend but was too delicate to mention it? She continued, 'Maybe then Elsa had hopes. She went to Kirkwall, got a job. But Thora came back and Dave Claydon married her, despite everything.'

She paused, remembering. 'We'd always been friends with the Harbister girls and I was a bit like a mother to them. But they changed. Once Thora married she hardly ever came to the Hope and Elsa was away to the mainland without a word to any of us.'

Her sad expression suggested that memory still hurt.

'When was that?'

'I can't mind exactly. A few years back. I'd been up in Shetland looking after my father and when I came back, she'd gone. She might have left me an address so that I could have written to her. But there was nothing.'

She shook her head sadly. 'Thora had looked in when I was away. Never stayed – perhaps she'd come wanting to make it up with Elsa and she was too late. I hoped she'd come back and see me, close like we were once.'

'What about Bet Traill, how did she take it?'

'I ken Bet well. We were friends. She's in a bad way, poor old soul. Loved those two girls, like they were her own. Never got over them both leaving. Seemed to take all the life out of her too. Taken to the asylum up the hill yonder a while back. Some of us look in and take her things to eat but,' she shook her head, 'she never talks, just sits there staring into space. It's awful to see her like that.'

She stopped, looked at him and said, 'You've come all this way from Kirkwall for nothing. Thora's the one you should talk to, if it's urgent business about this relative from Edinburgh.' Pausing, she sighed and added, 'Tell her that Molly Bain's still here and that she'll always be welcome for a visit.'

Thanking her, Faro went into the local inn, and over a pie and a pint of ale decided to fill in the waiting time to the next ferry by a visit to the asylum up the hill. It dominated the skyline. A grim, dark, depressing building with barred windows, more like a whisky distillery than a welcome retreat for folks who had mental problems.

The door was opened by a tall, thin woman, grim of face and tight-mouthed. He wondered if she had been specially chosen to suit the building's exterior. Responding to his request, she said, 'Mrs Traill doesn't receive visitors.'

Faro put his foot against the door before it could be closed in his face and said firmly, 'I have a message, an urgent one from her nephew, Jimmy Traill.'

The woman looked at him. 'The newspaperman? Is he a friend of yours?' Faro said he was and she nodded, 'You'd better come in, then.'

Following her down a long, dark corridor and up a flight of ill-lit stairs, she turned and said, 'Her nephew never comes near these days, so don't expect too much of her. Gets very upset, very wandered in her mind. And look out, she can use her fists and be quite violent sometimes.'

With these timely warnings, she opened a door, stood aside for him and called, 'A visitor for you, Bet.'

She was sitting by the barred window, a wisp of white hair visible above the chair. Turning as he approached, she said, 'Thora, is it you – at last?'

'No, Mrs Traill. I've come from Jimmy. He wants to know how you are?'

'Jimmy?' She sounded bewildered. 'Jimmy.'

'Your nephew Jimmy in Kirkwall.'

'Oh him!' she said contemptuously. 'It's

Thora I want. Why does she never come and see me anymore?' she wailed.

'I'll tell her when I see her,' Faro said lamely.

'That's not enough. I have to see her. Talk to her again.'

Faro was at a loss how to continue with this obsessive conversation. 'I'll do what I can. But Jimmy would like to know that I've seen you. Have you any message for him?'

'Thora. It's Thora I want.' Her voice was like a drumbeat. 'Thora and I have secrets. I was there – she needn't ever forget that.'

'When was that?' Faro asked patiently. Had he found the person who knew the secret of Thora's disappearance, her missing year?

Mrs Traill was shouting, 'The night Elsa – Elsa left us for good.'

'Tell me what happened?' he asked gently.

She narrowed her eyes, as if aware of him for the first time.

'None of your business!' A violent gesture of her fist. Had she been stronger, she would have struck him, her face a distorted mask of anger.

'I can't get her out of my mind. Can't sleep for it! Thora!' Her voice rose to a shrill scream. The door opened to the attendant who had let him in who said, 'Didn't I warn you not to upset her? See what you've done? You'd better go.' And to the old woman, 'Now, now, Bet, everything's all right.'

He left unobserved, as she sat mutely staring at the blank window. He followed the attendant downstairs. 'What's all that about the sisters?'

'Take no notice. Apparently she was devoted to them, like her own bairns. Never forgave the one who went away back to the mainland.'

'Elsa?'

'Was that her name? Keeps on wanting this Thora to come back. Lonely old soul. Doubt whether she'll last much longer. Best thing too.'

Feeling very depressed by the visit, with an hour in hand he returned to the inn and a lugubrious innkeeper, who soon revealed an entire vocabulary comprising only the words 'yes' or 'no'.

At last, Faro sighted the approaching ferry. As he stepped aboard, Amos grinned. 'Enjoy your visit?'

'Good to see the Hope again,' said Faro, which wasn't strictly true. There was no chance to talk to the ferryman this time as two sailors, who were obviously mates, joined him at the wheel, smoking their pipes, chatting and laughing.

Faro took a seat among the other passengers watching the Hope slowly disappear. His thoughts were dismal. If only he had been able to meet Elsa Harbister or find out something more about why she had left her home for the mainland and cut herself off from everyone, especially Molly Bain, without any explanation. He should have heeded Jimmy's warning. If her nephew and the local residents failed in their approach to Bet Traill, then he would fare no better.

As he stepped off the ferry, Amos said, 'See your old friends, did you?'

Faro smiled. 'Not at home this time.'

'Thora's sister?'

'No. Seems she left a long while ago.'

'Who told you that?'

'Molly Bain. They were very close once.'

Amos sighed, shook his head. 'Pity that. A wasted journey for you.' And flinging the anchor rope deftly towards the capstan, he gave Faro a mocking glance. 'Hope our wee voyage wasn't too uncomfortable for you.'

'It was quite an experience,' said Faro.

And saying good day, he wondered why on that first meeting Amos had seemed so likeable, someone he would enjoy getting to know. All that had suddenly gone sour. He wasn't quite sure, but the Amos of the second meeting was a different person.

CHAPTER FOURTEEN

Faced with the prospect of a long walk back to Scarthbreck, he was delighted to meet the carriage on the Stromness road. There was hardly room for him inside. His mother, surrounded by parcels and boxes, was tired to exhaustion.

Her shopping successfully concluded, she had seized the opportunity to visit a friend for a more-than-welcome cup of tea. Meanwhile Tom, the coachman, had been grateful to anchor the carriage outside the local tavern.

Mary Faro was only mildly interested in his activities, for which Faro was grateful not to be faced with questions for which he had no answers. Utterly worn out, she yawned, closed her eyes almost immediately and slept with her head resting comfortably on his shoulder, his arm tenderly around her as often in childhood he had slept, their roles now reversed by time.

A message from Stavely awaited him. He was requested to come to Hal's croft after breakfast early next morning.

Mary Faro, refreshed after her sleep in the carriage, her energy restored, provided an excellent supper. As he downed ham pie and a warmed-up apple dumpling, he came to a decision. Taking out his logbook, he added the abortive visit to the Hope, Mrs Traill and his failure to locate Elsa Harbister, all of which had convinced him to abandon any hope of solving the tantalising mystery surrounding Thora Claydon as the seal king's bride.

Rereading all that he had discovered concerning Dave Claydon's accidental drowning for Macfie's benefit, he resolved that, from now on, he must devote all his energies to the present, by finding Celia Prentiss-Grant and answering the questions posed by the abandoned clothes and a possible pregnancy.

As he finished writing, he put down the pen, certain there was something missing, something he had heard or overheard, a vital clue. But try as he might, his usually excellent memory let him down. Perhaps he was too tired, too disappointed at this negative result.

Laying aside the logbook, he went to bed and slept soundly, to awake at six, hearing his mother already up and preparing a substantial breakfast.

An hour later he knocked on the door of Hal's croft, whose signally grimy exterior and the overgrown wilderness that had replaced the garden told their own sorry tale.

The door was opened by Ed, tousled and unkempt. At the sight of Faro his face underwent a transformation: he turned white and almost staggered back. 'What do you want?' he gasped. 'What's happened now?'

At that moment, before Faro could utter any reassurance, Stavely appeared. Thrusting Ed roughly aside, he said shortly, 'Oh, here you are – I didn't mean this early,' and to his son, 'Aren't you going to invite Constable Faro in?'

Ed stood back, and as Faro squeezed past him in the narrow opening to the kitchen, he sensed that the boy was trembling violently.

'Hal's already away, cutting peat; he gets up at dawn.'

The boy disappeared into the bedroom and Stavely, unshaven and weary after a night's restless discomfort on a temporary bed, evaded by sleep and filled with tortuous misgivings, regarded Faro reproachfully.

'Mind coming back in an hour? Haven't

had my breakfast yet. We'll decide what to do next. The Prentiss-Grants want a daily report. I suppose that's their right in the circumstances.'

Faro left deep in thought and unable to rid himself of that vision of Ed's strange behaviour. In his experience of crime and criminals he had encountered guilt and innocence many times, and was well aware of the symptoms displayed by guilty men and women. Especially the very young who had not yet learnt to dissemble. And after that morning's encounter, he was certain that Ed Stavely had something to hide.

Returning to the croft an hour later, Stavely was ready and his behaviour almost confirmed those suspicions when Faro asked, 'How's young Ed taking all this?'

Stavely stopped, turned sharply. Preoccupied with thoughts regarding his son, he wondered uneasily if Faro was reading his mind. 'What do you mean – "all this"?' he demanded.

'Oh, living with his uncle here, missing all his friends in Kirkwall. It's a long way to go,' Faro said cheerfully, trying to sound casual.

Stavely hardly suppressed a sigh of relief. Of course Faro couldn't possibly know of Ed's missing hours coinciding with Celia's disappearance.

'He's always wanted to work here with Hal, they get along very well. Hal's fifteen years younger than Lily, much nearer Ed in age.'

Faro interpreted his sad shake of the head. 'Both a bit on the wild side, are they?'

Stavely gave him a hard look as he went on, 'We've all been there. Young fellows sowing their wild oats, that sort of thing.' He hoped he sounded understanding and sympathetic.

Stavely grunted disapprovingly, afraid that he had given himself away. And he was right. Stavely was no great actor, and Faro guessed that he knew, or at least suspected, that something was amiss with his son.

He needed an excuse to get the boy on his own and put to him a few well-rehearsed but carefully contrived questions, which he hoped might produce interesting answers regarding any illegal activities Ed was anxious to conceal from his policeman father.

Faro was left standing at the front door while Stavely went in to deliver the first of his daily reports. The audience only took minutes but he emerged looking ruffled and cross, mumbled something about things to attend to in Kirkwall. Mounting one of Hal's horses, generously provided as his transport, he said, 'Be back in a couple of hours. I leave you to your own devices, Faro. Find out anything you can.'

Without the faintest idea how he was to

carry out Stavely's instructions or where to start, apart from walking the shore, which had already been searched inch by inch for clues, Faro had a sudden desperate need of fresh air and fresh company, the latter hopefully in the comely shape of Inga St Ola.

Heading towards Spanish Cove, where there was plenty of the former in evidence, blowing directly across the firth, Faro met Mr West, the amateur botanist whose company he had once shared on the farmers' carts to Kirkwall, and who was now a familiar solitary figure searching for plant specimens on the cliff's edge.

Today he was walking down the road, binoculars swinging around his neck. As they met Faro said, 'You're not using the trowel today.'

West laughed. 'It's a pleasant change to spot the nesting seabirds. You can hear them – lively aren't they? And I enjoy exploring the horizons for interesting foreign ships, far out, heading in our direction.'

Pleasantries exchanged, Faro hurried on. His route taking him past the stables, he decided, without a great deal of hope, to make enquiries regarding the hiring of gigs.

The stableman looked up eagerly, and was obviously disappointed that this was not a customer as Faro asked if he kept any records.

'Aye, we have to do that, sir, to make sure we get our animals and the carriages back again. We have an arrangement for their return at stables in Stromness and Kirkwall.'

'Did you by any chance have anyone hiring a gig three nights ago?'

The lad frowned, thought for a moment and produced a grubby notebook. 'A gentleman hired a gig to Stromness in the morning and in the evening a chap took a horse for Kirkwall.'

'No young lady customers?'

The lad scratched his head. 'Very rare, sir. Miss Inga St Ola sometimes, or a few of the older ladies.'

Disappointed, Faro thanked him and walked on to find that the main reason for his chilly walk, Inga, was not at home. The door remained firmly closed and, disappointed, he was about to walk away when he heard a swishing sound, like a broom on a floor.

The door slowly opened and there was Baubie Finn.

She looked surprised but pleased to see him, and saying that Inga was away, she stood aside.

'Please – if you aren't in a hurry, do come in. I won't ask you to wait as I have no idea when Inga will be back. She's away seeing one of the ladies she's sewing petticoats for.'

Following her into the tiny parlour, Faro

realised he had only seen her sitting in the Orkney chair and was now aware of her curious shape. Walking seemed to be a problem and perhaps accounted for the gown that trailed on the floor behind her, her feet invisible. It did not conceal the fact that her body was shapeless, with extremely narrow shoulders so that her head looked out of proportion. When she turned, smiled and invited him to sit down, he was again struck by the roundness of her face, her sleek pulled-back straight hair, her face contourless by the lack of defined eyebrows. Only the huge, luminous eyes were remarkable, the sole vestige of female beauty.

Watching those odd gliding steps, ashamedly the selkie image, cruel but undeniable, immediately came to mind, arousing feelings of compassion for what this poor woman must have suffered throughout her life, almost a freak of nature, but gentle and wise.

The conversation was polite, conventional remarks about weather and whether he was enjoying his stay.

He found himself telling her about his visit to St Margaret's Hope.

'I know it well,' she said. 'My home is quite nearby. Some day, soon, I must go back. I have enjoyed Inga's hospitality long enough.'

No cause, no further explanation, and Faro

went on to say that the object of his visit was to see the house where he once lived.

Baubie nodded. She knew that house.

Suddenly hopeful, Faro added that he had been hoping to meet Elsa Harbister and that he had visited Mrs Traill, who was now in the asylum. Did she know her?

'I know of her, of course.' She looked at him curiously, and as he hastily explained Macfie's connection with the family, she nodded. 'I knew Thora and Elsa well as children. They had such a tragic life. I was sorry for them, we all were, neighbours wanted to help. And Bet Traill more or less adopted them.' Pausing, she shook her head. 'I think they were afraid of me, though,' she added candidly.

Poor Baubie Finn. Faro saw it all: wanting to be kind, her odd appearance, whispers of a selkie, a witch, must have terrified children. What must her life have been like all those years ago and even now?

He decided to mention Sibella Scarth.

She mouthed the name as if savouring it, then she just looked at him, shook her head.

'You never knew her?'

Again that shake of her head. Nothing more to be said on that topic. Faro was disappointed as she put in quickly, 'Inga has been very good to me. I had been quite ill.' Delicately touching the region of her chest, she sighed. 'I might not have survived, but she brought me here, nursed me back to life again.'

As she spoke, he noticed her hands, mittened almost to the fingertips, and he avoided contemplating the shape and colour of her nails – long, oddly curved. Like talons.

There was a sudden, bleak silence between them. Nothing left to say or too much said already.

Faro stood up, bowed, said he must leave. She followed him to the door and he turned. 'I hope we might meet again before I leave.'

She smiled, nodded, her expression suddenly wistful. 'I am sure we will, Jeremy.'

CHAPTER FIFTEEN

Leaving Inga's house, Amos was emerging three doors away – the home of Rob, his assistant ferryman.

'Hello again,' he greeted Faro, holding up his hand indicating the weather. 'Good sailor, are you? Fancy a trip round the coast to Stromness?' he asked mockingly, pointing to a tiny boat bobbing up and down at the pier.

It was a challenge that Faro accepted. 'Now that you ask, I was considering it.'

'Right you are. Off we go, then.'

Amos donned oilskins and sou'wester and threw a raincape across to Faro. A heavy sea made Faro regret his decision as he recognised that the ferryman needed all his skills as an oarsman to manoeuvre the small boat round the skerry, keeping as close as he dare to the shore, making slow headway in what promised to be an uncomfortable crossing.

Heaving a sigh of relief at the sight of Stromness, he parted company with Amos, who grinned.

'Well done. You are a good sailor. There were moments when I thought we might have to swim for it.'

'You perhaps, but I can't swim.'

'An island lad? Incredible!' Amos whistled. 'You are game, then.' Saluting him mockingly, he anchored his small boat and boarded the ferry.

Walking through the twisting streets, Faro observed that the police had been busy. Posters for the missing girl were on display, but now that he had made the sea trip as a kind of dare, Faro realised it was a fair distance back to Scarthbreck.

A mile further on, he turned at the sound of a gig approaching. Standing aside to let it pass, a man leant out.

'Saw you on the ferry, mate. Where are you heading?' Faro said 'Scarthbreck' and the man grinned.

'You're in luck. We pass the very door. Jump in.'

Faro was grateful, especially when he learnt

that the man was a neighbour of Hal's, polite but disinclined to conversation. His mention of the poster of the missing girl aroused no interest or curiosity, his companion's attentions solemnly devoted to a whisky bottle. Disappointed that his passenger declined his invitation to sample the contents, the journey continued in silence.

Mary Faro was only mildly interested in his morning's activities, flustered and a little excited by notice of a visitor expected shortly at Scarthbreck.

'A youngish man, Jeremy. The maids know him already. A remote cousin of the Prentiss-Grants, has an estate near theirs.' And lowering her voice to a whisper as if she might be overheard, 'I'm told that he's sweet on Miss Celia. Only gossip, of course, but the hints were that they all expected she would marry him some day.'

Standing back to see the effect on Faro, she said, 'Well, what do you think of that? He's come all the way here from Sussex, too early for the shooting. I expect it's just to help them find her.'

A deep sigh which threatened more tears, then she went on, 'We've had such a time preparing a room for him. Sir Arnold is so particular that he is to be made comfortable after such a journey.'

While Faro assimilated this new information, a tap on the door announced Sergeant Stavely, who followed Mary into the kitchen. His apologies for arriving at such an inconvenient hour were accompanied by wistful glances at a meal in preparation, which Mary Faro interpreted correctly. Always hospitable, she asked if he would care to join them.

Stavely beamed upon her, a quite emotional response, and taking a seat at the table opposite Faro he said, 'Very kind of your mother. I just wanted to know if you had anything to report.' That wasn't quite true, but understandable considering the dismal meal he had anticipated at Hal's. This visit had been very slyly timed.

Faro mentioned the posters at Stromness and Stavely nodded eagerly. 'Our men in Kirkwall have been very efficient, too, and they are now being distributed at various points across the island.'

When Faro mentioned his call at the stables regarding travellers on the night Celia disappeared, Stavely was pleased. He smiled, a rare occurrence, and said, 'Results may take a day or two. We must be patient, and I am now authorised to rent Hal's gig, for which I am extremely grateful. He only needs it for market days, normally prefers a horse, so it lies unused in the barn. It will make travelling much easier –

I am no great horseman. Walking the confines of Kirkwall is enough for me.'

Faro was also grateful for this alternative means of transport, being no great horseman himself, and accordingly the next morning they set off in the gig. Although open to the elements, it was able to accommodate four passengers comfortably and was a decided improvement in speed compared to walking weary miles in the rain and wind.

In Stromness, Stavely seized the opportunity to buy some hot pies, an agreeable supplement to his last meal, while sending Faro in search of the ferryman.

'I should like to have a description of anyone resembling Miss Celia who was on the ferry that night.'

Faro had earlier dismissed that as unlikely. The last ferry departed at eight o'clock. And at that hour, he had been walking with her along the shore.

Instead of Amos, another ferryman, taller, older – presumably Rob – was on duty. His face almost invisible under the woollen cap, he was chatting with two companions as the passengers boarded.

'Amos?' he said in reply to Faro's question. 'Having a day off.'

Faro said he needed to see him urgently.

Rob gave him a curious glance. 'He'll be at home – his brother's poorly. You'll find the house easily, in Bridge Street next to the Lamb & Flag.'

Back at the gig, Stavely waded into hot pies like a starving man, which according to his assessment of his lodging, he was indeed.

'Animals feed better than we do,' he grumbled and Faro took over the reins.

On the outskirts of Kirkwall they came across the first of the posters. Stavely halted the gig and they paused to read it.

The sketch was certainly like the photograph, but with only a verbal description of the girl's colouring and height Faro felt it was vague enough to apply to many females of her age. There was no description of the clothes she was 'last seen wearing', as 'in her underclothes' would have been extremely difficult to add.

Stavely had no such misgivings regarding the results. 'I have great hopes – they made a nice job,' he added with a sigh of satisfaction. 'If these don't bring about a ransom note, then the reward offered will,' he whistled. 'One hundred pounds – that's a fortune for most folk.'

Faro had a sudden idea. 'Was any reward offered for the return of the artefacts that Dave Claydon was carrying when he drowned?'

Stavely looked at him in astonishment. 'Hardly.

They obviously went to the bottom of the sea.' Then a quizzical look. 'Are you hinting that someone found them?'

'I think that is a distinct possibility.'

'Have to have proof of that, Faro. It's a bit of a waste of time and definitely not police business without someone coming forward claiming ownership.'

'What about the archaeologists?'

Stavely shrugged. 'They denied all knowledge of treasure. Stuck to their story of a few beads and a beaker.'

As Faro left the gig outside Amos's house across the road from the cathedral, he remembered Inga's cynical words about a reward expected to be shared by many.

He had a lengthy wait at the door and was wondering if Amos was at home. When the door opened, the ferryman seemed surprised, and not too pleased to see his visitor.

Perhaps, thought Faro charitably as he was somewhat reluctantly asked to come in, his evident displeasure was because of the hour of the day and the state of his invalid brother.

The parlour was dark, but the glow of a peat fire touched the man who was shrouded in shawls and huddled close to it. It was obvious that he felt the cold, as his bonnet was pulled down well over his eyes. Faro, sensitive to atmospheres, had the feeling a task had been left unfinished and hastily put aside.

Presumably Amos had been attending to some personal matters involving the invalid and the scene had been speedily rearranged. However, it reminded Faro of a feeling he had often experienced. Although it seemed impossible in this particular connection, he felt that he had been the subject of an interrupted conversation, and the words still hung precariously in the air.

'That's Josh, my brother,' said Amos, with an anxious look in his direction. Josh merely nodded in acknowledgement of this introduction, and, as if lifting his head involved considerable effort, he was seized by a fit of coughing.

The two men waited politely, with an exchange of sympathetic glances until this sad interlude ended. But when Amos spoke at last, Faro was aware that no trace remained of his former friendly manner. Hardly able to conceal his impatience, he asked, 'What can I do for you, Mr Faro?'

Faro, made to feel embarrassed and uncomfortable at this intrusion, endeavoured to re-establish his official policeman role with an explanation about the posters and enquired whether Amos could remember having seen anyone resembling the missing girl among his passengers.

Amos listened to him, shook his head and said in mocking terms, 'Mr Faro, don't you realise that what you ask is well-nigh impossible. I carry dozens – maybe hundreds – of passengers every day. Boarding is a busy, hectic time and even a pretty girl like the one in the posters might slip by without a second glance. Sorry I can't be of more help.' His accompanying look towards his brother, who was breathing heavily and was in obvious need of attention, was a clear dismissal.

Turning at the door, Faro said, 'Now that you have seen the poster, may I ask you to be extra vigilant?'

Amos smiled. 'You have my assurance on that, Mr Faro. Now I must bid you good day.'

Leaving the house, Faro headed towards the police station to be informed that the sergeant was away in the gig and expected to be back at about four o'clock when his business was completed.

What business? Did it concern the posters, or was Stavely seizing the opportunity of a couple of hours to visit his wife? Faro wondered, as he toured the streets and made a note of an impressive number of posters on display. Kirkwall was taking the matter seriously, with many shop windows displaying the artist's sketch, with 'One Hundred Pounds for Information' heavily stressed in large black letters. A great deal more than most folk could hope to earn for a year's hard work on the island, it was a substantial and tempting reward.

On his way back he looked into *The Orcadian*, its walls well plastered with the poster. He was out of luck: Jimmy was absent, away on one of his investigations. There was a certain reluctance from the lad behind the desk to tell him more than that. However, Faro left hoping it concerned the missing girl.

As he approached Kirk Green, with several hours in hand, and a dark rain cloud overhead accompanied by an unseasonable shrill wind, he decided to seek refuge in the rose-red cathedral. As always, the first impression when he set foot inside was one of infinity. Its immensity diminished him, an illusion due to the perfect proportions of the interior, to which the narrowness of the nave contributed an effect of loftiness.

Besides the grandeur, what most seized his heartstrings was the beauty of mellow stonework: grey flags, combined with the warm reds and yellow of sandstone. This was comparatively new, and in the original parts of the church, walls and pillars alike had been richly painted, glowing with colour. As a child he had spent many hours looking at the paintings of angels and saints, eagerly searching the walls for any traces of this ancient pattern.

Named after the patron saint of Kirkwall and all of Orkney, and more than seven centuries old, the cathedral's history had always fascinated him, believing it to be named after his own father, Magnus.

The story of the martyred saint, whose bones were first laid to rest in the chapel at Birsay and then transferred to the newly built cathedral, intrigued young Jeremy. Many years later, when a pillar was being repaired on the south side of the original altar, a skull came to light. Experts of Norse history recognised that the skull was cleft in the fashion used when a victim was of noble birth, according to the ancient *Orkneyinga Saga*.

Enjoying the tranquillity and serenity of its ancient splendour, Faro was suddenly aware that he was not alone. The line of empty pews stretching toward the altar had an occupant.

A man knelt in prayer, his face hidden by a large bonnet. Not wishing to disturb him, Faro continued his walk sheltered by the massive pillars. Glancing towards the figure something about him was familiar. A closer look, and he knew they had met before, less than an hour ago. The man was Josh Flett.

Poor fellow, thought Faro, overwhelmed with compassion for that lonely, doomed man. Were his prayers for recovery? As his home was only a short distance away across the road, did he come here every day when the cathedral was empty, to sit alone and pray?

Footsteps, and suddenly the man was alone no longer. A woman slid into the pew beside him. This time Faro had no difficulty in recognising the newcomer as Thora Claydon.

Anxious not to intrude on a private moment, aware that his presence would embarrass them, he remained where he was, hidden by the pillar. To an unseen observer, it was obvious that they knew each other and, although he could distinguish no words exchanged between them, they sat close, their shoulders touching and as if they were holding hands.

Her head nestled against his shoulder, her face turned towards him in earnest whispered conversation, her attitude pleading.

Their closeness intrigued him, opened new avenues of thought. Friends, even lovers? Was it possible that he had stumbled on another tragedy in the making? That Thora Claydon, widowed, was in love with a dying man?

At that moment, a door opened, voices

announced new arrivals and, from his vantage point, Faro saw the two spring guiltily apart. She touched his arm and walked, head down, quickly towards the entrance. She could not, however, escape the newcomers, apparently choristers ready for practice, who obviously knew her, and greetings were exchanged.

Faro looked back towards the now-empty pew. Josh was a shadow moving towards a side exit, swiftly for such a sick man, and one not wishing to be recognised.

He was accosted at the entrance by the fellow Faro recognised as Rob, Amos Flett's assistant. Faro stood back as the two exchanged a few urgent words, before Josh pushed past the ferryman.

He had to stand aside quickly as Rob went into the nearest pew and knelt down in prayer. He realised that the delay had cost him the opportunity of following Josh. Outside he was nowhere to be seen and was presumably back home again.

On the Kirk Green, Faro lingered until Thora appeared, freed of the choristers. Bowing as though this was an accidental encounter, he greeted her. She looked at him quickly and with no change of expression, wished him good day and hurried away, her eyes brimming with unshed tears.

He watched her go. He had stumbled accidently on a tragic tale. Having just gone through the agonies of a drowned husband, recently buried, it appeared Thora was now without any hope of a happy ending with the ferryman's brother, whose fate was sealed by the scourge of consumption.

Poor Thora, his heart went out to her. This meeting with Josh must have caused her indescribable distress.

With time on his hands before meeting Stavely, there seemed little more to be done until the posters worked and man's high principles or greed for a reward blossomed into revealing the present whereabouts of a missing girl.

He walked towards Tankerness House, remarkably well preserved for its three hundred years. Progress, in the shape of a modern town hall and post office, had mercifully passed it by. With a splendid ancient gateway and crow-stepped gable ends, characteristic of Kirkwall's architecture, its paved quadrangle retained the charm and dignity of a historic university.

His contemplation was interrupted as a familiar figure emerged in the comely shape of Inga. Their delight in this unexpected meeting was mutual and regardless of passers-by they hugged one another, and at Inga's suggestion adjourned to the Lamb & Flag for a pot of tea.

Seated at a table, Inga demanded, 'What brings you here?'

Faro explained about the posters, to which Inga reiterated her cynical response that everyone who knew the informer would want a share of the reward.

'Where do you think she is?' Faro asked.

Inga laughed. 'If I knew the answer to that I wouldn't be wasting time talking to you. I'd be heading to Scarthbreck and claiming the reward.'

Faro ignored that and went on, 'Do you think she is hiding, or is she being held by a kidnapper?'

Inga nodded. 'I see you have wisely abandoned the suicide idea, the pregnant girl putting an end to it all.'

'I think there is a darker side to all this.'

Inga laughed. 'That's dark enough for most folk.'

'I'm sure no one will believe me, but I'm certain there is a link somewhere with Thora Claydon.'

Inga laughed. 'Are you considering that the seal king has claimed a second bride? That handsome reward wouldn't be much use in his kingdom under the waves, would it?'

'I'm being serious, Inga.' And he told how he had witnessed the meeting of Thora and Josh in the cathedral and how intimate they looked.

Inga looked puzzled. 'I can't imagine Thora wanting to take up with Josh Flett. It's a miracle he's still here. Been consumptive for years. According to Amos, just weeks ago he was on his deathbed.'

And Faro thought again of the dying man in prayer. Perhaps his miracle was happening, although he didn't expect Inga to believe that as she continued, 'Doesn't sound like Thora at all. More likely, with Dave gone, she'd be on the lookout for a rich gentleman. Hardly likely to waste her charms on Josh Flett, unless he'd leave her a wealthy widow, second time round.'

'Was she happy with Dave?' Faro asked, remembering the circumstances of that strange marriage.

Inga shrugged. 'They were fairly comfortably off with Dave as an excise officer, but there were no bairns and Dave was fond of the bottle and had a reputation as a keen gambler who'd bet on anything.' Pausing she smiled. 'But who knows? Josh is quite different. He doesn't drink or gamble and he's always been a bookish sort of lad. Maybe second time lucky.'

Faro remembered Thora outside the cathedral in obvious distress as he said, 'You're very cynical, Inga. Don't you believe in true love?'

She nodded eagerly. 'Oh yes, I believe in true love. That certainly exists, a bonus in our frail human lives. But marriages are more often calculated on a financial basis. It has always been that way, history will tell you so if you have any doubts.' Touching his arm gently, she whispered, 'Don't look so shocked, Jeremy dear. You still have a lot to learn if you think that true love ends happily ever after with the wedding bells.'

After listening to her words, Faro decided that he was learning a lot more about Inga ten years after he left the island lovesick and yearning for her. Now, before his eyes, many of his illusions were being destroyed. He had loved her so much, all the other women he ever met paled before his dream of her, his first love. A love that had seemed to be mutual.

Now he knew that, had he stayed in Orkney, it would not have ended in a lifetime together. But had he been a rich man, instead of a poor youth with nothing to offer but his love and a struggling existence as a policeman's wife in Edinburgh, what then?

Suddenly the laughter and delight of this unexpected meeting had turned sour. Wounded by this new Inga, he decided to change the subject. 'I called yesterday and was pleasantly surprised when Baubie Finn answered the door.

You were the subject of our conversation, your kindness nursing her back to health when she had been so ill.'

Inga shrugged. 'What else could I do? Fever that was going into pneumonia. There was no one to take care of her, and I was glad to help. I couldn't just leave her at death's door. She was – and is – quite frail, and I've loved sharing my little house with her.'

Faro was silent, wondering how to phrase his feelings regarding Baubie. 'Do you find her quite strange sometimes?'

Inga looked at him frowning. 'What do you mean "quite strange"?'

Embarrassed, Faro said, 'I had only seen her seated in the Orkney chair. Walking, she seemed quite different, very slow-moving.' He thought of those oddly sliding footsteps. 'She's an odd shape for a female, I mean.' He stopped there and Inga laughed.

'Men notice such things, but I've never given it a second thought. Now that you mention it, I can understand why people think she's a selkie.' She paused. 'She has webbed toes and fingers, incidentally – hence the mittens she always wears.'

Faro thrust away the remembrance of fingers with odd-shaped, claw-like nails as Inga continued, 'Do you know she never mentioned your visit? Not a word that you had called when I was out.'

It was a chance to mention the memory of one incident that bothered him. 'You do get a lot of visitors, Inga. The first time I called on you, I met Amos just leaving.'

Inga looked at him and smiled. Rather secretively, he thought.

'Tell me about him,' he said lightly.

'What do you mean?'

'What do you think of Amos?'

She shrugged. 'What I think of Amos is no one's concern to anyone but Amos and me.'

Seeing the look on Faro's face, she relented and sighed. 'I hardly think of Amos at all, except that he's a very caring man devoted to an invalid brother. That's the reason he's never married. Because he's very handsome all the lasses love him. Men like him too. If he had more than a ferryman's pay to offer, he'd be the most eligible bachelor in Kirkwall.' She looked at him again, head on one side. 'Why do you ask?'

'You never mention him; I wondered if you were friends when I saw him leaving your house.'

She gave him a scornful glance. 'We are. Rob, his friend, lives a few doors away.' She paused. 'If you really want to know why he was in my house that day, although it's no business of yours, Jeremy Faro, I make his shirts and he'd come about that. I'm a seamstress, remember, that's how I earn a living.' She paused and added slowly, 'I am also a free spirit, no man owns me – or ever will.'

There was no doubt that this held a warning note not lost on Faro as she continued, 'I doubt that I will ever marry. I have no inclination to be a slave to any man.' And, echoing his earlier misgivings, 'Or to be a policeman's wife living in a dusty city far from the island.' Then wagging a finger at him, 'So don't waste any sleep getting ideas about a future for us. It doesn't exist and never will. I'm very fond of you, Jeremy, but fondness isn't enough for marriage. The most we could have is just a pleasant interlude together.'

Pausing to allow him to assimilate what amounted to a proposition, when he did not respond, she shrugged, 'If that doesn't satisfy you, you'd better go back to Edinburgh and forget all about me.'

'I assure you, I won't ever do that.'

With a shrug of unmistakeable indifference she said, 'Maybe. But I can see you married to your Lizzie, who's probably waiting patiently for you to ask her. She sounds the right kind of woman to make you happy in a way I never could. I'd soon get bored and I couldn't guarantee to be faithful to one man for ever.'

And on that fateful note, their conversation ended with the abrupt appearance of Sergeant Stavely, who said impatiently, 'I've been waiting for you at the station and I guessed you'd be here.'

A glance at the teacups and acknowledging Inga with a slight bow, 'Ready to leave now. Gig's outside'.

Faro and Inga exchanged polite 'good days' and Faro was silent on that drive, telling himself that she was right to warn him, and that sensibly putting aside this infatuation was long overdue. His return to Orkney, and meeting her again, had aroused all those emotions of first love. Now he knew he must see it through her eyes and cast aside all hopes that she would suddenly change her mind. Having solved the mystery of Dave Claydon for Macfie's satisfaction, the main reason for this visit, all his efforts must now be directed to help solve the sinister disappearance of Celia Prentiss-Grant. Then he would be free to return to his duties in Edinburgh.

The last hour had sadly convinced him that he would have liked to leave tomorrow, but he was trapped. As the last person to see Celia, if the worst had happened and the girl had met with a violent end, the reason for his restraint was a sobering thought.

Even if the killer's identity came to light, he felt certain that having momentarily been a prime suspect in Stavely's report would cast a shadow on his future career in the Edinburgh City Police.

CHAPTER SIXTEEN

The posters for the missing girl took immediate effect. The police station in Kirkwall had a small queue next morning. Harassed constables busily taking down details, overseen by Stavely, who had set up a reception area to interview claimants, it soon became obvious that their information had little hope of revealing the present whereabouts of the missing girl.

'A lass like that walked past our farm last week.' Dismissed by Stavely since Celia had not even arrived in Orkney last week.

'Saw a lass walking past the cathedral here last night.' Further details revealed that she had red hair and walked with a limp.

Next, 'A woman moved in next door last

week, a stranger she is, and looks like the poster.' This woman was about thirty-five, dark hair going grey, and she had a husband.

'Saw a lass with a bairn down by the Peerie Sea. Age? About twenty. Aye, plump she was. I didna' ken her hair colour, she was wearing a bonnet.'

And so it continued. All prospective claimants had one thing in common: they were eager to know if the reward was to be given before or after their valuable information had been revealed.

Stavely threw down his pen. He was fairly certain that the sightings were a waste of his time, as each disappointed claimant was turned away with the stern instruction that further proof was necessary.

While the Kirkwall constables were so employed, Faro was to remain at Scarthbreck, as Stavely believed there was a strong possibility that further claimants might descend directly on the Prentiss-Grants with their demands for the reward offered.

By lunchtime that day none had appeared. The only gig to drive up to Scarthbreck had been the Hon. Gerald Binsley, from Binsley Hall in East Sussex.

His arrival had Mary Faro in a great state

of excitement. A room had been prepared, the maids rushing to and fro under her guidance, menus were to be approved and Mary, breathless at last, sat down at the kitchen table and beamed on Faro, who had laid aside his notebook.

'Is this man a prospective claimant for the reward?'

'Of course not, Jeremy. He's a friend of the family. According to the maids, that is. He often accompanies them on their travels.' And in a conspiratorial whisper, 'And what is more, like I told you, rumour is that he's sweet on Miss Celia. Well, what do you think of that?'

Faro's immediate thought – one he was not prepared to share with his mother – was that, considering what might well be Miss Celia's unfortunate condition, the Hon. Gerald had rushed up from the south of England in order to make an honest woman of her.

At the house, he made a brief appearance before the anxious parents to inform them that Sergeant Stavely was in Kirkwall and at this moment would be testing the success of the missing-person poster – hastily rephrased 'missing young lady' – returning immediately to report any success.

Sir Arnold received this information in his usual unyielding manner with a brief dismissal gesture, while Lady Millicent wrung her hands in a manner Lady Macbeth would have envied.

Informing them that he would remain in the vicinity of the servants' lodge and would be available at any time, Faro left wondering how he could negotiate a meeting with the Hon. Gerald, and in particular how he might delicately phrase a few private words with that gentleman on a possible reason for Miss Celia's disappearance.

He was in luck. As he walked down the front steps, a tall, thin man, not handsome or even particularly young, but kindly looking, appeared heading in the direction of the stables, leading a handsome chestnut mare.

He bowed and introduced himself as Gerald Binsley. 'How do. You must be Detective Constable Faro,' and as they shook hands, he said anxiously, 'Any news?'

'Not so far, sir, but it is early days.' Faro tried to sound reassuring as he added, 'The posters were only distributed yesterday.'

Binsley shook his head, bit his lip and looked very worried.

'We had hoped there might be some response already, if only to claim the reward direct from Sir Arnold.'

'It is more likely any news will come from Kirkwall. Most people who had sightings to report would go to the police station there, and

Sergeant Stavely will be arriving with the results so far.'

Binsley smiled wanly and said, 'This is such a worry for the parents, as you can imagine. Only child and all that.'

Faro was suddenly hopeful. 'You have a long acquaintance with the family?'

'I have indeed. Known young Celia all her life. Taught her to ride.' And patting the mare, 'Started with ponies, but Blossom here in Orkney is her favourite. Bit wild sometimes.'

Intercepting Faro's sharp look, Binsley laughed. 'Yes, both of them suit each other. Celia's born to the saddle. No horse she can't break. Rides like a man, hates all that side-saddle ladies' rubbish.'

Again he laughed, remembering, then soberly shook his head. 'Dear God. I hope she is all right, that nothing has happened to her.'

'We all hope that, sir.'

'I've heard it all from the parents.'

All except the abandoned clothes, Faro thought, wondering what Gerald Binsley would make of that, as he went on, 'Just like Celia to decide to go for a swim – and to hell with the conventions. She has absolutely no fear at all, never had. Bravest little girl I ever met.' Suddenly silent, he bit his lip and looked ready to burst into tears.

A moment's silence, then, aware that Binsley knew considerably more about Celia than her shocked parents would care to recognise, Faro said, 'We are all close to these distressing circumstances, sir, but as a friend of the family, have you any idea why Miss Celia should have chosen to come to Orkney alone, and then immediately disappear?'

Binsley shook his head sadly. 'None at all. She loved practical jokes, even as a child, loved to terrify her parents. Should have been a boy, y'know, but this behaviour is beyond a joke.'

A difficult, spoilt, indulgent only child, were the words that Binsley's remark conjured up as he continued, 'I thought I knew her very well. She confided in me quite often, when she had rows with her parents, which was often enough. As a little girl, she was always threatening to run away, join a circus. Tried it once before, when she was about fourteen. Left them a note.'

He laughed harshly. 'Didn't get far that time. Found her hiding in an old cottage on the edge of the estate.' He sighed. 'A crisis all about nothing, just to make her parents sorry they hadn't given in to some whim – I forget what – possibly some trinket she wanted.'

'What about tickets, sir? Where did she come by the money to travel, hiring a carriage from their London home down to the docks, to board a ship leaving for Kirkwall?'

'We don't know for sure. Parents are a little reticent about that. Seems she had a small monthly allowance, but her father admitted that there were several guineas missing from his desk drawer – he was about to raise ructions and blame a thieving servant. Then, of course, fortunately, he found a note in the drawer from Celia that she would pay him back.'

A less than pleasant picture of the missing girl was emerging, and even the possible reason of pregnancy was fading, with Binsley in the extremely unlikely role of father to her child. Binsley was obviously a very worried man, which, Faro decided, accounted for his manner, eager to be friendly, seeking a stranger's reassurance.

Taking advantage of gathering useful information, Faro asked, 'Did she have a wide circle of London friends?'

'The usual group of young females all presented at court and on the hunt for husbands.' He shook his head. 'But not Celia, she had little interest in marriage – as I found out too late.'

'Too late, sir?'

'Indeed. We had been friends all her life. She trusted me, even loved me in a way – however, as I would learn, as one would love an uncle.' With a bitter sigh he added, 'The parents were getting worried and wished her to settle down, finding highly eligible young men in the prospective-husband role.'

Momentarily silent, he glanced at Faro. 'I knew she hated all this. I loved her, had always loved her, and suddenly what seemed like a brilliant idea came to me. I proposed to her. I asked her to marry me. And she laughed. She laughed. Thought I was having a joke with her.'

And shaking his head violently as if the memory was too much to bear, '"How can I marry you?" That was what she said. "You're my friend. I don't love you."'

He sighed deeply. 'And that seems to have put an end to our friendship, too. She became suspicious, regarded me as part of her parents' conspiracy to marry her off.'

'Was this some time ago, sir?'

'No, in June – it was her birthday, but I realised she no longer shared confidences and avoided being alone with me. I understood her behaviour all too well. She had trusted me with her secrets and I had betrayed her.'

Another silence. Then Faro said, without a great deal of hope, considering the parallel of his own disastrous relationship with Inga, and her harsh words, 'When we find her again, maybe—'

Binsley shook his head firmly. 'No, absolutely

not. I have lost her. I know that. But I shall never cease to love her and that is the reason why I had to come to Orkney to help to find her, whatever happens . . .'

They had reached the stable block where a lad waited. Handing the mare over to him, Binsley turned again to Faro. 'Thank you for listening to my tale of woe, sir. It is such a relief to talk to someone. Forgive me for troubling you in this manner.'

'Not at all, sir. I do understand such problems.'

Binsley smiled. 'And yet you are still young.'

'I have lived long enough, with enough experience to realise that it is often easier to talk to a stranger than those closest to us by blood.'

Binsley's eyebrows raised. 'D'ye know, that is absolutely true.'

And as they walked back in the direction of the house, he added, 'I'm afraid Celia's parents can be difficult sometimes. They seem quite out of touch with how young people think and behave these days. They live in a cosy time lock, quite unaware that the world has moved on since Victoria came to the throne.'

He sighed. 'They have known me all my life, since I was four years old, like second parents, but I have never really got to know them at all. Always a bit in awe, never at ease with them as I am with Celia.' Pausing, he gave Faro a curious glance. 'And as I appear to be with you on the merest acquaintance.'

He got no further. 'Gerald – so this is where you are.' Two spaniels and the formidable figure of Sir Arnold bore down on them. Cracking his whip against his riding boots he said irritably, 'Thought we might have a morning ride together, but it seems you have forestalled me.'

'I took Blossom out, she needed exercising. Celia was very particular about such things.'

Sir Arnold pondered on this for a moment and said briskly, 'That's what we keep stable boys for. Mare's too meek and mild for me, I like an animal with spirit,' he said, pointing to the powerful black stallion being led from the stables.

Faro thought cynically that Sir Arnold's feelings obviously did not include spirited daughters.

Gerald turned and said, 'Good day, Faro. Good to meet you.' As he held out his hand, Sir Arnold looked astonished and stared at Faro as if seeing him for the first time and Binsley had spoken to a brick wall.

As far as he was concerned Gerald was alone. The policeman did not exist.

CHAPTER SEVENTEEN

Returning to his room in the servants' lodge, Faro's conversation with Gerald Binsley had given cause for considerable thought and reassessment and, in the kind of desperation he was enduring, in Binsley he had found it easier to talk to a perfect stranger.

One thing was clear. If Celia was indeed pregnant, then the man responsible was certainly not her old friend and confidant who was also quite unaware of this possible rival's existence.

Using his remarkable ability of total recall Faro went over every detail of what Binsley had revealed about Celia's rebellious nature – in the eyes of her parents, a tomboyish unnatural girl.

It confirmed Faro's theory that womankind

in general was also on the move, undergoing a metamorphosis – evidence provided by the fact that a curious coincidence linked Celia Prentiss-Grant and Inga St Ola, two young women belonging to different strata of society who had nothing in common, except for one element. They represented a new kind of woman who no longer considered themselves as mere breeding machines or men's chattels, but were preparing to face a future of sturdy independence; the words 'free spirit' came to mind.

If he married and had daughters, Faro wondered if they would, in turn, seem outrageous, bewildering, in attitudes which he would fail to understand, almost as if they belonged to a different species of women from his mother and her generation, upon whose ideals and beliefs he had been reared.

His own acquaintance contained one woman of this new breed. Lizzie had shown courage and proved herself indifferent to what society considered her shame. With Vince, a child the result of rape, she had not given in to despair or taken her own life, nor had she allowed society to brand her or put her into an asylum, as was the fate of so many unmarried mothers, with babies taken away from them and cast into the workhouse, doomed to a future of slave labour.

Lizzie had fought single-handed to survive

for herself and her child. She had refused to sell herself into prostitution but had sought menial jobs instead, determined that her baby should thrive and survive the stigma of illegitimacy.

Once again it seemed so unfair to Detective Constable Faro, who knew so much from his daily beat in Edinburgh's Leith Walk of the behaviour of respectable upper-class men who could defy the rules, patronise brothels, take a mistress, and often as a result of their indulgences, pass on, while laying claim to their conjugal rights, venereal disease to an innocent wife. All this and still they kept their heads high in Edinburgh society, a man's world where women remained an inferior species.

Faro shook his head. If Inga, Celia and Lizzie were three prime examples of new women from completely different classes, then there was a wind of change on the horizon, a change much overdue.

Stavely came back later that day, his arrival in Mary's kitchen timed to a well-cooked supper; an excuse to see what results Faro had to report. His watchful regard for his son while residing under his uncle Hal's roof was in temporary abeyance. Lily had gone down with summer fever and the devoted son had returned home to Kirkwall to take care of mother and siblings.

It was enough to endure the disappearance of Celia Prentiss-Grant without the anxiety of a son who might have criminal leanings. Stavely suspected that his brother-in-law indulged in a little smuggling, an activity regarded as harmless and almost a way of life by most of the inhabitants. He was not prepared to investigate further, bearing in mind the discredit its revelations might throw up by association. A smear on the reputation of a respectable sergeant with the Orkney Constabulary, to say nothing of Lily's concerns for his future promotion.

Faro's report of no claimants for the reward at Scarthbreck did not surprise him, as none but the bravest would have dared approach the formidable questioning of Sir Arnold.

Faro mentioned that he had met Gerald Binsley.

'What was he doing here? Could he be—?' asked Stavely eagerly. And darting a look at Mary Faro's back attending to the stove, he whispered, 'Could he be . . . er . . . responsible for her condition?'

Faro shook his head emphatically. 'According to him, he is regarded by her merely as an uncle.'

'An uncle, eh?' And ignoring that cynical snort, Faro went on, 'He's a long-time family friend, known Celia since childhood, here to help them find her.'

Stavely was disappointed in this result. Sighing, he sat back in his chair, patted his stomach and hoped there was room for a second helping of potatoes and beefsteak pudding. He would stay the night with Hal and take the gig back to Kirkwall in the morning.

'The lads back at the station can take care of any new developments.' Considering that very unlikely, he regaled Faro with an account of the far-fetched sightings of claimants that morning, eager for the reward.

'Up to now,' he added diving happily into treacle pudding, 'all we have to do is wait. The ransom note, that'll be the next thing.'

It was indeed. Stavely rode across, ready to depart for Kirkwall, when they were summoned to Scarthbreck. The ransom note had arrived by the morning mail, posted in Kirkwall the day before.

Written in block letters on a map showing the interior of St Magnus Cathedral offered as a visitors' guide, a pillar was marked with a cross. 'After Sunday morning service, hidden under the adjacent pew, deposit an envelope containing one thousand pounds in promissory notes. Do not fail if you wish to see your daughter alive again.'

Sir Arnold's face was even redder than usual.

He said hoarsely, 'This is worse than we expected.' And to his wife, hand-wringing, in floods of tears, 'Try to be calm, my dear.'

'Calm!' She screeched with terror, thrusting the note at Stavely, 'This note is in our daughter's handwriting. Do you understand what that means? God only knows the indignities she has had to suffer writing this, with a pistol at her head.'

'You are certain that this is in her hand?' Stavely asked Sir Arnold.

'No doubt about that. We fear that she has been forced by her kidnappers to write it,' he added, accompanied by howls of terror from Lady Millicent.

This was indeed a grave situation. While Stavely assured the terrified parents that there would be every available constable stationed in the vicinity in plain clothes ready to make an arrest, he obviously had not thought of the difficulties involved.

Faro considered the reality of attempting to catch the kidnappers in a cathedral with the congregation milling out after morning service. One man could easily lurk and make his escape.

The note also revealed something of the kidnapper's identity. He obviously knew the cathedral well, also the placing of the side chapels, and might well be one of the Sunday worshippers. Aware that the Prentiss-Grants would expect a solitary lonely stretch of road, perhaps with a few trees, favoured by kidnappers when collecting ransoms, he had also taken into account the precaution that, most likely, the police would be lurking somewhere out of sight.

As for the constables, they were well known to everyone locally and, even out of uniform and in their Sunday best, would be readily identifiable.

The kidnapper was clever. What better place than his choice of a crowded Sunday morning service at the cathedral, which would conceal his identity and make the uplifting of the ransom easier? Even with uniformed constables stationed outside the doors, ready to search everyone who emerged, this unexplained activity would not be kindly received. Consternation, anger and indignation would reign from those innocent churchgoers delayed and eager to get home to Sunday dinners.

To Stavely, examining the note, Faro said, 'This is no spur-of-the moment ransom demand. We are dealing with someone local, who has worked it out very carefully, down to the last detail.'

Stavely sighed. 'You're right about that. Well, we won't have long to wait until tomorrow morning.'

They would both be in place at the service, the plain-clothes constables in position, and Stavely decided that Faro and one of the strongest constables, Willy, known for his prowess in the prize ring, should sit together in a pew concealed by the pillar, ready to leap out and arrest the kidnapper.

As agreed with Sir Arnold despite Lady Millicent's pleas, there would be no money, only an empty packet.

It was going to be a long morning service, Faro decided, keeping a close eye on the pillar from the pew across the aisle. Those nearest were a family with five somewhat unruly children of assorted ages, the eldest at the end of the line, a lad in the traditional woollen bonnet. The adjacent pews were occupied by better-behaved small families, young and elderly couples, and two black-clad widows. Perhaps one was Thora, impossible to identify under the heavy veils.

The ferryman, Rob, came in alone, and quickly knelt in an adjacent pew across the aisle, motionless, praying earnestly until the service began. Of his friend, Amos, there was no sign, perhaps the demands of his invalid brother excluded churchgoing on Sunday mornings.

Watching the family with the naughty children took Faro back to his own early days, constantly admonished to sit still. At his side now, her mother's tender sideways glance said she, too, was remembering his childhood days. She had insisted on accompanying him in the carriage which Sir Arnold, aware of the plan to capture the kidnapper, had placed at the disposal of Faro and Stavely.

Faro feared there might be danger but could think of no plausible excuse to make her stay behind at Scarthbreck, since other arrangements had been made for the servants to go to the local church escorted by the factor's wife.

Mary sighed: she did so miss morning service at the cathedral and this was an unmissable chance of an extra day off; an excuse for calling on the artist Emil to collect her overdue rent.

'Even on Sunday?' said Faro, but she refused to be shocked by his admonishing tone.

'I'll look in on some of the neighbours, have a cup of tea with them.'

And no doubt, thought Faro, she would be eagerly received for the latest gossip about Scarthbreck's owners and the posters of the missing girl displayed everywhere.

As they made their way into the cathedral, she did not have to go in search of Emil Latour. He was there already seated in an adjoining pew. He bowed cordially.

'Strange, seeing him here,' she whispered to

Faro. 'I thought he'd be a Catholic, that crucifix in the bedroom and everything.'

The sermon seemed longer than any Faro remembered. Over at last, the congregation stood for the last hymn. The procession of choir and ministers moved towards the nave, and as the worshippers filed out, among them were Faro and prizefighter Willy, who edged closer to the pillar.

There was no movement towards the pew and as the cathedral emptied, Stavely rushed over. Regardless of holy ground, he cursed softly. Their wait and their preparations had been in vain. The packet was still there. Their plan foiled.

They exchanged glances. The kidnapper must have guessed, or been warned in advance.

At least Mary Faro's visit had not been in vain. Emil had awaited her outside and had handed over his monthly rent with sincere apologies.

'Wasn't that thoughtful? Nice chap,' said Mary. 'He has invited me to have luncheon with him.'

She sounded delighted. 'I might as well seize the chance of such a nice invitation. Not often I get a Sunday off.'

'How will you get back?'

'Don't worry about me, dear. Mistress Blake's

man has the local stable. He'll see me right.'

Kissing her and telling her to take care, advising the Scarthbreck coachman where to wait for him, he hurried towards a side entrance of the cathedral where Stavely, having dismissed the constables, including Faro's colleague, was pretending to examine the tombstones, anxious to escape to a family Sunday dinner: an afternoon with Lily and the children, and in particular some carefully phrased questioning regarding any dubious activities of his wayward son.

'There's nothing to be gained by lingering, Faro,' he said shortly. 'Our man must have guessed. We'll have to think of something else. Go back and tell Sir Arnold – he won't be best pleased. Take the carriage.'

'I think I'll remain here for a while longer.'

Somewhere a clock struck the hour. Stavely stared at him. 'Please yourself, lad, but it's a waste of time.'

'Nevertheless, just an idea, Sergeant.' He shook his head. 'Maybe we're looking for the wrong person.'

Stavely regarded him sternly. 'Well, you're on your own; if there's a fight, you're not armed, remember.'

'I'll survive, without a gun.'

Stavely shook his head and repeated, 'A complete

waste of time.' And with a contemptuous shrug, watching Faro vanish into the side door of the now-empty cathedral, strode briskly homewards.

Taking up a position concealed by the pillar near the pew, Faro prepared to wait, aware that he was taking a gamble, but his instinct had never failed him, nor had his remarkable memory.

He had made careful notes, right back to the fatal night of Celia's disappearance. The curious fact that Celia had vanished into thin air without her clothes; why? And more important, how?

Certain that she had not gone into the sea, or that any boat would have risked the dangers of such a fog to collect her at the fragile Scarthbreck landing, and certain that she had not taken refuge in the nearest croft, which was Hal's, where Stavely would have found her, he thought she could have returned to pick up Blossom. But the mare had never left the stable.

If not by sea, then the only other exit from the area would be heading in the direction of Stromness and Kirkwall, but the hiring stable at Spanish Cove had verified that no young woman came in that night. For Faro's benefit, the stableman had described the elderly gentleman who had booked a gig, and the young man who had hired a horse. He had watched them each leave, and checked that the equipages and the horse were duly paid for, and as was the custom, had been returned safely from the Kirkwall stable.

Second on Faro's list, the handwriting on the ransom note, and the terrifying implications suggested by Lady Millicent that Celia had been forced to write it, with a pistol held at her head by her kidnapper.

Thirdly, and perhaps most revealing, were details of his interesting conversation with Gerald Binsley which had revealed clues previously overlooked.

Finally, the foiled pickup of the ransom this morning. As Faro sat patiently in the empty cathedral, he knew he was staking all on a remote possibility, the discovery of the kidnapper's identity.

The minutes passed slowly, a clock chimed a half-hour, and another. He was cold and hungry. Observation and deduction had failed him, he had almost given up and was about to leave, when the sound of a door opening echoed unnaturally loud through the empty cathedral.

Footsteps approaching, he braced himself to confront Celia Prentiss-Grant's kidnapper.

CHAPTER EIGHTEEN

The footsteps were of the youth from the family with the unruly children who had been seated nearest to the pillar. Attired in shirt and breeches, he did not even look round. Unaware of Faro's hidden presence, bending down he began a search underneath the pew.

'Can I assist you?'

The lad jumped up and faced Faro. 'You startled me, sir.' His hands were trembling. 'I-I was looking for . . . for something that Mamma left behind.'

In reply, Faro held out the packet. 'Would this perhaps be—?'

He got no further before the youth jumped forward and seized the envelope. 'Thank you, thank—' then shaking it, 'But it is—'

A bewildered angry glance and Faro smiled. 'Empty. Yes, that is so.' As he said the words the youth turned quickly but the narrowness of the pew put a stop to his flight.

Faro seized his arm in a firm grip. He struggled to free himself, pounding his fists against Faro's chest. 'Let me go, sir – this instant.'

'In a moment – after we have had a little talk.'

'I have nothing to say to you.'

Faro laughed. 'Oh, I think you have a great deal to say to me. Is that not so? Surely you realise that gentlemen remove their head coverings in church. Allow me.' And so saying, he reached out and snatched off the woollen bonnet. A cloud of curls sprang from their confinement.

'Ah, Miss Celia, we meet once again.'

'You – you devil! How dare you! Release me at once.'

'No point in being high and mighty with me, miss. You are in a very dangerous situation – you could go to jail.'

She stared at him, biting her lip. 'What nonsense. Of course I can't go to jail. I haven't – I haven't hurt anyone,' she added doubtfully.

'Maybe not.'

'I just wanted to get away. A practical joke, that's all.'

Faro shook his head. 'You have created a criminal act of deception which had the whole constabulary out combing the shore near Scarthbreck, posters distributed everywhere and the whole of the island looking for you. Don't you think that is quite enough criminal activity, to say nothing of the distress and anguish you have caused to your parents?'

'I'm not sorry for them,' she said. 'Now may I go?'

'And where to, might I ask?'

'I shall leave the island – leave everyone.' A stifled sob as she attempted to shake off his restraining hold. 'Please let me go.'

'In a moment. Now sit down and listen.'

'I will not. You cannot make me.'

'Very well. But first of all, let me assure you that it will be better for you and for all concerned if you will sit down – here, in this quiet place where we are unlikely to be disturbed – and tell me the story, right from the beginning.'

She looked at him doubtfully. Removing his hand from her arm, he said gently, 'Do sit down, miss.'

Suddenly tears started. 'They wanted to marry me off and I wasn't going to stand for that – like a package auctioned to the highest bidder. Not likely. I had my own plans.' Her expression softened.

'Which were?'

'I had met someone – here, before we left for London. We were in love and I believed . . .' a shadow crossed her face. 'I believed truly that we would be together always and that I could persuade my parents to see that was best for me. There was a terrible row – threats – they were going to lock me in my room. I had to escape, so I stole some money out of Pappa's desk. I knew all about the ships for Orkney, we often travelled that way.'

She paused and Faro asked, 'What happened when you arrived, after we walked on the shore together?'

She laughed softly. 'I had it all worked out. I knew about the seal king legend, I'd been fascinated by it as a child. The maids used to tell me, especially about that local woman, Thora somebody, who had been taken by him and survived, and returned after a year and a day.'

She gave a romantic sigh. 'It gave me an idea – I would make it look as if that had happened to me, give them something more important to worry about than finding me a husband,' she added contemptuously. 'I wore . . . these,' she said, indicating breeches and shirt. 'Easy to conceal under a loose gown and my winter cloak. I was grateful for that heavy mist, I can tell you. I walked back to Spanish Cove, hired a horse and rode into . . .'

'Kirkwall,' Faro prompted, remembering the description of the youth and the destination given by the stableman.

She gave him a sharp glance as he added, 'That is where your lover lives, is it not?'

Her eyes widened, then tearfully she groaned, 'Not is – was! Oh, he seemed delighted to see me but after . . . after that first night together, when I talked about our plans for the future – I'm not a fool. I had a feeling that marriage was not in his mind. Excuses in plenty: yes, he adored me, but surely I could see that he was too poor to support a wife as well as his invalid brother.'

Faro now knew the identity of this lover, Amos Flett. He was not particularly surprised considering the ferryman's reputation with the island women of which poor, misguided Celia had been quite unaware.

'If it was only money,' she continued, 'then that could be solved. I have a very rich father. So I got this brilliant plan, pretending I had been kidnapped and sending a ransom note. A thousand pounds was an absolute fortune, we could leave the island, start afresh and live happily ever after.'

She crumpled the empty envelope in her

hand. 'Even if it didn't change his mind about marrying me, I was going to take it anyway. It could change my whole life.'

'You would never have got away with it, miss, not once it was under investigation by the police. Kidnapping is a crime, the penalties could be hanging or transportation.'

She looked scared. 'Surely not if it wasn't serious – as I told you – just a joke.'

Faro shook his head. 'No joke, miss. In plain words, you were stealing, obtaining money by false pretences.'

'Rubbish! It couldn't be stealing – from my own father.'

Faro nodded. 'Oh yes, it could. It is still a crime, once the police are involved. You and your lover could both go to jail. Hanging or transportation, remember.'

'But A—' she stopped, and put a hand to her mouth.

'Amos is his name, am I correct?'

'Yes,' she admitted reluctantly. 'But Amos is innocent. He knew nothing of this—'

'A moment – did your parents know his identity?'

'Of course not. I wasn't going to tell them. They wanted to know, but I'm not an idiot – my father would have moved heaven and earth to remove him; he can be quite ruthless.'

Her words confirmed Faro's suspicions that the Prentiss-Grants knew more than they pretended about her reason for returning to Orkney: that, as he and Stavely also suspected, a man was involved. He said, 'Please continue.'

'A-Amos was taken aback – shocked – at what I had planned. When he saw the posters, then he panicked, and when I told him about my brilliant idea involving the ransom note I'd sent, he almost threw me out of the house.' Tearfully, she turned to Faro, 'What am I going to do?'

'First of all, your father's carriage is still waiting outside the local public house, to take you back to Scarthbreck.'

'Oh no!' she protested, springing to her feet.

'Oh yes, miss. You must face your parents.'

'They'll be furious. They have never forgiven me for not being a boy, you know. They desperately needed a son and heir.'

'I am sure you are wrong and that they love you.'

She shook her head. 'Oh, you don't know them. They will never forgive this . . .'

'They will be angry, but all will be forgiven in the relief of having you back home again. And Gerald will be delighted too—'

'Gerald?' Smiling, she clasped her hands delightedly. 'Is dear Gerald here too?'

'Indeed, he is. Came post-haste to help search for you.'

'Oh, that was kind!'

'He is very fond of you, and I am sure he will put in a good word for you.'

Her face softened again. 'Yes, he is kind, the one person who understands me. If only my parents hadn't been so determined when the wretched men they put in my way were horrible; they decided that I should marry Gerald. He proposed to me – they put him up to it. A last resort, after all those years of being my good friend. I couldn't believe it. I was disgusted.'

'I rather think it was his own idea, not your parents', although they would have approved.'

'It was the last straw.'

They were walking towards the entrance. At the door Faro said, 'May I suggest you replace the woollen cap, and hide your hair?'

As she did so, he added, 'A necessary precaution. I'm sure you don't want to attract attention and curious stares – a girl in a man's shirt and breeches, among Kirkwall's Sunday afternoon strollers.'

'Over here.' He led the way to the Lamb & Flag, where Tom, sitting at the window, quickly downed his ale and rushed out. His eyes wide in astonishment, he bowed as Faro handed her into the carriage. 'To the police station, if you please—'

She gave him an angry glance, pushed open the door and tried to leap out. 'You promised – you promised.'

Hauling her back as she wriggled in vain, he shouted to the driver, 'And then to Scarthbreck! Let me finish, miss, if you please. I have to let Sergeant Stavely know that Miss Celia has been found.' As they stopped, he said, 'Hand this in, if you please, Tom,' and hastily scribbled a note for Stavely to come to Scarthbreck immediately.

Tom returned, averting his eyes from the young mistress, and Celia said wearily to Faro, 'You can remove your hand from my arm now, Constable. I won't run away.'

Faro smiled at her. 'I wish I could be sure of that. Maybe I should have requested a pair of handcuffs at the police station.'

As they drove towards Stromness, she said, 'I won't be sorry to leave that awful house. I was always hungry.'

Faro smiled. 'Not quite what you were used to.'

She shuddered. 'Not in the least. I am not sure, now that I have come to my senses and am quite safely out of being madly in love, that I could have ever endured life in such a house. Always untidy, it even smelt rather dark and dreary. And I was expected to feed them both, cook for them. What an idea!

'I haven't the least notion about preparing meals, it has always been done for me. And then there was that brother of his. I was told that he was an invalid. He didn't seem to care for my presence, either, and always tried to avoid me. Never spoke a word.'

Faro had a vivid picture of Thora and Josh Flett and that lover-like meeting in the cathedral as she continued, 'Such ill manners, too. Never rose to his feet like a gentleman when I entered the room, just kept on huddled up by the fireplace as if it was a cold day, with his bonnet pulled down well over his eyes.'

She shook her head. 'Of course, I was sorry for him, knowing how ill he was and that making an effort to be polite was too much for him. He seemed much more lively at night, though. After I retired I used to hear them laughing and talking together – and I suspected that the whisky bottle was much in evidence.'

As they drove through Spanish Cove, she turned to Faro and smiled sadly, 'You have been so kind to me. You are a strange policeman. When we first met that night – just a few days, seems such a long time ago,' she added with a shudder, 'even then, you never seemed a stranger . . .'

She paused, a bewildered shrug, then she smiled, placing a hand on his arm. 'I have absolute trust in you, Constable, and whatever happens over there – at home – I'll always be grateful to you for listening to me. And I am sure you will do your very best to save me being sent to jail.'

A frowning maid opened the door to Constable Faro accompanied by a youth. Uncertain whether to admit them or not, shocked by the lad's somewhat scruffy attire, she clearly did not recognise her esteemed young mistress.

Celia suppressed a giggle and swept a manly bow to the astonished maid who said, 'I will see if Sir Arnold is at home.'

'No need. He is expecting us,' she said, striding towards the drawing room where faint voices could be distinguished.

The maid scuttled ahead, throwing open the door. 'Constable Faro here, sir, with . . . with . . . a gentleman.'

Celia marched in, and stood facing her parents. Sir Arnold rose to his feet, darting an angry glance at Faro. 'Another claimant, is this?'

'Not at all, Father.' And Celia took off the bonnet and shook free her curls.

'Celia!' her mother screamed. 'You are wearing breeches!' She promptly fell back in her chair, and in the consternation that followed no one even considered producing the required smelling salts.

'Celia, my dear.' It was Gerald who stepped forward and Celia threw herself sobbing into his arms.

Leaving her to explain as best she could the reason for this extraordinary reappearance, Faro chose not to be present, and before anyone could halt his exit, thankfully closed the door on what would doubtless prove to be a very painful and long-remembered domestic scene.

CHAPTER NINETEEN

Returning to the servants' lodge, an hour passed before a very angry, frustrated Stavely appeared. He had witnessed the amazing scene of Celia still in disguise and arguing furiously with her father, while her mother, weeping, implored her to retire immediately and put on a decent gown.

Celia ignored her, obstinately denying that she had come to Orkney to 'meet up with that fellow', whose identity she steadfastly refused to disclose. At least she owed him that. Now that the whole business might end in disaster for the hapless Amos Flett, she refused to take revenge upon an innocent man. Even angry with him, heartbroken by his rejection, she was sufficiently fair-minded to see clearly that she had been driven by her own impetuosity, and although she cringed at the thought, she had forced herself upon him.

The responsibility was hers. On the strength of some passionate kisses, she had believed that this was the love that would last a lifetime. Amos's only crime was that she had taken seriously his intentions and imagined that such overtures indicated that he was also wildly in love and intended marriage, when, in fact, this was his normal flirtatious behaviour as most of the young women on the island could have told her.

As for Stavely, having been reduced to a minor role in the drama of the missing heiress, he was not best pleased to realise that Constable Faro was receiving any praise that was going, for making the 'arrest' and unmasking the kidnapper single-handedly. It was most unjust, considering all the hard work the Orkney Constabulary had put in. And for himself in particular, bearing in mind the disruption of his comfortable home life by living near to Scarthbreck with his wretched brother-in-law.

Picking up the threads he was witnessing of the Prentiss-Grants' reconciliation with their daughter, Stavely was annoyed that he had never suspected Miss Celia's deception as he studied the 'youth', tall and slim in shirt and breeches, arguing with Sir Arnold. He had been deceived by the voluminous cloak, the loose gown discarded by the shore, and had taken for granted that they were to hide a pregnancy, and had he been a bit sharper than Constable Faro and more observant, then his success in solving this particular 'crime' would have weighted handsomely on the credit side of his speedy promotion, with an additional commendation from Sir Arnold.

Sitting at the kitchen table, ignoring Faro's pleas to calm himself, he shouted, 'Why didn't you inform me at the cathedral of your suspicions? As we have worked together on this case, didn't you think I was entitled to share them?'

'One can never be absolutely sure, Sergeant. I could have been wrong and I realised there might be a long wait ahead.' Remembering that Stavely was very short on patience, he added, 'A wait you would not have enjoyed, eager to get home where Mrs Stavely had dinner on the table for you.'

Stavely grunted, a happy fleeting memory of that feast now troubling his digestive system. 'I take exception to that message handed in at the station. You know where I live, you could have come to the house.'

Faro was becoming exasperated by a futile

argument and what promised to be a chronicle of 'what ifs?'. He said, 'The police station was nearest and I had to hold on firmly to Miss Celia, who was doing her utmost to escape. No means of restraining her. No handcuffs, alas, in the Scarthbreck carriage.'

They weren't getting anywhere and Stavely decided to change the subject. 'What about this man?'

'What man?' Faro remembered his promise and shook his head. 'There was a man – in London – her parents wanted her to marry. She rebelled and ran off, back to Orkney. Had this idea she'd scare them by pretending that the seal king had carried her off.'

No man and no pregnancy. All the wrong answers. Stavely sighed. 'What nonsense. As if any normal man like Sir Arnold would believe that story. How was this seal king able to write a ransom note?'

'We all knew it was written by Celia herself. Her mother was the one to seize on the terrible possibilities it indicated. And there was enough realism in the kidnapping story for Celia to try to extract one thousand pounds from her father. That was all she wanted. A vast sum of money.'

And remembering Celia's version, he added. 'She would be rich – indeed, it would have given her independence, a chance to escape a forced marriage and begin a new life.'

'Must be out of her mind – bad in the making and mad too – to want to leave that life of luxury every young lass would envy, with everything she wanted.'

Faro thought, not quite everything, but made no comment as Stavely continued, 'I'm going to have the devil of a job explaining it to the authorities, and she could be in big trouble, you know, breaking the law by this deception.'

'I am sure you're right, but Sir Arnold will no doubt pull a few strings and be eager to more than compensate for his embarrassment and the extra work involved for the local police.'

Stavely realised, with feelings of guilt, that this was indeed the case. As he was leaving Scarthbreck, the mollified Sir Arnold saw him to the door and suggested that the Orkney Constabulary accept a large sum of money to repay this costly mistake, his foolish daughter's behaviour which had caused such inconvenience to everyone concerned. He had even added, clearing his throat, that the fault was his, imagining that his daughter had been kidnapped, spreading alarm and despondency across the entire island, when it appeared she had merely been visiting old friends.

As a postscript and a piece of spur-of-the-moment invention, he added casually, 'Seems it wasn't entirely her fault. She did leave a note on her mother's dressing table. Got blown away . . . windy day, open window. That was how the alarm was raised.'

Stavely hoped his peers would believe it. Personally, he didn't believe one single word and neither did Faro, which was hardly surprising since he knew the whole truth regarding Celia Prentiss-Grant's disappearance.

One person, however, was delighted and excited by this fanciful embroidery of what had happened. Mary Faro never once questioned its authenticity, for it would never have occurred to her that the master of Scarthbreck, a peer of the realm, respected by all, would be capable of a deliberate lie.

Regaled by the misfortune of the missing message, she said stoutly that she never had faith in notes left precariously on dressing tables by open windows. She had a story about an acquaintance to fit such an occasion. The tragedy of a note on a mantelpiece which blew down into a blazing fire and almost set a room ablaze.

As for Sir Arnold, his generosity knew no bounds. Relieved beyond measure to have his daughter returned safely and unsullied, in what he presumed was still her virgin state, the servants were given an extra day off to compensate for sleepless nights and the stress of several days of needless anxiety.

Mary Faro, however, was less interested in the outcome of this piece of drama which had happened in her absence. She had a tale of her own, and Faro found himself listening to a prolonged version of her lunch with Emil Latour, from which every bite eaten was described in elaborate detail.

She looked flushed and glowing, a surprisingly youthful mamma, and he suspected she had sampled Emil's splendid French cuisine, which Faro learnt he was an expert in, along with an accompanying indulgence in excellent French wine.

Amused at first, he realised that he was also slightly shocked at somewhat unseemly behaviour more in keeping with a giddy eighteen-year-old than the lady he regarded as a stolid mother, at fifty beyond frivolity and interest in the opposite sex. Now it was alarmingly evident that after all these years of widowhood she did not consider herself beyond a little romance.

In all fairness, listening somewhat impatiently as she chattered so happily, he decided that it was always a little shocking to discover romantic tendencies in parents, considered from childhood as quite old by their offspring.

There was a pause. A gleam in her eye as she reached her tenant's plans for returning to Paris.

'He hoped – no, *insisted* that I should visit him there,' she added, with a look of triumph. 'Very soon. Without delay. Fancy that, now!'

Faro's eyebrows shot skyward at this revelation from the mother who had stoutly refused to leave the island for Edinburgh, which she had abandoned after his father's death, not consenting even now to visit him.

Pleased with her conquest, she giggled girlishly and Faro's lack of comment in this monologue needed no comment or interruption. All her occasional glances were directed at him to establish that he was still paying attention and interested. There was an occasional wry movement of his lips, hardly a smile but eagerly interpreted by his mother as a gesture of approval.

Dismayed, he realised that she was quite moonstruck, something new and fortunately rare – flirting with an artist twenty years her junior. Well, well, he thought, after all these years devoted to mourning her beloved Magnus, it had just taken a couple of hours and a rather flashy Frenchman to break the spell.

But Faro was soon to learn that he had not heard or seen the last of Emil and neither, to her delight, had Mary Faro. A horseman cantered up the drive to Scarthbreck and Emil dismounted, accompanied by artist's materials and a large easel strapped to the saddle.

Mary looked out of the window, and with a small exclamation, quickly removed her apron, straightened her skirts and glanced in the mirror, tidying hair that was immaculate beyond reproach, before rushing out to greet him.

Faro watched, fascinated, as the tall Frenchman bowed over her and kissed her hand. The indications of luggage hinted that this was not to be a brief visit for afternoon tea. He was right. Emil had come to stay.

Bewildered, he wondered what on earth was happening to his practical down-to-earth mother as, full of laughter, her face glowing at some whispered flattery, she led Emil into her kitchen.

Seeing Faro, he bowed, and Mary said, 'Emil is to stay here for a few days. You'll never guess, Jeremy.' And to Emil, 'Do please tell him.'

Bowing gravely, Emil made a gesture of dismissal, 'Sir Arnold was most impressed by my quick sketch of his daughter and he now wishes her to sit for her portrait in oils.'

This, Faro later learnt, was a commission to celebrate what her parents hoped and prayed for, a forthcoming engagement to the Hon. Gerald Binsley. Mary said, 'Emil is to have a room in the lodge here. I will leave him with you, Jeremy, while I see that a suitable room is available.'

Faro decided wryly that Inga would enjoy this story regarding his mother's transformation. Emil was not in any hurry. Several preliminary sketches must be made, as the artist solemnly declared that it was his usual procedure to get to know his model before the actual painting began.

As Mary eagerly rejoined them, for Faro suddenly the roles of mother and son were reversed and he felt like a father sternly regarding the skittish behaviour of a lovesick daughter. He wondered what would be the outcome, anxious about leaving her unchaperoned in Emil's society after he left Scarthbreck.

For Stavely, at least, there was some relief that Constable Faro need no longer stay to gloat over him – although gloating was not one of Faro's failings.

'You can go back to your duties in Edinburgh, now that this matter has been cleared up and filed away to everyone's satisfaction.'

Faro smiled. 'I am no longer a prime suspect.'

Stavely moved uncomfortably. 'It wasn't my doing. In the regulations, which you know as well as any of us, the last person that is seen in the company of someone who disappears under suspicious circumstances should remain accessible until the case is solved.

'Unlike yourself, normally such a person doesn't happen to live in a part of the British Isles with easy access to the scene. So we could hardly let you go back to Edinburgh, could we now? Fortunately for you, and for the police, it wasn't a dead body after all.'

Or not quite after all, as the following days were to reveal.

CHAPTER TWENTY

The prospect of returning to Edinburgh should have left Faro with a sense of triumph after solving the mystery of Celia Prentiss-Grant's disappearance. But after a week of unexpectedly intense activity with the Orkney Constabulary rather than a holiday, it would seem tame indeed to pick up the threads of his life at the Central Office.

He might now summon up courage to ask Lizzie to marry him, although he was no longer wholly certain about this, or even that she would eagerly accept. Meeting Inga again had raised doubts that he knew anything at all about women, to say nothing of their extraordinary behaviour as personified by Celia and, now, even by his own mother.

You knew where you were with men, he thought, by comparison. They seemed uncomplicated, straightforward creatures.

He would have ended his Orkney visit with a lighter heart had there not been a couple of riddles still unsolved: his negative report to Macfie on Dave Claydon's accident and the artefacts he was carrying to Edinburgh.

Or what intrigued him most, the missing year and a day from Thora Claydon's life a decade ago.

He was unable to accept the popular island version of the seal king's bride which gave her a kind of legendary aura: although the islanders might prefer to shake their heads and add it eagerly to their recorded legends of trolls, selkies and magic, this one would continue to haunt him.

Common sense told him that every mystery has an explanation, and the only magic for Faro was the occasional miracle by which, against all the odds, a dying man like Josh Flett was wooing Dave Claydon's widow.

He thought again of the similarities between Celia and Thora. The latter reconciled to Dave who had accepted her lack of memory for those missing months and promptly married her. Celia had been reconciled to her parents, and it seemed very likely that she would marry her faithful Gerald, who would dismiss the fleeting incident of her amour with Amos Flett.

The reply to his letter to Macfie, which he had been expecting daily, arrived next day and its contents reopened the mystery of Dave Claydon's drowning.

Macfie wrote, 'Hope this reaches you in time. I have been in touch with the authorities concerned and they are unable to trace any correspondence with Dave in their files relating to priceless artefacts which he claimed were being brought by him to Edinburgh on their orders. What is even more baffling is that there was no trace of a Leith-registered ship leaving Kirkwall that evening. This information has caused me grave concern that Dave was using his situation as an excise officer to engage in some criminal activity such as smuggling. I realise that this information will not be of much use with your visit at an end, which is a pity because we are never likely to know the truth.'

Faro put down the letter which threw new light on the events of that fatal night. Amos had problems aplenty grappling with his small boat in wild seas that night and could have mistaken a merchant vessel looming towards them in heavy fog as the Leith-bound ship Dave Claydon informed him that he intended boarding. If he was not carrying the artefacts to Edinburgh, why was he boarding the ship in the first place? The answer that came readily was that he had in mind a private buyer in some other place abroad.

Macfie's information had come too late. Faro had no time left to open another investigation suggested by its contents. As for the artefacts, the truth lay buried with Dave in Kirkwall cemetery.

Then a thought. Unless Thora had been told.

Before he left he would make a final visit. An excuse to ask if she had any message for Macfie. He would also call on Amos, negotiate a chat to Josh, and aware of his romantic dalliance with Dave's widow, summon up opportunity to mention Claydon's unfortunate accident.

Finally, although he had little hope of success, there was a possibility that when he went to book a passage to Edinburgh, the shipping office might have on record details of vessels leaving Kirkwall on the night of Claydon's drowning.

Too late, alas, for any successful action and he could not imagine stirring up interest from Stavely, or even Jimmy, with new light on a closed case and a dead man.

There was one other person he could not leave Orkney without seeing once more. And that was Inga. Despite his shattered illusions – and indeed his forlorn hopes – he would always care deeply for her. She had an indestructible place in his heart, part of the youth he had left ten years ago, part of his growing-up.

As for his mother, she had promised to come and visit him this time. He had refrained from asking, 'Would that be before or after going to Paris to see Emil Latour?' He could sympathise with her. She had no friends or connections in Edinburgh that did not revive dismal memories of her heartbreak over Magnus's death.

Faro knew he would not be coming back to Orkney in the foreseeable future and began planning his remaining few days.

'Must you go so soon?' his mother demanded. 'I've got used to having you. I'll miss you. It seems like only yesterday that you arrived. You could get a transfer to the Orkney Constabulary,' she added wistfully. 'It would be great having you home for good and I'm sure Sergeant Stavely would give you a fine recommendation. He would be so pleased to have you working with him.'

Faro wasn't at all sure about that and shuddered at the prospect she was suggesting, as she said, 'We shall all miss you, you belong here.'

That much was true. He did belong, from the very roots of his being. He could not deny that. His selkie blood called to him. Body and soul might be Orcadian but his heart needed escape from the confines of island traditions. Ambition yearned for enlightenment, for a larger canvas to explore.

There was no immediate transport to Kirkwall available, so he decided, although an indifferent horseman, he would hire a mount from the stables at Spanish Cove. First the shipping office, then Thora and a call on Amos.

Would the ferryman be shocked that Dave Claydon had deceived him regarding the identity of the ship bound for Edinburgh? Or would he argue that it had been a natural mistake?

Whether Amos knew the truth or not, it was understandable that he did not wish to admit to any involvement in the illegal practice of taking passengers to board departing vessels, their credentials cleared by the port authorities.

As Faro walked the short distance to Spanish Cove he decided to look in on Inga, but the door remained closed. She was not at home. Nor was the stableman. A note on the door said 'Back at 2'.

With more than an hour to wait but hardly worth returning to Scarthbreck, he decided to explore the local store which had an engaging 'Teas served' notice in the window.

He doubted there would be many customers, with only two small tables covered with checked cloths and vases of wilting wild flowers, a gallant attempt at lightening a dark, uninviting corner.

One table was occupied. A cheery greeting from the botanist, Mr West. 'My housemaid is away for the day. She looks after me very well, cooks and cleans. All quite adequate but I decided to treat myself to a little luxury.' And indicating the chair opposite, 'Do please join me in a little celebrative lunch. I come here quite regularly and I recommend the soup and the bannocks and cheese.'

Their order placed, the conversation switched from the present availability of botanical specimens and the unreliable weather to the book West had laid aside.

Faro said, 'I'm afraid I interrupted your reading.'

West smiled. '*A Tale of Two Cities*, Mr Dickens' latest and a great book. Apart from *Barnaby Rudge* dealing with the Gordon riots, all his novels so far have dealt with present-day topics – and how excellently he brings injustices to light. This one, however, set in the French Revolution, is his first venture into historical fiction.'

When Faro said that he was also a great admirer of Mr Dickens, the botanist beamed on him, and indicating the book again, 'The plot intrigues me, the whole story hangs on two men in love with the same woman, one taking the other's place and making the supreme sacrifice. Unlikely, I fear, in real life, and relying on the Bastille guards being either unobservant or stupid. But Mr Dickens writes with such authority that his readers are called on for a suspension of disbelief. For myself, I greatly enjoy an adventure or a mystery.'

And the real-life mystery Faro had been trying to solve sprang into mind as West enquired politely, 'May I ask what is your profession, sir?'

Replying that he was a policeman, Mr West, fascinated, clapped his hands together. 'Would you believe it? That is exactly what I would have chosen had I not gone in for botany. Quite a difference, an interest in innocent flowers to violent crimes. And yet, there is something we have in common. And that is finding out what is behind it all, what makes things happen!'

Pausing, he gave Faro a look of triumph. 'Most intriguing! What is inside a plant to make it grow and what is inside a criminal to prompt him to commit violent deeds?'

Faro did not see all the logic behind these statements and was not called upon to unravel any of the botanist's theories, as the stableman walked past the window.

He stood up, explaining his journey to Kirkwall and the need for a horse. Handing over coins for his share of the lunch, they were sternly rejected.

As they shook hands West said, 'I trust we will meet again and continue this discussion. If not here, I shall be in Edinburgh in November to deliver a paper to the Royal Botanic Society.'

'That would be splendid,' said Faro, tearing out a sheet from his notebook and scribbling down his address. 'I shall look forward to seeing and hearing you, sir.'

A likeable and intelligent old gentleman, Faro thought as, armed with instructions from the stableman, who regarded his attempts to mount the mare with growing concern, he was asked, 'Are you sure you ever rode a horse before, sir?'

Treating the remark with a non-committal but embarrassed nod, Faro did not add that it was some considerable time since he had sat upon a horse in Orkney. An unnecessary qualification for police work where constables used their feet to patrol the streets of Edinburgh, any equestrian expertise he had was most certainly lost.

Now he rode out, unsteadily at first, watched by the stableman anxious for the welfare of his horse. However, a couple of miles down the road and he had the hang of it, firmly in the saddle and managing to trot at a steady pace, rather enjoying the novel experience.

* * *

At Stromness he watched the ferry approaching but decided not to wait for a word with Amos. An opportunity, while he was absent, to call on Josh Flett, and Faro wondered whether his wooing of Thora began during Dave's lifetime, a secret affair, or if it had grown out of compassion for the widow.

There were present all the ingredients of a tragic, doomed love about this relationship, and his thoughts returned to the discussion with Mr West and their mutual admiration for Mr Charles Dickens, for this was a subplot quite worthy of one of his novels.

Riding through a quilted landscape stretching to the horizon, he realised that the best of summer was past. Change was already in the air, a mature, mellow look to the fields, greens fading and the hint of harvests soon to be garnered.

He rode into Kirkwall, with a breeze never completely absent from that stretch of the road in his face. A pleasant, invigorating ride, although he had not the least doubt he would pay for this unusual exercise with aching muscles and stiff joints when he awoke next morning. Leaving the mare at the stable, with arrangements to take her back to Spanish Cove later that day, he was surprised to realise that he had grown quite fond of this new companion.

His first call was at the shipping office by the quay. And his first disappointment, to be informed that the next sailing to Leith was several days hence; a hiatus just as he was looking forward to being in Edinburgh again.

Making the booking and giving his name, the head of the clerk jerked up, looked at him and said, 'I know you, you're that Jeremy Faro who went to be a policeman.' And throwing down his pen, he leant across the desk and chuckled. 'Well now, I'd never have believed that of you. You never seemed that clever when we were at the school together . . .'

'Really?' Faro had not the slightest remembrance of the rather chubby, balding young man who was grinning amicably at him.

'That's correct. In the same class. We sat together one term and you were hopeless at sums, always getting the strap. I always beat you, got good marks, stars even. The teacher thought I'd go far.'

There was a hint of bitterness in his pride. 'I'm Tod Raine, don't you remember me?'

He had indeed changed and Faro barely recognised Raine as one of the bullies who had tormented his lame friend Erland Flett. Raine had maybe beaten him at sums, but did he remember that he had been no match for Faro in fisticuffs?

Doubtless this Tod Raine had forgotten such events, even the bloody nose he had received, and now seemed eager to be regarded as an old chum.

He was married, two great wee lads, he said. 'What about you?'

'I'm here on holiday, seeing my mother.'

'Not married yet?' When Faro shook his head, Raine gave him a look of contempt. 'Better get down to it, mate. Look sharp. You're not getting any younger, you know.'

Faro ignored that as Raine went on to boast that he was now head clerk with exceptional responsibilities, informed by his bosses that he was in line for promotion to a top situation in their Glasgow or Edinburgh offices.

Listening, Faro made the expected sounds of approval, his mind toying with other possibilities – if this was the right person to give him reliable information concerning the registration of the ship that Claydon had been boarding the night he drowned.

He decided to broach the subject by again producing the Edinburgh relative of Dave Claydon.

'Did I know Dave? Everyone knew Dave.'

He wagged a finger at Faro. 'The newspapers made a mistake.' And that was what Faro wanted to hear.

'Wasn't the Leith ship that night. The skipper's a grand, conscientious man. He would never tolerate those illegal goings-on. He protested, made quite a fuss about anyone believing it was his ship, but that never got into the papers, did it? Flett insisted that was what Dave had told him. But on such a terrible night anyone could have made a mistake.'

He shrugged. There was a pause and Faro asked, 'Have you any ideas about what ship it was, leaving that night?'

Raine looked at him and grinned. 'Is this one of your cases, Jeremy?'

Faro shrugged. 'Not at all. Just interested.'

'Then I can tell you there was only one ship – a Norwegian-registered merchantman bound for Hamburg – leaving that night.'

'Indeed? And it was never followed up – the mistake, I mean?'

'Of course not. No one wanted to involve the skipper. He didn't have much English and there would have been a rare court case, cost a lot of money. So they just kept quiet, let the newspaper report be taken for granted. Strictly illegal, this boarding out of harbour waters, but we all know it goes on.' And leaning further over the counter, he tapped his nose and whispered, 'Between you and me, there's quite a bit of smuggling involved. Always has been, it's nothing new and everyone knows – many get a share in it. Maybe Amos Flett, too. Who can tell? But money changing hands is great for keeping lips sealed. If you've got the money you can change the world these days.'

Faro guessed that the procedure of illegal boarding also provided splendid opportunities for smuggling artefacts abroad and he left Raine very thoughtfully.

Was Claydon's intended appointment with a buyer in Hamburg and were Stavely and the Orkney Constabulary aware of what was going on beneath their noses? Or did they turn a blind eye to a criminal activity which filled various pockets to satisfaction?

CHAPTER TWENTY-ONE

Walking past the cathedral, Faro's next stop was at *The Orcadian*, where he hoped that Jimmy Traill would not be absent in pursuit of one of his news stories. His luck was in.

Jimmy sat huddled over a desk, his pen scratching furiously over what must have been a very trying and long article for the next edition. The pile of screwed-up pieces of paper littering the floor beside him indicated the gravity of this mind-searching task.

Turning and seeing Faro, he called, 'Come away in,' and obviously eager to abandon the task at hand, he left his desk, shook hands and gave Faro a friendly grin.

'Good to see you again. No, no, you're not

interrupting,' and pointing to the forlorn proof of his labours, he groaned.

'This is an infernally boring piece I have to write for tomorrow. Sheriff court procedures. So boring, not my style at all. I like plenty of action.' And rubbing his hands together, 'I was quite disappointed, I have to tell you, that the Celia Prentiss-Grant case fizzled out so soon.'

'All that fuss over a lost note,' he added in disgust. 'And I was all prepared for something really sensational after those posters. A kidnapping with a dramatic rescue. I could have guaranteed to keep our readers agog for weeks on that. How's your holiday?'

Hearing that he was taking the next Leith sailing and had come in to say farewell, Jimmy sighed. 'How I envy you, old chap. My ambition is to work on a national newspaper. One like *The Scotsman* where there must be interesting news to report every single day.'

Jimmy's problem, Faro thought cynically, was most aptly defined as the grass being always greener on the other side of the fence. He could have disillusioned him about the Edinburgh press. Readers wearied of information from the Indian wars on the North-West Frontier – unless some member of the family was a soldier, for most folk it was too remote to connect with their ordinary lives – and reports on the health of the

Royal Family, particularly those regarding Prince Albert, who was a lot less fit than his queen.

It was not unknown for journalists faced with blank pages for tomorrow's edition to desperately approach Edinburgh's Central Office in search of some police business, minor crimes or criminals that might be stretched out to fill a column or two.

'I should have told you before, but for circumstances back at Scarthbreck,' Faro said, 'about my visit to your auntie Bet.'

'How was she?' Jimmy's facial expression showed a lack of interest and enthusiasm.

'We did not have a great deal of conversation.'

'That doesn't surprise me.'

'She seemed a little confused.'

'Don't tell me – you weren't Thora. She's the only person Auntie ever expects or wants to see.' He laughed bitterly. 'Don't I just know. That's the reason I stopped going to visit her. Used to go regularly. But it's a long way, as you'll appreciate, and she wasn't in the least grateful, just resentful that I wasn't Thora or hadn't brought her with me. It was Thora this and Thora that and where was she?'

Pausing, he scowled. 'As if I knew or cared after the first and only time I took Thora with me, a wee while back while Auntie was still managing fine in her own home. What a disaster

– I might as well have been a piece of furniture – a table or chair would have had more attention than they paid to me. Auntie was getting very deaf, Thora had to sit close and hold her hand, listening to her going on about dear Elsa and the happy days they had long ago.

'It was very embarrassing for Thora with me present. In fact, she tended to avoid me after that. Even now, living just streets away, we can't help meeting but she'll cross to the other side of the street and pretend not to see me.'

'The last time we met was at Dave's funeral. A polite but chilly greeting, never invited me back to the house afterwards, nothing like that. Truth is, like I told you before, Auntie never liked me,' he added sadly. 'And now that she's lost her mind, I'm sorry for the poor old soul, but honestly haven't time to go all that way to listen to her rambling on about dear Elsa and Thora.'

'She seemed very upset about Elsa leaving them and going to the mainland,' Faro put in, and Jimmy shook his head.

'That daft sort of talk is too much for me. I got the impression that Elsa wasn't ever coming back and that Auntie was responsible.'

Faro shook hands and promised to keep him in touch with any events in Edinburgh that would make a column or two for *The Orcadian* readers. Jimmy said wistfully that if Faro heard of any post for an experienced journalist on *The Scotsman*, he would be greatly obliged.

As they parted, Faro wondered if he would have time to pay one more visit to Mrs Traill. Remembering her words about Elsa, his conversation with Jimmy had made her distress abundantly clear. And this might indicate that she knew the secret of Thora's year-long sojourn as the seal king's bride.

Six o'clock was striking as Faro made his way across Kirk Green towards Amos Flett's house. There was no response. A disappointment, as he was hoping to have a word with Josh alone, but presumably he did not answer the door in his brother's absence

Walking past the cathedral, where the faint sounds of a choir practice lilted through the air like the voices of angels, he was led towards the Earl's Palace, now a magnificent ruin, built by Robert Stewart. Created Earl of Orkney by his half-sister, Mary Queen of Scots, his reign of terror, penury and slavery was still remembered and Faro found it curious to understand why his mother and many like the Sinclairs and Scarths were proud to claim descent from the monster who, with his band of illegitimate sons, had peopled the length and breadth of the islands with their bastard offspring.

He would have preferred to claim descent from the selkies and Finn folk, the original inglorious inhabitants of the island. In his childhood years, Mary Faro, who took him to church twice on Sundays, would have been horrified by his fascination with the pagan gods who had pre-dated the birth of the Saviour of the world, remembered in the unchronicled history of brochs and the Ring of Brodgar, mysteries which continued to intrigue Faro – puzzles and riddles without hope of explanation.

If only his selkie grandmother had not died before he was born. If he could have had a chance to know her, he was sure she would have understood. They would have shared a bond that was lacking with his mother. No matter how much he loved her, they were poles apart in their understanding. But walking through places once dear brought a longing to return to the peace and safety of that long-lost family who had given him birth.

Sadly, he could no longer identify with the Jeremy Faro of those early years, a shadowy figure growing fainter with the passing years, the frail thread broken. It was as if he looked back on someone else, a strange child from one of Mary Faro's bedtime stories.

Hopefully, he returned to Amos's house. As

he waited, considering whether he should delay any longer, the door was opened by Amos, who did not look pleased to see him. He looked preoccupied, but courtesy demanded that he should be invited in and made welcome, making Faro feel guiltily that his excuse was feeble.

Leaving on Wednesday, could he have a timetable of ferry times? It all sounded very false, which it was.

Amos went ahead of him and was glancing around the room as if to establish that all was in order, and Faro had that strange feeling, so frequent on entering an empty room, that it needed a moment or two to rearrange itself.

Invited to sit down, Faro saw that the table had been set for two, but the empty dishes were not yet cleared.

Following his glance, Amos said apologetically, 'My day off – Rob's in charge of the ferry. I've been out and about.' Again that anxious look round the room. 'Domestic matters to attend to.' And opening a drawer he handed over a timetable. 'Here you are. This is what you need.'

His silent regard and faint smile as Faro studied it, hinted that he no longer had any excuse to prolong this visit.

Preparing to leave, Faro asked politely, 'How is your brother?'

Amos stared at Faro, whose mind was obviously elsewhere. 'Josh? Josh is upstairs in his bed.' He added, 'One of his bad days, I'm afraid.' Faro nodded sympathetically but he found it odd that the room was full of recent cigar smoke, a very expensive and exclusive brand Faro recognised as prevalent in the gentleman's clubs and best restaurants in Edinburgh, and Amos had declared emphatically that he was not a smoker. At their first meeting on the ferry, Faro was lighting a pipe and Amos had smilingly declined the fill of tobacco he offered. Then, with an impish glance, 'Not one of my vices, but I have plenty less virtuous to make up for it.'

Now following him to the door, Amos said, 'I hope you will have a storm-free voyage. Have you enjoyed your holiday?'

'Yes, indeed. Although I also had a mission from a relative of Dave Claydon.'

He paused and Amos said rather brusquely, 'You told me about it.' His bleak expression said that he did not want any further discussion on that topic. 'Look, I told you all I know,' he added desperately. 'Is this an official investigation?'

All friendliness had vanished as Faro replied, 'Of course not, but I have heard that it was not the Leith ship he was attempting to board.'

Amos shrugged. 'So I gathered later, but

that's what he told me. It made no difference whether he was going to Leith or Timbuktu. He had hired my boat, handed over the money. That was all I needed to know.' A weary sigh indicated that he had told this story many, many times and was heartily sick of yet another reiteration. 'I told you what I told the police, the divers and anyone else involved. He fell in the water and I couldn't rescue him. That was the end of it.'

Faro didn't want to end his visit on this sour note. 'I'm sorry to have troubled you, Amos. I wish you well . . . and your brother,' he added hesitantly, aware of the odds facing Josh.

Amos smiled again. 'I just wish I could have been of some help. Anyway, I expect you'll be coming back next year to see your mother again.'

'Possibly. I'm always trying to persuade her to come and visit me.'

Amos smiled wryly. 'It must be nice having a mother – or a father. Ours went long ago, hardly had time to get to know them or remember them,' he added sadly.

Then came the unexpected: 'We are related you know, the Faros and the Fletts. On your next visit, perhaps we'll have the opportunity to spend a little more time together.'

And as an afterthought, 'On Tuesday, I am

to take a small group of visitors on a cruise of the islands. Come with us, if you can spare the time.'

Faro was pleased, remembering how the friendly Amos had distanced himself at their second meeting on the ferry to the Hope. Without knowing the reason for his displeasure, he had now been reinstated, presumably on the grounds of distant relationship.

Amos smiled and held out his hand. 'Fare ye well.' A handsome young man with a devil-may-care attitude to life which Faro guessed led to his success with the island women, who he wooed ruthlessly while skillfully managing to evade the responsibility of any relationship crossing the boundary into marriage.

It was a progress most men would have envied and Faro had felt pangs of jealousy where Inga was concerned. She had been evasive about Amos and he now wondered if, a declared free spirit, who could indulge in brief love affairs, she had also been one of his conquests and fallen for his undoubted charms. She had certainly been very vinegary, perhaps guilty, regarding Faro's remarks.

In Amos's social strata, he would remain free of domestic ties as long as gullible girls would accept that he could not commit himself, with the responsibility of an invalid brother, which few young lasses would wish to share. Once Josh was no longer an excuse, however, it would be a very different matter.

And Amos had almost been hoist with his own petard, in the wooing of Celia Prentiss-Grant. He must have concealed the vital excuse from his agenda with her until the full horror of his domestic situation was revealed in her brief few days under his roof.

Faro was glad that Amos had not been her kidnapper and could understand his shock at a young woman taking advantage of what had seemed a perfectly normal brief infatuation, which no island girl would have taken seriously. Amos had been the first lover of the heiress of Scarthbreck and she had presumed from her sheltered life that this was to be the prelude to marriage.

Approaching Thora's door, he found it hard to understand that the widow would prefer the frail invalid to his handsome virile brother, and his thoughts drifted to that lover's meeting in the cathedral. Had it been Amos and Thora he could have understood. He tapped on the door and waited. There was some delay and he was considering that the lady was not at home. Then the sound of footsteps. The door opened to a repetition of the scene at Amos's house. She did not look pleased to see him – aghast was perhaps too strong a word for her expression, but puzzlement and anxiety were mild descriptions.

For the last time, he hoped, he was bringing out the excuse, worn deplorably thin, of the Macfie connection. Each time it sounded more feeble, even to his own ears, as he said, 'I am leaving for Edinburgh soon, and as I was in Kirkwall I thought I might call on you in case you have a message for Mr Macfie.'

'Mr Macfie,' she repeated, frowning, looking at him as if she had never heard the name before.

Faro smiled politely. This time he was being kept on the doorstep regardless of the rules of the island's hospitality. And there was a reason. Once, twice, she glanced over her shoulder and he was certain she had a guest and that this was an inconvenient intrusion.

He began, 'I am sorry to trouble you—'

'Not at all. It is quite all right. I am usually alone at this time of the evening.'

Dismissal implied, and anxious to extend the moment, he said, 'I was in the Hope last week and visited Mrs Traill.'

'Mrs Traill,' she repeated, and with something akin to fear in a nervous laugh, 'I was not aware that you were acquainted with Mrs Traill.'

'I am not. But she is Jimmy Traill's aunt, and

I was to convey a message from him.'

Thora nodded vaguely as he said, 'She has few visitors but she spoke very warmly of yourself.'

Thora studied him intently. 'Indeed.'

Her voice was expressionless and Faro went on, 'A worthy lady, thought highly of by the locals. I gathered she had been a foster mother to you and your sister Elsa.'

Thora's eyes searched wildly. There was panic in her face as she bit her lip and leant against the doorpost as if she might fall down.

Faro felt ashamed that he had caused such distress. Obviously any mention of her sister opened old wounds and renewed bitter grief. He wished he had not mentioned Elsa at all, but now felt that he could not leave it on that unhappy note.

'She talked about you both most fondly and how sad it was about Elsa leaving.'

The panic in her eyes was clear now. She closed them tightly and abruptly, as if to cut off some unbearable vision, and Faro realised he could no longer prolong this conversation, fast becoming a monologue. He ended lamely, 'She was anxious for your welfare and would much appreciate a visit some time,' he added, thinking there was little hope of that. 'I promised I would pass on the message should we happen to meet.'

Thora recovered, straightened her shoulders and said lightly, 'That was very kind of you, Mr Faro. I am grateful. Thank you for coming to see me.' A brief smile and she closed the door firmly, but not before Faro was very aware that the same pungent smell he had encountered in Amos's house was again in evidence.

The smell of very expensive cigars. In the unlikely event of Thora being a cigar smoker, his guess was that the unseen visitor she was so anxious he should avoid meeting was, in fact, her lover, Josh Flett.

As he closed the garden gate, had he been gifted with eyes in the back of his head, he would have seen the curtain twitch and two heads staring out, watching his progress.

'He knows,' she whispered tearfully. 'He knows!'

And without a word, only a sigh, he took her in his arms and held her.

CHAPTER TWENTY-TWO

On his way back to the stables to ride the mare back to Spanish Cove, Faro walked through the kirkyard and looked at the raw, upturned earth of Dave Claydon's grave, not yet prepared for a headstone.

If only Dave had been alive, he doubtless could have obliged with solutions to the mysteries that were troubling Faro, in particular what was contained in the artefacts he was carrying at the time of his drowning and perhaps, also, the secret of his wife Thora's missing year.

Finding a shop still open on the main street, he bought chocolates and a couple of carrots, rewarded for the latter by a whinny from the mare who, he was gratified to observe, recognised him again. She munched happily as the saddle was set upon her, while Faro signed the documents. The stableman grinned.

'She's a good, gentle beast, knows people who are kind to her. Never forgets a face this one, and she enjoys a gallop along the road to Kirkwall. Nothing like a good workout for keeping the beasts happy and in fine condition.'

It was an uneventful return journey, and although Faro's muscles were showing signs of reaction to this unusual activity, having mastered trotting and galloping over the long, empty stretches by the peat bogs, he decided horse riding was an exhilarating exercise on a fine summer evening. Especially with an agreeable mount who seemed to enjoy responding to his commands.

What would it be like to ride in Edinburgh? He toyed with the thought. There were fewer horsemen in Princes Street these days, mostly country folk too poor to own or hire carriages, while farmers continued to use carts to deliver and collect supplies from town and sea. For the ordinary citizens, the convenience of the horse-drawn omnibus combined with railway trains, no longer a novelty, promised to extend services to the ever-growing suburbs.

Clattering through the twisting streets of Stromness against a darkening horizon, Faro decided to stay close to the coast road. Below, a glimpse of sea shone in the mellow evening light, with seals heads bobbing in the waves or reclining on rocks. He noticed once again how their numbers increased as Spanish Cove came in sight. The divers and foreign fishing boats were not the only enthusiasts for its safe waters.

Leaving the mare with another carrot, he patted her nose and was rewarded by having his cheek nuzzled. He felt pleased: this was a new experience as he had never been drawn to horses. Now he realised that, from childhood, he had been a little afraid of them, a feeling doubtless intensified after the death of his father under the wheels of a horse-drawn carriage.

Settled ideas and prejudices can change quickly, and after a couple of hours riding hard, Faro felt as if he was parting from a friend and understood the attachment folk had to domestic pets, something he could never hope to enjoy in his police lodgings. But one day he would love to own a dog, a very big dog, that he could take for walks on Arthur's Seat.

Before heading for Scarthbreck he would look in on Inga. She was at home. And contrary to his two visits in Kirkwall, he was greeted with no long delay, no frown of dismay. The door opened promptly and, delighted to see him, Inga stood on tiptoe and hugged him, giving him a fond kiss.

'Good to see you, Jeremy. What an unexpected pleasure. Come in, come in.' When he told her he had been in Kirkwall and proudly boasted about his horsemanship, she laughed.

'There's a first time for everything, even for an Edinburgh policeman who avoids horses.' Head on one side, she asked, 'Have you time for a cup of tea or are you in a great hurry to get back?' She paused, smiling. 'Baubie's still with me.'

Following her into the parlour, he decided that this was one guest whose presence did not require being kept secret from visitors.

Baubie was seated in the Orkney chair and stretched out a mittened hand. 'I am glad to see you again.'

'Baubie's going back to South Ronaldsay soon. I shall miss you,' said Inga, giving the older woman an affectionate glance.

'You've looked after me long enough, my dear. I can't impose on you any longer.'

'It's no imposition,' Inga protested.

Baubie shook her head. 'I am quite well now. Well enough to go back to my old life again, thanks to your good nursing.'

'Thanks to your herbs,' said Inga.

'All the herbs in the world can't take the place or make up for one person's loving care,' said Baubie, taking Inga's hand and laying it against her cheek.

Inga smiled and planted a kiss on the smooth, unfurrowed forehead. 'You are so good for me.'

And suddenly aware of Jeremy again, she said, 'Do sit down. You're not a stranger here.'

In the tiny kitchen, he watched while she prepared a pot of tea. Through the window the sound of seals barking drifted upward from the bottom of the cliffs far below.

'They are very noisy tonight. How do you ever sleep through that racket?'

She shrugged. 'I can sleep through anything.'

Faro found that hard to believe. 'They're very loud – and shrill.'

'Very excited. I expect they know that Baubie is about to leave. And they're planning to follow her.'

As Faro's eyebrows raised at this extraordinary explanation, she said, 'I shouldn't have to tell you that. Forgotten your folklore, Jeremy? Remember, the seals always follow a selkie, keep as close a watch as they can from the sea. At least that's the popular belief,' she added hurriedly at his quizzical expression.

He carried the tray of bannocks and cheese into the parlour where Inga served Baubie, buttering a couple and handing her the plate, saying reproachfully, 'She eats very little, Jeremy, just enough to survive. I can't get her to eat any animal flesh or fish.'

Jeremy shuddered and Inga laughed, remembering that he wouldn't touch fish either, despite it being the main source of food on the islands, caught in plenty. A daily catch fresh from the sea.

'I would rather starve,' he said.

'Still? Even in Edinburgh?'

While Baubie looked at him in silent approval, he said, 'Even in Edinburgh. Or anywhere else in the world.'

Inga glanced at them and shook her head. 'You don't know what you're missing. Selkie blood, they say,' she added casually, aware from days long gone of the rumour concerning his grandmother.

Munching a bannock, she asked, 'Have you ever learnt to swim by any chance?'

He shook his head and Inga turned to Baubie. 'An island lad who couldn't – or can't – swim,' she said mockingly. 'No one would believe it.'

Baubie smiled. 'I sympathise. I don't like water much.'

'What a pair! Missing all the good things on offer,' Inga laughed, embracing them both in one affectionate glance.

'I do eat meat now,' said Jeremy defensively.

'Good. That will keep you strong and in fine shape to fight off criminals,' said Inga. As he drained his cup of tea, she turned to Baubie. 'Can you tell his fortune, what is waiting for him on the mainland? And his future,' she added teasingly. 'Who he's going to marry?'

Baubie said nothing, but merely held out her hand for his cup, her face expressionless.

Faro, he had no belief in fortune-telling and despised its rise to popularity, the fashion for seances which was sweeping through Edinburgh.

Cross with Inga, he could hardly refuse. However, if Baubie Finn had supernatural powers, there were many hidden truths about this Orkney visit that he wouldn't mind hearing, besides those more personal things he was not eager for her to discover.

He prepared to listen. She touched on his childhood which Inga could have told her about, as well as other details of his life, while what he really wanted to know was what had happened to his grandmother Sibella and why his parents had steadfastly refused to talk about her, or how she had died. He often wondered if Sibella had gone back to the sea, a bit of a family scandal, very hard to explain to curious neighbours. Maybe they thought they had the seal skin she shed hidden away safely and, as so often happened in the island's folk tales, one day Sibella had discovered it in a cupboard and turned back into a seal and swam away to her own people.

It was nonsense, really, and he tried to

concentrate on Baubie, who was twisting the cup and studying the leaves intently. Shaking her head, she sighed and handed the cup back to him.

'There's nothing I can tell you about your future that you don't already know, or any action that you haven't already decided upon.'

Inga looked disappointed. 'Is that all? I thought you'd see something. Are you sure, Baubie?'

Baubie was sitting back in her chair. She looked suddenly old, drained and exhausted.

'It's past your bedtime,' Inga said, and Faro recognised the signal that it was time for him to go. He took Baubie's hand, and feeling as if he was leaving an old friend, he leant over and said, 'May I?' She smiled and he kissed her forehead.

She squeezed his hand. 'Thank you, Jeremy. I shall remember that most gratefully.'

And following Inga to the door, Faro was confused, for that kiss had triggered off a distant memory struggling to the surface of his mind. Sometime long ago, that same tender scene had been played out before.

Inga was saying, 'I'll see you on your way,' and they walked arm in arm along the cliff edge and sat on a boulder overlooking the watchful, noisy seals, all heads turned towards them.

'She did see something in your cup, Jeremy,' Inga said solemnly. 'I know. I can tell. You will take care, back in Edinburgh, won't you?'

'As if you care.'

'Of course I care, don't be silly. I can't help it if we're destined to walk different roads.'

'That's nonsense. We can decide our destiny.'

She shook her head. 'No, we can't. I would know, feel it somehow, if there was any prospect of a lifetime together.'

Changing the subject, which was so painful, he took a packet of chocolates out of his pocket, and said, 'Almost forgot, these are for you.'

Thanking him, she pecked at his cheek and, ignoring that, he said, 'I wish I had a gift – something to give Baubie. She has so little.'

'She is content.'

'What does one give a selkie, Inga?'

'Only love and understanding, Jeremy. That's all a selkie needs.'

'Or anyone else,' he whispered and put his arm around her shoulders. He had to be content with this gesture, and suppress the overwhelming longing to make love to her. He felt such longing for fulfilment, so lost without flesh to flesh, the ultimate giving and receiving of love.

In the sudden laden silence between them, as Inga looked down at the seals regarding them with such intent, Faro said, 'I wonder which one is the seal king?'

Inga laughed. 'I couldn't tell you that. Did you expect him to be wearing a golden crown or something? I expect there's only one male down there with a harem of females.'

Lucky man, thought Faro. No problems of what to say to a lady when you want her. Nature made everything so simple, except for men like him.

Inga, watching his serious face, said, 'Find anything interesting in Kirkwall?'

'I saw Thora, and that story of the seal king's bride haunts me. What did he look like when he lured her into his kingdom of the sea? Did he rise from the waves as the handsomest man she'd ever dreamt of, and did she wade out into his arms, ready to leave the world behind?'

Inga chuckled. 'Well, he was certainly better looking than that lot down there. And the handsomest man I've ever met is right here on the island.'

He gave her a quizzical look. 'Who could that be?'

'Amos Flett, of course, from what I hear.' She smiled. 'He might have had a rival if you'd stayed. Did you know the Fletts and Faros are related?'

'So Amos tells me.'

She looked at him intently. 'Distant cousins. You're rather alike, apart from the hair colour . . . same bone structure. Good looks must run in the family.'

Faro shrugged. Perhaps this remote kinship was the reason why Amos had not seemed like a stranger when they first met on the ferry, as Inga continued lightly, 'And how was Thora?'

'She had a visitor. I think she has a lover. Remember I told you about Josh Flett and their secret meeting in the cathedral?'

Inga's eyes widened. 'I don't understand that at all. Thora has never struck any of us as the sympathetic type and Josh is on his deathbed. Where does he get the energy?'

'You'd better ask her. He also smokes very expensive cigars.'

Inga shook her head. 'You must be mistaken, Jeremy. That would kill him, his lungs have rotted away. Besides he has never smoked, neither has Amos. Way they were brought up. Grandfather was very stern, religious. Considered smoking and drinking the Devil's work, first step on the way to damnation; he would have had the hide off them.'

When he explained about the brand, she smiled. 'Smugglers' stuff, of course. Well known, but no one admits to it. Dave was also into that, being on the spot as it were, as a gauger.

Everyone guessed he did a little on the side.'

And Faro remembered the luxurious Claydon house, that possibly explained artefacts other than those which had supposedly gone to the bottom of the sea with him.

He felt frustrated, he had failed in his mission. No one would ever know the truth now as Inga went on, 'Amos must be delighted at Josh's new lease of life – amazing what love can do.' She laughed. 'It's incredible – a dying man resurrected. Grandfather Flett would have loved that. Praise the Lord, praise the Lord.'

Again she shook her head. 'I'd like to hear Amos's thoughts on this Thora affair. Y'know he never talks about Josh these days, maybe that's why. Disapproval. At one time he was obsessed by Josh, devoted to caring for him, which was the reason he had – so he said – for never getting married.'

Faro knew that too. He would never have anything like Amos's success with females. A few interludes to keep pace with his unmarried, or unhappily married acquaintances, but never a woman he really wanted to spend the rest of his life with.

He looked at Inga. Except for her, and maybe Lizzie.

He sighed. It was getting late and Inga moved from the shelter of his arm. 'I must go. Baubie will be in bed. I like to give her a glass of hot milk.'

'You're very fond of her,' Faro said.

Inga smiled. 'She's the strangest, most wonderful person I have ever known – and the very first selkie, for that matter.'

'You really believe that?'

'Don't you? Anyone looking at her would have doubts that she is a usual island person.'

As they stood up, still holding hands, he said anxiously, 'Will I see you again, before I go?'

'Of course, Jeremy. You're just along the road. And Amos is planning an evening cruise around the islands.'

'He mentioned it. Invited me to come along.'

'He does it every year at Lammastide, fireworks on the shore, too. Come along, you'd enjoy it. Amos is a great organiser.'

He looked at her. 'You're very fond of him, aren't you?'

'What sort of question is that?' she asked gently.

'All right. I'm jealous. He has you all year and I see you for a week in ten years.'

She kissed him and laughed. 'Don't be daft, Jeremy. Time doesn't matter where affection is concerned.' And giving him an admonitory shove, 'Come on, you surely know that – you're sensible enough to have worked that one out.'

He kissed her again, holding her, not wanting her to say she loved Amos and wishing he had that magic with girls. Still he lingered, wishing he could go back to Spanish Cove and hold her in his arms all night, waking to find her beside him, her head on the pillow.

His longing was a steady physical ache to possess her utterly, to prove to her that he was no longer the callow seventeen-year-old she had seduced, but a strong virile man who loved her with every fibre of his being. Not for a night, but passionately and for ever. Her shadow would always fall between him and any other woman he ever made love to.

He left her feeling as if his heart had been wrenched from his body. This tortured relationship could not go on. Time he was away from this land of magic where anything could happen and seal kings could take a human bride from the shore. Yes, about time he was back in Edinburgh, his sanity restored. Lizzie never aroused these violent emotions and he was careful never to allow her to become aware of a man's natural response, afraid that such arousal might scare her off for ever, reviving terrible memories of being taken by force.

And then there was Vince, conceived by rape all those years ago. He didn't like the boy but felt sympathy for his need for a father who didn't exist for him.

There was a faint moon rising and as he walked along the cliff edge, the sky fading into twilight – a smouldering twilight, for it never got really dark in summer – the seals were keeping pace with him, watching eagerly, their excited barking echoing from the rocks.

Wondering again who was their king, he laughed.

CHAPTER TWENTY-THREE

As Faro reached the servants' lodge, Emil Latour was heading towards the stable, leading a fine horse, his progress watched by a smiling Mary holding a lamp, and he thought cynically that Emil was getting his feet well under her kitchen table.

Following her inside, Faro decided that she was looking very pleased with herself, obviously making much greater progress with her love life than her unfortunate son.

She pointed to a book on the sideboard, 'That kind Mr West left this for you. Finished it, said it might be good company for your journey. There's an Edinburgh address for you to leave it for him.'

Weary and depressed, Faro declined supper and went off to his room. Before he fell asleep he read a chapter of *A Tale of Two Cities*. Remembering the conversation with West, falling asleep, something clicked into his mind about that discussion. Something important. What was it? But his eyes were heavy and sleep overcame him.

Next morning there were other matters to engage his mind. Emil was outside, overseeing a carriage unloading framed paintings.

Mary Faro took off her apron and rushed out offering assistance. 'Looks like he's moving in permanently,' Faro observed drily.

She smiled. 'He wanted them here with him. They're very valuable, quite irreplaceable and he's scared they may get stolen from my house. The very idea,' she added indignantly.

Emil drifted over and, looking at him rather pityingly, she went on, 'I've told him, Jeremy, but he won't believe me, how safe it is in Kirkwall. But it worries him that we never lock our doors.'

Listening, Emil's face was expressionless. 'That is the problem, Mary,' (he pronounced it as the French 'Marie'). 'No keys. No locks. That worries me deeply.'

As he shook his head, Mary's glance changed from pitying to fond. She smiled. 'No one locks doors here, Emil. I wish I could convince you.

It isn't necessary and it would seem an insult to friends looking in casually, and the postman would be most upset.'

Emil's eyes were riveted on the final canvasses being unloaded. 'I wish to have them with me at all times.' With a shrug he added, 'Do not distress yourself, it is only for a few days. I cannot carry them in my luggage as I travel back to France, and an arrangement has been made for a ship to come here. Excuse me.'

Bowing, he went over to the driver and Mary led Faro indoors. 'These French gentlemen, they do take on,' she giggled.

'Where will he put all those canvases?'

'Into my rooms, of course.' As Faro's eyebrows raised at this intrusion, she said apologetically, 'His room is tiny, all the servants' are. Just a bed, a chair and a press. You've seen them. He wouldn't be able to get in the door and I have lots of space.'

Faro thought of his bedroom, and at his expression she squeezed his arm. 'Emil is such a nice, kind man, although he is a bit solemn sometimes, and I'm glad to help him.' She sighed. 'He is all alone in the world. No family, poor man, never married. No one to care for him.'

Except you, Faro thought, as later it seemed that Emil and the driver had cluttered every available space with canvasses, framed and unframed.

Mary leant over Faro's shoulder as he looked out of the window to see the artist riding briskly along the shore towards Spanish Cove.

She sighed. 'He likes his daily exercise. So good for him. Sitting painting Miss Celia all day must be very wearisome.' And Faro would have been very interested to know what handsome commission he was receiving to accommodate such fatigue.

He had an unexpected visitor that morning: Gerald Binsley returning from an early ride.

Mary was across at the house with menus of Celia's favourite dishes. 'She's always hungry: those friends she was staying with forgot to feed her. Pity that message to her mother went astray, what a lot of trouble that would have saved everyone,' she added.

This was the publicised version of Celia's disappearance, but those who knew the true events of that evening found it extremely difficult to accept and reconcile with the neatly folded abandoned clothes.

Gerald dismounted to shake hands with Faro. 'We are so much in your debt. Wanted to thank you personally for all you did for Celia, helping her out of a deuced difficult situation like that.'

'Not at all, sir. In fact, it was a remark in our conversation that gave me a clue to what had happened.'

Gerald looked amazed. 'And what was that?'

'Miss Celia's love of horses or her riding like a man. Wanting to be a boy. And that voluminous winter cloak in the height of summer troubled me. It suggested she had something to conceal, and for such a slender young lady, a boy's shirt and breeches could be hidden underneath a loose gown. A chat with the stableman at Scarthbreck confirmed my suspicions.'

Gerald shook his head in disbelief. 'That's amazing. Never occurred to me, although I've known her all these years.'

And Faro remembered the more obvious conclusion of a secret pregnancy as Binsley continued, 'All is now forgiven. The parents are so relieved to have her back safely, Sir Arnold has even forgiven her for stealing money from his desk in London and throwing the shadow of suspicion of a thief among the servants.' He paused to smile at Faro. 'Her father is grateful. He would like a word with you.'

Faro made no comment. He was not looking forward to that. As they spoke, Emil rode in and, saluting them, dismounted before heading for the stables.

'How is the portrait?' Faro asked.

Gerald sighed. 'Come to a full stop, I'm afraid. Celia and her mother leave for Brighton tomorrow. Sir Arnold enjoys Orkney and will stay on for the shooting, of course. House guests and that sort of thing demand his presence.'

And more employment for his mother, Faro thought. Something to occupy her when both himself and Emil had departed.

'So the portrait will be abandoned, after all.'

'Not quite. Merely a change of direction. Latour has promised to come to England next year and finish it. Meantime, a series of sketches and a daguerreotype, very popular with the last generation, and Celia has an excellent profile . . .' Gerald paused to smile broadly. 'As for the immediate future, I have proposed again – and have definite hopes of success.'

'That is good news. Please accept my congratulations, sir.'

Gerald put a finger to his lips and said wryly, 'Not quite yet, but when I promised not to raise the subject again she looked quite disappointed, until I said that should the idea ever appeal to her, then we might discuss the possible success of a marriage built on the solid ground of a long and trusting friendship.'

Faro thought sadly of no such hopes of a happy-ever-after future with Inga, as Gerald went on, 'I am sure there will be difficulties, but I hope I can promise her a less restricted life outside the parental home that will meet with her approval. She will be able to travel, to develop her cultural interests and to learn to appreciate the better parts of this new world of progress we are witnessing. Nor will I expect her wifely duties to be limited to being hostess at endless dreary parties and producing a baby each year.'

Frowning across at the house, he said, 'I will have to be content with irregular visits, meantime.'

'London does seem a fair distance,' Faro said sympathetically, remembering how far from Scotland Kent had appeared, like entering another world. Gerald then said, 'Not really. My place in Sussex is on the South Downs. Excellent riding country and I shall continue to hope that needs for those visits will end with Celia living under my roof.'

Gerald's mount was getting restive. Patting his nose, Gerald said, 'Past his breakfast time.' He whistled, a boy approached and led the horse to the stables.

'I wonder if I might impose on you? If you have a few spare moments, perhaps you would accompany me to see Sir Arnold? He will be at home at this hour.'

Faro had no excuse to refuse and followed

him into the house. Tapping on the study door, Gerald announced, 'Constable Faro to see you, sir.'

'Come in, come in. Thank you, Gerald.' As he bowed and departed, the man who stood up and leant across the desk to shake Faro's hand was a very different Sir Arnold from the irate parent of their first meeting.

'Take a seat, Constable. I wish to express my gratitude regarding the . . . er . . . unfortunate business of my daughter's disappearance.' Clearing his throat and studying the inkwells on the desk, he said, 'She tells me you behaved in an exemplary manner throughout, very understanding, discreet, and careful that no one should know the truth. You not only protected her reputation, but you also protected her family and shielded them from appalling consequences should the real story have ever reached the press.'

Pausing for a moment to shake his head at the awful thought of what might have been, he continued, 'A scandal that might well have signalled the end of my family's association with this island, which I am very fond of. Distant ancestors apart, I do not want to become an absentee landlord, coming only for the annual shooting.'

An expansive gesture accompanied his words. 'I feel most strongly that these are my people and I want to be the best of lairds for them.'

It was quite a speech and Faro did not doubt he meant every word as he went on, 'I have already donated to the local constabulary,' and pushing a purse across the table, 'Now it is your turn, Constable. I should like you to accept this – the reward for information, to which you are entitled, in fact.'

In answer, Faro shook his head. 'Thank you, sir, for your generous gift, but I cannot accept it for merely doing my duty by solving such a distressing problem. I am glad that there was no lasting damage and that your daughter will have a happy and settled future.'

Sir Arnold smiled. 'If Gerald Binsley has any influence, then I think we can be assured on that score.' He frowned. 'As for this young man she placed in such an embarrassing position . . .' Pausing, head on one side, he regarded Faro. 'I expect you are aware of his identity. I don't wish to know,' he added hastily, 'but I admire his gentlemanly qualities for not taking advantage of a silly girl throwing herself at his feet – which a less scrupulous and honest fellow could well have exploited for its monetary gain.' Pausing, he added heavily, 'I mean blackmail, of course.'

Returning to the servants' lodge, with Emil's paintings strewn everywhere in his mother's parlour, Faro considered that, the daily sittings for Celia's portrait abandoned, Emil no longer had any excuse to remain at Scarthbreck, a fact he had not thought fit to convey to Mary Faro.

The thought of his remaining indefinitely was disturbing. Faro did not feel like leaving his vulnerable, sentimental mother at the mercy of the Frenchman who, whatever his romantic appeal to women, did not quite ring true.

Faro did not trust him, especially after taking a quick look at the paintings stacked against the walls. They seemed quite unexceptional, and 'mediocre' was the word that sprang readily to mind as he replaced the final one. True, perhaps knowing nothing about art, he was doing Latour an injustice by passing judgement, measuring all artists by the same yardstick of excellence set by the Pre-Raphaelites whom he had encountered last year.

Heading to his bedroom door, he almost tripped over the latest addition to the servants' lodge.

A small and very excitable black puppy slid along the corridor and gave him a rapturous welcome, head and tail wagging vigorously. He was soon to learn that Emil had decided Marie should have an animal which, when fully grown, would protect her in that unlocked Kirkwall house.

He had found a stray puppy on the shore when he was out riding. It had decided to adopt him, and being an animal lover, however unlikely that seemed, he had brought it back as a gift for Mrs Faro after requesting Sir Arnold's permission to keep it in the servants' lodge.

Sir Arnold had no objections. He shrugged and declared it most likely to be a mongrel sired by one of his two dogs, which accompanied him everywhere. 'She may have it, by all means. If she decides not to take it back with her, there's always room for a good retriever in the kennels here.'

The puppy, appropriately named Beau, proceeded to gnaw Faro's bootlaces, setting the pattern of mischief personified, with a remarkable taste for sharpening its teeth on anything visible at its own height, with a particular fondness for wood. In no time at all, the pup's devoted slave, Mary Faro, obliging with sticks, reminded Faro when he went out of doors to bring back wood for Beau.

Faro did not object. He was pleased, and decided that his mother needed an animal to fuss over. Beau was a good idea to ease the loneliness of her return home, not knowing when she would see her son again, and in the case of Emil, if ever.

CHAPTER TWENTY-FOUR

Faced with the almost novel prospect of having time on his hands at last, Faro decided to put from his mind the two insoluble mysteries which had engaged his attention and enjoy to the full the undemanding remainder of his holiday.

He planned to rise early in the morning, and with three days ahead a pleasant blank, decide how best to fill them in. A day in Kirkwall, perhaps another visit to St Margaret's Hope, and then Amos's island cruise.

His hopes of being refreshed by a good night's sleep failed as he lay awake, his mind refusing to settle, and finally he decided to pick up Mr West's kindly loan of *A Tale of Two Cities* once more. As a hopeful remedy for insomnia, it defeated its purpose, he became more wakeful than ever, desperate to know the fate of the characters, of Sidney Carton's noble sacrifice in taking the place of Charles Darnay, his rival in love, and going to the guillotine in his stead.

He concluded that novels make the success of such impostures – impossible in real life – so plausible, and when at last his eyes rebelled against the lamplight, he shut the book. But that question remained, of how Carton had got away with his deception undetected by Citizen Defarge.

He awoke next morning, breakfasted with his mother, busy and shining-eyed and waiting on Emil. Faro smiled tolerantly, just wishing he liked the Frenchman better or could imagine him in the unlikely role of a future stepfather.

Gathering up Beau, he decided on a brisk walk along the cliffs as a prelude to the day's activities, in the forefront of his mind to show the puppy to Inga – a valid excuse, although he was by no means certain that she was a dog lover.

The delighted puppy bounced along the cliff walk, sniffing happily at everything in this new world, and cocking his leg with a frequency that suggested a remarkable bladder for the necessary marking of his territorial claims.

Inga's door, alas, remained firmly closed, and disappointed, he set off on the return journey along the cliffs, where a sudden burst of brilliant sunshine tempted him to sit down by a large boulder while Beau, given a delectable piece of driftwood, gnawed happy and content at his feet.

Stroking the dog's head absent-mindedly, Faro regarded the seals, who now took a special interest in this new animal perched far above their heads.

Faro sighed. What a holiday. He had turned from detective into dog-walker and seal-watcher in a visit which had become a missing persons enquiry, with himself the main suspect.

He was inordinately pleased to have solved that mystery quite unaided, with a little observation and some imaginative deduction, to everyone's satisfaction. Perhaps with the single exception of Sergeant Stavely.

He opened his logbook, quickly closed it again, refusing to be lured into what was now stale reading with its unanswered questions, dull words and theories which he knew almost by heart. He thrust it back into his pocket and, determined to enjoy the warm sunshine, he took out Lizzie's pocket telescope and gazed back towards the street of Spanish Cove with its bleak houses bordered by stables at one end and a shop at the other, as though firmly held together by a pair of mammoth bookends.

They had a closed-in look: no curtains twitched at windows and each time he had passed through there had never been signs of life. No open door, or children in evidence. No washing hanging out, no smoke from chimneys.

Which was Mr West's home? He hadn't seen the botanist again. Inga had mentioned Amos's friend Rob, also a fisherman and his wife as neighbours, but she was not on social terms with them. As for the others, she had shrugged, 'People come and go. Amos has a house next to Rob and brings Josh for a breath of sea air in summer. City folk rent for the fishing and shooting. Scarthbreck beaters need extra accommodation then. Divers often stay over as a convenient assembly place and there's a coastguard, in case the lifeboat needs to be taken out.' He had glimpsed it, rocking nervously at the water's edge.

Surveying the prospect from his sheltered spot above the high cliffs, Inga's house must have appeared bleak before she put her magic touch to work. Had he not experienced the hospitality of the traditional Orkney home, he would have been inclined to regard Spanish Cove as a monstrous figment of the imagination, designed by an architect with a grudge against humanity, its solitude and desolation at the mercy of fierce weather, where every gale force wind struck a chord of sinister melancholy.

He focused on the steep and narrow set of steps roughly hewn out of the rock, a stiff climb communicating with the shore. A tiny pier with no sign of solid anchorage, nor evidence of nets and fishing boats. Doubtless the permanent residents found employment in the peat fields or on neighbouring crofts.

Faro shook his head. For him, there had to be a reason for everything, and Spanish Cove, a street which gave the impression of having been lifted bodily from the poor area of any big city, made no sense at all. He was forced to admit, however, that it was an improvement on the murky, overcrowded closes off Edinburgh's High Street, whose residents would have loved a glimpse of that wild sea and benefited greatly from an abundance of the fresh health-giving air.

Along past Scarthbreck was the Neolithic settlement far along the shore, a distant rubble of stones, which the telescope brought into focus, so close that he could almost reach out and touch the sparkling waves of the incoming tide, with the seals basking on the rocks near enough to be resting at his feet.

And the seals reminded him that as well as

failing to accomplish his mission for Macfie for his own satisfaction, he had not found a convincing answer to Dave's wife's legendary role as the seal king's bride. But determined to enjoy the warm sunshine, he shrugged both issues aside, and regretting that he had not brought a book to read, his mind drifted back to Mr Dickens' latest novel. The sun's warmth on his eyelids was seductive and soothing. He closed his eyes, as his mind drifted towards sleep. Once again, something from the back of his mind clicked into place.

He had it – the answer!

A moment later it was lost. A shrill bark from Beau made him open his eyes to see that the puppy had slipped the lead anchored under a stone and was racing down the cliff face.

Angrily, Faro stood up, whistled, and when that had no effect he yelled, 'Come back, come back!' Useless. Beau neither heard him, nor cared. He was in pursuit of something. The seals were indifferent, they regarded him enigmatically. The presence of a dog barking ferociously on land had no fears for them.

Faro was exasperated. What to do? He called in vain and the tide was coming in fast now, hiding the wretched animal from view. He took out the pocket telescope, impatiently scanning the shoreline. Boulders, smaller stones, perhaps they too had once shaped furniture, beds and shelves in the homes of the island's first inhabitants, their history for ever lost.

Suddenly he was aware that alongside the stones, in sharp focus, a boulder moved. It was Beau, tail wagging, bending over something that twitched.

A dark shape – a dead seal? Or a bundle of abandoned clothes? His heart sank at the remembrance of that discovery.

Beau had found his quarry. A glimpse of flesh. Pink, naked human flesh. An arm raised. Was it a man, alive and injured?

With no thought but of how he was to get down there as fast as possible, he considered the descent to the shore. Steep, dangerous, with no certain footholds, the steps cut into the cliff at Spanish Cove. It was the only access but too distant; the landing beyond Hal's croft too far.

If the man was still alive, then this was a life-or-death emergency. He gazed over the cliff edge, took a deep breath and scrambled down, seizing whatever footholds existed, jutting rocks and clumps of coarse grass. Slipping, falling, sliding down on his backside, bruised and sore and aching in every limb, at last his feet touched solid ground and he ran towards the body.

Beau looked up at his approach and gave a yelp of triumph.

Faro knelt down. A man still barely alive, face down, not completely naked, wearing trousers.

Who was he? Faro turned him over by his shoulders. He had a shattered, broken face. His bloody lips moved. The man was dying.

He stared into Faro's face, trying to speak. And Faro had seen too many dying men in his ten years as a policeman not to recognise that he was too late. Garbled, whispered words told of a murderous attack, but the words made no sense, choked out of the blood, lost in the wind.

His eyes closed in death and Faro remained kneeling beside him. A youngish, strong-looking man, not much past thirty. Amos's friend and fellow ferryman, Rob, glimpsed a couple of times as a resident of Spanish Cove.

He had not been swept in by the tide, nor drowned. His trousers, coated with sand, were dry. So was his thick fair hair, and when Faro's hand came away from his head, it was wet not from the sea, but from blood oozing out of a head wound.

Faro physically restrained Beau from licking the blood which had doubtless alerted him to the scene. Thus reproached, the dog was no longer interested. His retrieving instincts satisfied, he lay down, gnawing happily at a piece of driftwood.

Faro looked round. How long had Rob lain there, thrown down the cliff face? More important, how was he to be transported up again?

Dragging him from the lapping water edge into the shelter of a large rock, safe from the tide, despite safety no longer being any earthly concern for this poor lad, Faro set off at a run along the shore. Beau was well ahead, believing this was another exciting game, while he clambered over rocks and leapt over sea pools and seaweed.

Stumbling, falling and cutting his knee, he reached the steps at Spanish Cove and remembered that Rob lived alone.

With Beau waiting, tail wagging, at the top, he arrived breathless. Gasping, his first thought was that Stavely must be informed. But of what use was urgency now?

Then the sound of hoof beats, and from the direction of Scarthbreck, a man riding hard, his arrival greeted by a delighted Beau.

Faro rushed forward waving his arms frantically.

'Hello there, what's the trouble?'

It was Hal, Stavely's brother-in-law. He dismounted. 'God, what on earth's happened to you?' He glanced down at Beau preparing a slight repast on his bootlaces. 'Clear off!' And to Faro, 'Had an accident while you were walking the dog?'

'Found a dead man – down on the shore a quarter of a mile back there.' Still breathless, winded by the steep climb, Faro pointed.

'What?' Hal looked him over in disbelief, taking in his dishevelled appearance but mostly dwelling on his bloodstained hands. 'A dead man?' he repeated. 'Who killed him?'

Faro shook his head. 'How would I know that? I've only just found him.'

A wry glance from Hal. 'Wasn't you killed him, then? Looks like you got into a fight.'

'No!' Faro shouted indignantly. 'I saw him from the cliff top, he was moving, still alive. I scrambled down.'

'From the cliffs,' Hal said heavily, gazing along and shaking his head. 'No one could do that. You must have been mad.'

Faro took a deep breath. 'Never mind me – ride into Stromness, get hold of somebody. Sergeant Stavely—'

Hal nodded. 'He's at cousin Pete's, down the road. Lily and him. Birthday party. I'm on my way to meet them.'

'Get him, bring him and anyone else who can help.'

Hal, aware of the urgency, leapt back on to his horse. 'Right, you stay here. We'll need someone to take them to the right place. Can you see it from here?'

'No – just go, quick as you can.'

Watching Hal disappear, Faro realised all this was going to take some time. He sat down, put Beau back on the rope lead, and with the aid of the telescope was able to keep an eye on shore and sea and the incoming tide. Nothing moved, no one came or went, and the eventual sight of Hal riding alongside a carriage with Pete, two slightly inebriated friends from the party and Stavely inside the carriage, was for Faro the most welcome sight in the world.

It was a one-sided welcome. Stavely was not best pleased at being dragged away from an excellent celebration meal which was about to make its appearance on the table. He'd already had a few drams in preparation and now this crisis was too much.

He was heartily sick of Detective Constable Faro, wishing he had never come to Orkney. Delighted to hear that he was going back to Edinburgh imminently, Stavely had breathed a sigh of relief, still smarting over the way he had effortlessly solved the Prentiss-Grant case with quick thinking that would have been such a feather in his own promotion cap. Lily was going on about it, wouldn't let it drop. 'Why didn't you think of that?' she demanded. 'Only a man would have thought of pregnancy as the answer.'

Now he stared at Faro's woebegone appearance in disbelief. 'God, what has happened to you? Hal told me you'd found a dead man.'

Faro shook his head. He was suddenly weary, sick at heart and exhausted as he never remembered having been in his life before. 'Down there. We can go by the steps, a quarter mile along the shore.'

The sun had gone, dark clouds moved in from the horizon. A storm was on its way.

As he prepared to lead the way, Stavely said to him, 'You look awful.'

'Try scrambling down a cliff face some time.'

Stavely shook his head. 'Incredible! Looks as if you've been in a right old tussle – and come off worst.'

Faro ignored that and headed towards the steps.

'You can leave the dog in the carriage.'

'No, he comes with us. He'll remember the place.'

Stavely grunted and said doubtfully, 'Hope you're right. Give over, I'll take him.'

Faro needed all his efforts to concentrate on the steep uneven steps. Painful indeed, his bruises making themselves felt with a vengeance. At last, on the strand, Beau let off the rope, racing ahead, with Stavely and the other men running towards the spot where Faro had left the dead man.

The sheltering boulder came in sight, Beau sniffing eagerly at what remained of it above water. But there was no body, living or dead. Nothing.

'Are you sure?' Stavely asked.

'Of course I'm sure.'

Hal's comrades stared at him resentfully, wandered around looking here and there in a desultory fashion, finding nothing.

Stavely joined them, giving directions. Grumbling, they walked back and forth, a hundred yards in each direction.

Faro looked on helplessly, unbelieving. He sat down heavily. He had to think but his head ached more than his bruises.

There had been a body, a dead man.

'You knew who it was?'

'The ferryman Rob; don't know his second name, lives up there at Spanish Cove.'

All heads turned towards the distant group of houses. 'You knew him?' Stavely repeated.

He sounded quite eager, Faro thought, as he said, 'I only met him once briefly, but yes, I'm sure.'

The men watched him expressionless. Stavely sighed, 'You could have been mistaken, he maybe fell from the cliff, only injured. Walked away.'

Faro shook his head. 'He was dead, I'm sure of that. I've had experience of dead men, Sergeant, make no mistake about that.'

As he spoke, all heads swivelled upwards to the cliff face. Climbing up would have been even more impossible than scrambling down. An injured man bleeding profusely from a head wound could never have reached the Spanish Cove steps.

'The only other way is the landing stage past my croft,' said Hal.

'That's a mile away,' Stavely put in, looking at the sea. 'Tide's coming in fast now, he could have slipped back again.'

'He didn't drown,' Faro said sharply.

'And how do you know that?' Stavely's flushed and angry countenance led Faro to decide to repeat Rob's dying words.

'His trousers were dry, covered in sand. He said he had been attacked, pushed down the cliff face.'

Stavely stared at him. 'He told you that?'

'Yes, before he died.'

'What else did he tell you?'

Faro pretended not to hear and for Stavely

334

alarm bells were again ringing. Another missing body brought bitter thoughts of Celia Prentiss-Grant. Was this the work of another practical joker? Or was Faro behind it, for some obscure reason of his own?

CHAPTER TWENTY-FIVE

Stavely recovered his equilibrium and asked more suspicious questions, none of which Faro could answer, so weary that he was almost oblivious to the strange glances and suppositions his bloodstains brought forth.

He groaned as Stavely said, 'I'm afraid you'll have to come into Kirkwall and make an official report. But we'd better get you home first, change your clothes.'

Not those steps again, but that was the only way.

He managed somehow, on the threshold of exhaustion. Stavely, regarding the houses said, 'Which one is where this fellow lives?'

'I have no idea,' Faro replied, as Stavely

marched ahead and tapped on one of the doors.

It was opened by Mr West, blinking against the light as if he had been asleep.

'Ah, hello, Stavely,' he said brightly, obviously recognising him, but the sergeant held up a hand as if to cut short any further conversation.

'I'm looking for a man called Rob, who I understand lives hereabouts.'

West pursed his lips and pointed. 'Ah yes, Rob Powers. Two doors along. But he'll be at work.'

Stavely's anxious expression suggested urgency, and glancing nervously at Faro's bloodstained hands and face, he added helpfully, 'His colleague, Amos Flett and his brother have just arrived – in the house next door.'

Turning to leave, Stavely said to the botanist, 'How are the pigeons doing?'

West smiled. 'Very well, Sergeant, very well indeed.'

Faro was slightly ahead but his acute hearing caught a whispered 'Keep you informed' speedily stifled by a nod from Stavely, who was heading briskly towards Rob's house.

West shouted after them, 'There'll be no answer,' and repeated, 'He lives alone.'

But Stavely either didn't hear or didn't intend to listen. He gestured to Hal and the other two men to remain outside and, with Faro at his heels, he pushed open the door which was without key or lock in the usual island tradition.

A dismal scene greeted them inside. It was obvious from the untidy dusty state of the tiny parlour that Rob did indeed live alone. A sink full of dishes, a musty stale smell of multiple odours followed them into a bedroom, the bed unmade and above it a crucifix, on the walls a series of religious portraits. A large family Bible was his obvious bedtime reading.

Stavely gave the rooms a cursory inspection. 'There's nothing to indicate that this fellow didn't leave for work as usual, is there now? No evidence of violence, nothing to suggest an accident. Seems likely that his fall down the cliff knocked him out. After you found him, he recovered and will turn up, a little worse for wear.' And regarding Faro intently, 'Something like yourself, in fact.'

Faro stared at him. Stavely was refusing to believe that murder had been committed and a man's dying words would be dismissed as circumstantial evidence.

Stavely's next words were ominous. 'However, until he does appear, we had better make an official report.' Weary and unsympathetic, he'd missed that feast he had been looking forward to, his only reason for coming to the family party, knowing how boring it would be. And although he didn't believe Faro's story, there was something odd about it, as well as his dishevelled appearance, and Stavely, still bruised by being shown up in the Prentiss-Grant case by Faro's quick thinking, wasn't taking any chances on being made to look a fool this time.

'I'll tell Amos Flett. He'll need to be informed,' Faro said.

Stavely nodded, 'Very well, you do that.'

Hal was riding off to inform Lily of the delays and Pete and the two party guests, unwilling companions on their fruitless search for the missing man, were sitting in the carriage, muttering together, their remarks full of anger and resentment at having being dragged into this farce.

Stavely gestured towards them. 'I'll see these lads get back safely. It's not far. Back for you in twenty minutes,' he added, hoping there would be some remnants of the festive meal still available.

Observing that Faro's forlorn appearance suggested he was on the verge of collapse and in no state to walk back to Scarthbreck, Stavely thought that he had better be tidied up before the journey into the police station.

'Stay right here. Don't go away.'

Faro's weary shrug indicated that was not his intention, and sighing, Stavely again decided that Constable Faro was just a damned nuisance and he asked somewhat impatiently, 'When is it you intended leaving us?'

'Wednesday.'

With one foot in the carriage, Stavely nodded grimly. 'You might have to postpone that again. If neither this Rob nor his body has turned up there'll need to be an enquiry, once you've set this missing person business in motion.'

Watching Stavely drive off, Faro groaned not only for his aches and bruises. Was this another case with all the elements of the Prentiss-Grant incident? If only he had caught the last boat to Edinburgh instead of now being forced to remain indefinitely, once again a prime suspect in the case of a man whose body had disappeared. But Faro was certain that he had indeed been murdered.

Walking back along the street, a tap on Amos's door had an immediate response. Quick, light footsteps approached and the door opened. Not by Amos, but his brother. Faro caught a glimpse, a smile of welcome quickly suppressed as he stepped back into the shadows.

Obviously Faro was not his expected visitor.

'May I have a word with Amos?'

'He's not here. Probably at the ferry.'

'Very well. But if you should see him, I have

a message.' He hesitated. 'About Rob. There's been an accident.'

'What?' Josh wasn't listening. He was looking anxiously beyond Faro who, glancing over his shoulder, observed a carriage approaching. Thora stepped down and when Faro turned again, the door had been firmly shut.

Thora also seemed dismayed at his sudden appearance, as the driver of the gig helped her unload several pieces of luggage. She was not intending to delay and, ignoring Faro's polite greeting as the door was opened once again, and grappling with her luggage, she went swiftly inside.

Obviously she had come to stay. The couple's behaviour baffled him. Did Amos not approve of their association, and did the lovers always have to meet when he was absent? Was time precious?

He thought of those quick, firm footsteps hurrying to open the door. Hardly those of a dying man.

Returning along the street, West was at his window, binoculars trained on the horizon. Hearing footsteps outside he nodded, smiled and Faro stopped in his tracks, overwhelmed by a possibility so outrageous that it left him completely stunned.

Imperative to sit down and sort out his thoughts, he couldn't just stand there and wait to tell Stavely what he had discovered, and passing the tea shop, he went in, sat at a table and ordered a pot of tea, when what he was needing most at that moment was something infinitely stronger, like a very large dram.

Seeing West had triggered off what had been at the back of his mind, half-remembered since he read *A Tale of Two Cities*.

A man who takes another man's place.

And there it was being played out before him.

He did not need his logbook to recall the facts. Dave was a good swimmer. But the same night that his supposedly drowned body had been washed ashore, Josh Flett, long on his deathbed, had breathed his last.

The switch was made. Josh was buried as the drowned man and Dave became the dying invalid confined to the house, any glimpse of him swathed in bonnet and mufflers. There must have been complications, and a criminal organisation involved; for Amos's identification of the nonexistent body discovered by a conveniently 'passing' tourist with a substantial bribe for his statement changing hands.

There had to be a death certificate. But from Edinburgh police records, Faro knew that for clever criminals doors could be opened and forged documents readily obtained.

And then there was Thora. As Dave's wife she had to be part of the plot. Faro remembered the Claydon house, the table kept as a shrine to her 'dead' husband. The meeting in the cathedral, those precious stolen minutes. Small wonder Inga had been taken aback that Thora the widow had chosen Josh rather than his handsome brother.

It all made sense, but what was the motive? How was it to end? The Claydons could never live openly together in Kirkwall. They would have to move to another island and start anew. It was a fragile situation.

What was the delay? What were they waiting for? Dave as Josh had to die again. No, that would be an added complication. The logical answer lay with the missing artefacts, that mysterious treasure trove waiting to be handed over to a buyer with enough cash to make their exile worthwhile.

Exile. He looked down at the harbour, West watching the horizon. That was the answer. They were waiting for a boat to arrive, and that was why Thora was also in Spanish Cove.

And what about Amos? A fellow conspirator, what did he stand to gain?

'So this is where you are?'

And he looked up into the face of Amos, unable to find the words that would bring things back to normality, as he sat down opposite.

'Josh tells me you were looking for me. I was having a rest. Was it something urgent?'

'Rob is dead.'

'What! What are you talking about? Rob's at the ferry today.'

Faro stared at him and shook his head. 'I found Rob at the bottom of the cliffs beside Spanish Cove. His head was bleeding. He was dying.'

Amos opened his mouth, closed it again. 'That can't be. Where is he now?'

'I don't know. Has he any family? We called in at his house.'

Amos shook his head. 'He hasn't anyone. Lives alone.' He looked stunned and angry. 'Didn't you go back for him? Make sure?'

'I left him. Got help and went back. He had disappeared.'

'Disappeared?'

'The tide was coming in, perhaps he had been swept into the water.'

Amos sprang up. 'Maybe you just *thought* he was dying.'

Sergeant Stavely had said that too. Now Faro remembered the blood from Rob's mouth, choking on four whispered words, 'Attacked me . . . gave . . . gosh . . .'

Then the silence of death. But now those words took on a new meaning.

They were not 'gave . . . gosh'.

Rob had been trying to tell him that Dave Claydon was Josh Flett.

CHAPTER TWENTY-SIX

'So that's where you are!' This time it was Stavely, red-faced and indignant, his eyes on the set table. 'You were supposed to be waiting outside,' he said, ignoring Amos completely.

Amos, who stood up white-faced, bewildered, and without a word, hurried out of the tea shop.

Faro watched him. Aware of his agony, of one thing he was certain, he was innocent of Rob's death.

'Amos was very upset. Rob was his friend.'

'Did he have anything constructive to say?' Stavely demanded.

'Just that Rob lived alone. But I have something to tell you, Sergeant, something very important.'

Stavely shook his head. 'Not now. It can wait. We'll go to Scarthbreck first. Get you cleaned up. Into the carriage, if you please.'

Faro was pleased. He didn't fancy the walk back to the servants' lodge. When they reached it, taking in Faro's exhausted appearance, Stavely had a moment of compassion.

He said rather curtly, 'We'll get you back once you've made a statement, described the man you apparently found,' and pointing to Beau, who had never left Faro's side and now leapt on to his knee, 'And take that animal in with you.'

Faro hoped that he would not meet his mother. He did not relish her despairing looks and anxious questions about his appalling appearance. He had one answer prepared, but it was Emil he met on the way in and he looked only mildly interested.

'Chasing Beau, fell down the cliff,' Faro said in a cheerful voice which he hoped was also casual enough.

Emil shrugged, shook his head with a disbelieving smile, a slightly mocking bow and hurried across the courtyard.

From the window Faro saw the Frenchman talking to Stavely and wondered if the sergeant was an art lover. Washing his bloodstained hands and face at the kitchen sink, dabbing at cuts and bruises, and brushing his clothes, he left Beau with an affectionate pat and hurried out to the waiting carriage, where Stavely signalled his impatience. 'At last. Let's go.'

Apart from asking how long the Frenchman was staying, Stavely resumed his enquiries about Rob. Faro, wanting to discuss his theory concerning Dave Claydon, found himself repeating the story in great detail but Stavely's lack of comment suggested that his mind was elsewhere, and in weary acceptance, Faro knew he would have the whole version to repeat once again and a statement to sign.

As the carriage moved swiftly in the direction of Kirkwall, he said, 'I've just made a very important discovery, Sergeant, which I think I should share with you.'

'Another one?' said Stavely with a mocking laugh. 'Don't tell me this fellow is about to appear and pretend it was all a practical joke.'

Faro cut him short. 'Josh Flett—'

'Josh Flett,' Stavely interrupted. 'What in God's name has that poor soul to do with all this?'

'Nothing, but Dave Claydon might have.'

'Dave Claydon!' Stavely shouted. 'Another drowned man. Been in his grave for weeks. So the dead are walking now!' Pausing, he looked intently at Faro. 'I think you must have damaged your brains falling down that cliff.'

'I didn't fall, I climbed down,' Faro said. 'And if you'd spare the time to listen instead of yelling at me, what I'm trying to tell you is that Dave Claydon is still alive. The man they buried in his place was Josh Flett.'

Stavely's mouth opened and closed again. 'Detective Constable you might be, but you're quite, quite mad. This is absolute nonsense.'

'I am not mad. And I have proof.'

'Proof!' Stavely snorted. 'I'd like to hear that.'

So Faro patiently went through all the details of the imposture for Stavely's benefit. The sergeant held up his hand, shook his head once or twice and tried to interrupt with, 'But how . . . ? And why . . . ?'

All were swept aside, Faro ending with his visit to Amos and Josh rushing to the door.

At mention of the appearance of Thora, Stavely lost his patience. 'So what! The grieving widow is in love with the poor invalid. I don't find that astonishing. You're not a married man, Faro, so I can't expect you to understand such emotions. Very complicated they are,' he added, remembering how sometimes he felt he hardly knew Lily at all. After all these years of marriage she could still surprise him.

Faro sat back, conscious that he had been wasting his time. 'So you don't believe any of it?'

Stavely shook his head. 'All seems a bit pointless to me. There's one serious flaw. You need a death certificate before you bury anyone, and in an accidental death in Edinburgh you'd need the fiscal's report.'

'And here?'

'Not always for accidental drownings. Depends. With the fishing boats and such storms as we get, they're a daily hazard, often so frequent that the fiscal would have to live permanently on the scene.' Pausing, he added, 'Incidentally, for your information, there was a death certificate signed by a doctor.'

'The local doctor who attended Josh?'

Stavely shook his head, and said uneasily, 'No, he was away on holiday.'

'Very convenient.'

'Amos got hold of a doctor from somewhere, I expect.'

Amos, very helpful again, thought Faro, as Stavely went on.

'Helped in every way he could, even identified the body, to save Thora a gruesome task.'

'Or to save anyone realising that the body was not that of Dave Claydon, recently drowned man, but of Amos's brother Josh, who had conveniently died that day,' Faro replied, grimly aware that whatever was going on, Amos was deeply involved.

Stavely regarded him stolidly.

'Your theories are all very interesting but where's your proof of a word of it?'

'I haven't any except that all this could be part of something much bigger – they could all be in a conspiracy.'

'Such as?'

'Smuggling artefacts abroad comes readily to mind.'

A faint gleam in Stavely's eye, then he shook his head. 'Too far-fetched. They'd never get away with it.'

They had arrived in Kirkwall. 'Now, if you will be so good as to accompany me . . .'

Feeling suspiciously as if he was under arrest rather than making a statement that no one was going to believe anyway, Faro went into the police station. Once the words were taken down and duly signed in the presence of Stavely, a silent witness, he prepared to leave.

Stavely escorted him to the door and indicated the waiting carriage. 'I can take you part of the way back, as far as Pete's.'

He was not eager to do so, having had more than enough of Constable Faro to last him a lifetime. It was a tedious, dismal journey, with no attempts to resurrect the topic of Josh Flett.

Faro was overcome by exhaustion and in no mood for further argument, so both men, absorbed by their own very different thoughts, were relieved when, at last, the carriage clattered through the twisted streets of Stromness and headed in the direction of Scarthbreck.

As Faro was leaving outside the cousin's house, Stavely leant out and said, 'If I were you, I'd abandon all those fantastic notions and concentrate on staying out of trouble.'

The following morning, Faro realised there was one man who would have been eager to believe his dramatic disclosure regarding Dave Claydon's resurrection and that was Jimmy Traill, but instead he had accepted Stavely's offer of transport and was now regretting having overcome the temptation to look in at the newspaper office before leaving Kirkwall.

In despair, he felt that no one would believe him, and as Stavely had been eager to point out, the deception was merely a theory, and he wouldn't ever be likely to be able to prove that the man buried in the kirkyard in Dave Claydon's grave was Josh Flett.

The only ones who could supply that evidence were Amos Flett and Thora. As both were in this conspiracy, whatever its nature, that was a possibility remote indeed.

Faro knew there was one other person who might believe him, and that was Inga. Setting out for the walk to Scarthbreck and hoping that he might pick up a carter returning to Spanish Cove, he was fortunate. The farmer and his wife lived there, and driving back in a gig, offered him a lift.

They were polite, friendly but not inquisitive about his reasons for visiting Scarthbreck. They seemed a little in awe of the 'Big House' and conversation was restricted to his holiday on the island. They were relative newcomers from Burray and had not heard of his family connections.

Reaching their destination, there was a small crowd of people on the pier. Shouts indicated that a body had been washed up.

Faro raced down the steep steps. A glance at the body confirmed that it was Rob, and a horseman was speedily despatched to inform Sergeant Stavely who, Faro guessed, would not be pleased.

Inga was among those gathered. 'So he was swept away by the incoming tide, poor lad.'

Faro knew he could no longer be considered a prime suspect.

He was eager to tell Inga about Dave Claydon's imposture but there was no opportunity. She had a customer coming for a fitting and ran ahead up the steep steps, leaving Faro no option but to remain until Stavely arrived.

Neighbours who had hurried down to the scene suggested that Rob's body be taken to his house until the police arrived.

As Faro reached the top of the rough steps behind the sad cortège, Mr West emerged from his house. He had seen the crowd gathering from his window and guessed that something was amiss, but touching the region of his chest, he said, 'Alas, I am no longer able to go up or down to the pier, stairs of any kind are beyond me.' And regarding the men heading into Rob's house, observing Faro's anxious looks and curious to know the reason for his bloodstained appearance a short while ago, he said, 'A sad business.'

'Did you know him?' asked Faro.

West shook his head. 'Not really. I'm afraid we aren't very sociable here.'

Faro wasn't feeling sociable at that moment, either. 'I have to wait for the police to arrive.'

West nodded. 'Then perhaps you would care to come in and have a little refreshment.'

West's house was typical of the man. Glass jars containing small plant specimens fought for space on every surface, between stacks of books and papers. Scooping some aside to make a seat for Faro, West retreated into his little kitchen whose window connected with the pigeon loft.

At his entrance some of them perched expectantly

on the sill. Looking over his shoulder, he smiled at Faro, 'My little darlings . . .' and he went on to produce a list of names which Faro made no attempt to remember. There was one bird that fluttered down, identified by the ringed foot as a homing pigeon.

It immediately engaged West's attention, and his expression anxious, he turned his back on Faro, seized the bird and unfolded a small piece of paper. Whatever it contained obviously concerned him. A sharp intake of breath and 'Just a word from a loved one', combined with the grave expression which West could not conceal, failed to satisfy Faro that this was, in fact, the message that the pigeon had delivered.

Over the inevitable pot of tea, while Faro again thought longingly of something much stronger befitting his shattered nerves, he was able to enlighten West's curiosity regarding the drowned man. How he had, in fact, discovered him while walking Beau yesterday morning.

'He had fallen down the cliff?' said West.

'It looked like that,' said Faro, but some doubt in his voice prompted West's next question.

'He was still alive when you reached him?'

'He was, but died almost immediately. A severe head injury.'

West regarded Faro intently for a moment

and then said, 'Then he was unable to tell you exactly what had happened.'

Faro thought of the four whispered words the dying man uttered. He shook his head and West tut-tutted, looking thoughtful.

Thanking him again for *A Tale of Two Cities*, West nodded approvingly.

'I am delighted that you have enjoyed it. A most valuable addition to one's reading list.'

Faro smiled wryly with a sudden longing to tell the old man that it had been much more than a valuable addition, that it had in fact led him to solving one of the mysteries that had brought him to Orkney on this visit.

A shadow passed by the window and Faro recognised Amos with Inga at his side. Again, that fleeting shaft of jealousy that he had been her customer expected for a fitting.

West looked startled as he leapt up and excused himself, 'A friend I have to see.'

Outside, Inga was entering her house and Amos heading down the street. Faro caught up with him at the entrance.

'I am so sorry.' Amos turned towards him. His face a mask of anguish, and anger too, he nodded bleakly and through clenched teeth muttered, 'Someone will pay for this.' And brushing him aside, he went into Rob's house.

Faro considered following him but felt it

more urgent to talk to Inga who emerged with a basket over her arm.

'A bad business,' she said. 'Couldn't have come at a worse time.'

He looked at her questioningly and she said, 'This will make it particularly hard for Amos at tonight's Lammastide celebrations.'

Seeing his blank expression, 'Didn't Amos tell you?'

He shook his head. 'He said I was to give you a message. His boat will be at the pier down there, picking up passengers for his tour of the islands at eight o'clock. He'll collect you at the landing for Scarthbreck.'

'Are you coming?' he asked eagerly.

She shrugged. 'Maybe – I'm not sure. I have other things to do.'

'Maybe I have too, then.'

She gave an impatient shrug, obviously not making the same sentimental connection of a last evening together. 'Amos said you were leaving, that it was important for you. Anyway, make your own mind up. I'm off.'

Faro was baffled. West's door was still open and he decided he should go back and apologise for his hasty exit.

West smiled as he appeared but he had hardly got the words out when Stavely appeared in the street, breathless, on horseback.

As he stood with West at the door, Faro was aware that the two men exchanged a curious glance. What was their connection? he wondered as Stavely said impatiently, 'Accompany me, if you please, Faro. I'll need you to identify the drowned man as the one you found yesterday.'

CHAPTER TWENTY-SEVEN

Rob Powers identified, Faro was free to go and was no longer detained by Stavely. With his departure date imminent, all that remained was to bring his logbook up to date. All things considered, apart from one or two loose ends, he was relatively satisfied with the results, although what he was going to tell Macfie, he had not decided. Telling him the truth that Dave Claydon was still alive and involved in criminal activities was going to be tricky.

As for Thora and the couple's plans for the future, he remembered the packing cases behind her front door when he first called on her. That they were in preparation for a forthcoming journey was evident by her arrival at Spanish

Cove. Did that signify that they were about to take flight, escape to a new life when money changed hands for the stolen artefacts? Especially as Stavely had refused to take seriously Dave's imposture as Josh Flett.

The sinister implications suggested that he should reconsider the wisdom of that boat tour with Amos as foolhardy as well as dangerous. But ignoring danger, taking chances, he told himself, were what being a detective was all about. The irresistible temptation to unravel the final threads of Amos's involvement, his safety ensured by the presence of other passengers, was too strong for him to ignore.

Such were his thoughts as he approached the private landing pier, an indulgence by former owners of Scarthbreck. Rough seas, treacherous undercurrents and submerged rocks, however, made it extremely dangerous, and their ladies did so hate getting their feet or the hems of their gowns wet and considered it most undignified, if not indecent, having to be carried ashore by one of the male servants.

On the overgrown steep track which edged its way down the cliff face, he walked carefully, keeping a lookout for Amos and his boatload of visitors, wondering if anyone ever used the landing stage now. The archaeologists carrying their equipment and gear would have found it

unwieldy and hazardous, as Gerald Binsley had
been informed by Sir Arnold when he mentioned
that on a longer visit it might serve for a bit of
fishing.

Faro's view of the sea was shielded and it
was not until he managed the last stretch of rock
pools and reached the shore that he saw a boat.

It was a much smaller boat than he had
imagined, with Amos sitting in it alone, crouched
over the oars.

Faro hailed him and he responded, raising a
hand but obviously unwilling to come any closer,
no doubt with experience of those dangerous
currents, so there was nothing for it but to gain
access by scrambling across the rocks with their
covering of seaweed.

Amos was well clad against the weather,
huddled in a huge rain cape, a bonnet pulled
down well over his eyes. His face looked
pale and strained as Faro observed that there
were seats for no more than six, including the
oarsman.

Jumping down into the boat, he asked,
'Where are the rest?'

Amos raised his head, looked towards the
Neolithic settlement. 'Waiting round the corner
there.'

He began to row, as if it were an effort, and
considering that he had brought the tiny craft all

the way from Stromness, the original pickup spot
for the passengers, Faro, who was beginning to
have doubts about the successful outcome of this
pleasure cruise, gallantly offered to take an oar.

Amos nodded in agreement, and as they set
off again, regarding that pale, sad face, sympathy
for the loss of his friend replaced any of Faro's
growing premonitions of danger.

Staying well away from the rocks, they rowed
in the direction of the settlement, a melancholy,
deserted place. The sea was smooth as glass
but the boat was entering the area notorious
for submerged caves, and without a landing
stage there were considerable hazards for any
intending passengers, to say nothing of a soaking
should they wade out to the boat.

Surely Amos had realised this was not a good
meeting place, and Faro could see no evidence of
a landing stage or anyone waiting for them.

'No one there,' he said.

Amos ignored him. Having difficulty with
his oar, he seemed short of breath. 'Mistaken
directions,' he gasped. 'Pick them up, next stop.'

Faro's question as to where that was went
unheeded. There was one, however, that he was
determined Amos should answer.

'Where is Dave?'

Amos's head jerked upwards. 'Dave is dead.'

'No, Amos. Josh is dead.'

Amos's head turned towards him, 'How . . . what makes you think that?' he asked slowly.

Sitting side by side like comrades, as Faro told him what he knew, Amos shipped the oars, and as the boat drifted gently on the sea, he made no attempt to interrupt or comment.

Faro ended with the whispered words Rob had uttered before he died. 'What he was saying was not "gosh . . . gave" but that Josh was Dave.'

'Rob died for that.' Amos's voice was a whisper. 'That's why they killed him. He got in too deep and his religious principles made him want out.'

Faro found himself remembering Rob praying in the cathedral, and the Christian symbols in his house. 'It was all he had in a way. He believed in right and wrong, good and evil. At first it was just a lark, everyone accepted smuggled goods; then some minister or other made him see the evil of his ways. He wanted us all to believe too, and threatened to tell the truth for the good of our souls. Dave and Thora were in serious trouble. They had to lie low for a while. Me too.'

No longer rowing, the boat was drifting lazily seaward. It had shipped a little water too, lapping in the base at Faro's feet.

He asked cautiously, 'Why are you telling me all this?'

'I thought you should know. Inga said you were intrigued about Thora and the seal king, about that missing year. And her sister Elsa.' Pausing, he looked at him. 'You really wanted to know about Elsa, so I decided I would take you to meet her.'

This was news indeed. So Elsa was still alive. 'Where is she?'

'You will have to wait and see, Faro. Wait and see. I promise you won't be disappointed.'

Faro had already decided, perhaps he had known right from the start when Amos was waiting for him in the boat, that there were to be no other passengers. He had planned it all carefully and the thought made Faro conscious of his own danger as Amos said, 'Everyone wondered why Elsa didn't come to Dave's funeral.'

Looking towards the area of the caves, Faro had a sudden vision of Mrs Traill, her mind wandering, her guilt about Elsa, that she and Thora had a secret. He asked, 'Is Elsa still alive?'

'Didn't I tell you? I'm taking you to meet her.'

'Is it far?'

'Not very far now.'

Amos began to cough and Faro noticed the flecks of blood on his mouth. His first thought, a surge of pity. Was Amos dying like his brother, the same consumption?

It was at that moment he noticed the stain on Amos's cape, which he thought was seawater, had grown larger. Amos touched it, dragging the cape closer, and his hand came away red. It was blood.

'What happened to you?'

Amos looked at him. 'I've been shot. After they killed Rob, I was finished with them. I'd had enough of murders. Someone took a potshot at me from Spanish Cove. Not as serious as what it did to the boat.'

There was rising water in the base of the boat. Seeing the sudden alarm on his face, Amos managed a mocking smile.

'Good job it's a smooth sea, or we would have gone down by now. Fortunately I'm a good swimmer, I'll make it even with a bloodied shoulder. But I hear you can't swim. Boat sinks and you drown. However, you are so keen to know the truth and I can't deny you that before we part, especially seeing that we are almost kin – almost cousins. Shame really.'

Faro struggled towards an oar, got hold of it, but single-handedly he knew he could do nothing. Amos watched him, smiling gently, making no effort to help.

'It's useless, Faro. You'd be better off

listening to what I have to say. At least you'll go to eternity happy that you guessed right and smuggling artefacts is the name of the game. In this case thousands of doubloons from the *El Rosario*, with an eager buyer waiting on the Continent.

'As for Elsa . . .' Amos paused.

'Elsa is dead,' Faro said.

'That's right. Another good guess. And dear, devoted Thora killed her, killed her only sister. She claimed it was an accident, but they hated each other because of Dave. Both wanted him. Dave was there and so was I. A lad of sixteen, and I helped them dispose of her body in the caves over there. Weighed it down with rocks.

'And they have held that incident over my head ever since, made me do as I was told. Waiting for money from abroad for those artefacts Dave had appropriated, they had a bit of unbelievable good luck. My poor, brave brother died and they decided this was what they needed. Dave would take his place, become Josh, till the deal was settled. They thought it was a brilliant idea, couldn't have been better timed. As for my indignation, my disgust at what they intended, they laughed that aside. Told me not to forget that I was an accessory to Elsa's murder and if this plan failed, I'd go to jail too, probably hang.'

He pointed towards the submerged caves growing distant. 'Behold, Elsa's last resting place.' Then, with the water steadily rising around their feet, he added genially, 'And most probably yours, Faro. I was going to take you here personally, but not with a sinking boat. Anyway, you'll meet in the great beyond but I'm sure you've worked out all the answers.'

'I have now,' Faro said. 'Someone told me the sisters were as alike as two peas. They were, apart from the colour of their hair.'

Amos smiled. 'Useful, wasn't it? Thora panicked. It was Lammastide, and Dave convinced her that she would get away with Elsa's accidental death at her hands by becoming the seal king's bride. Disappear, put on a dark wig, take Elsa's place and no one would know the difference.'

'She couldn't carry on the deception for ever, so when she came back a year later, Elsa conveniently disappeared. Went off to the mainland, broken-hearted that Dave had chosen to wait for the seal king's bride. It all seemed simple, the perfect murder.'

Faro wanted to hear more, but the boat was no longer controllable. Swaying in the hidden undercurrent, the water had risen swirling round their knees. All of a sudden Faro was swept overboard.

Amos was smiling again. 'Won't be long now, old friend. I'll swim back, say the boat sank, you were lost, I tried to save you, just like I tried to save Dave when he fell boarding the ship that night.'

Faro tried to grip the side of the boat but his wet hands kept slipping.

'I'll make it easier for you. Take a grip of this.' And Amos tried to lift an oar. He managed to swing it over towards Faro.

As the boat veered and the sea took them both, he yelled, 'There's a rock over yonder – until the tide turns. Fare thee well.' A hand raised in grave salute, Amos shrugged off the cape and began swimming for the distant shore.

Faro hung on to the oar. If only he could drift towards that rock, still unsubmerged by the rising tide.

Then suddenly he was no longer alone.

Had Amos come back for him, taken pity?

Something was underneath him. Something solid, holding him above water, pushing his body towards the rock, still several feet away. Perhaps he could reach it.

Desperately, he stretched out an arm, but the movement lost him the oar. It drifted away and as he slithered back into the sea, a face appeared.

Amos, he thought again. No, not a man.
Human-eyed, beseeching, curious.
A seal.
The sea claimed him again.
So this was death.

CHAPTER TWENTY-EIGHT

Baubie Finn had been restless all that day. In the morning she had asked Inga to take her back to South Ronaldsay, her voice urgent, explaining that, although she had been so happy in Spanish Cove, she could wait no longer to return to her own home.

And then while Inga, always willing to help her friend, was discussing the arrangements, Baubie had shaken her head. 'Not today, my dear. I find I must stay here today.'

Inga made no comment. The discovery of the drowned man, whom she had never met, distressed Baubie, made her even more ill at ease, and as the day drifted towards evening, she wanted to go along the shore and watch the fireworks at Scarthbreck.

A curious request, thought Inga, and remembering how slowly Baubie walked, she would hire a gig from the stables.

Baubie was pleased. But with Scarthbreck in sight she decided no, she wanted to go further, on towards the old dwellings.

Inga was puzzled as she drove further along the shore, the seals keeping pace, their heads bobbing up and down in the water. Far from any fireworks now, the shore was empty except for the passing of a carriage bearing Thora with a companion, who, although she could not see him clearly, Inga assumed to be Josh, accompanied by the Frenchman Emil on horseback.

She called out a greeting. They turned away and pretended not to see her.

'Did they know about the fireworks?' she began, but Baubie wasn't listening. She didn't want to stop here after all.

Shaking her head she said, 'This isn't the place. Further, further along.'

Utterly confused, Inga drove on until Baubie seized her arm and said, 'Here. Stop here. This is it.'

She got out of the gig and walked, quickly and steadily, towards the water's edge. Inga followed, afraid that her friend would get her feet wet, and that it would bring back the pneumonia, sure as life.

'Baubie. Come back,' she called, but Baubie didn't seem to hear or care. The seals had moved nearer, clamouring, barking, and Baubie was holding out her hands towards them almost in supplication.

'Come back,' Inga called.

This time she heard her, turned round and said, 'Jeremy is out there. He's drowning.'

'What . . . ? How do you . . . ?' Inga stopped.

'The seals tell me. You must save him.'

'But where?'

Baubie pointed. 'Over there – where the waves are breaking . . . a rock.'

Inga shaded her eyes. 'But I don't see—'

'He is there. Go – please go.'

Inga waited no longer. She slipped off her gown and dashed into the sea. And it seemed, in case she was in danger of losing her direction, the seals were around her, guiding her ahead. Their presence was no consolation: she had never been so scared in her life before. She was an excellent swimmer but the undercurrent was strong.

At last, with the seals' heads bobbing in a circle around her, she saw the large rock and a still shape, spreadeagled and face down.

It was Jeremy. She pulled herself up the slippery surface and turned him over. He was alive. His eyes opened.

'Is this heaven?'

'You bloody fool,' she swore and wrapping an arm around him, managed to dog-paddle him to the shore.

Baubie was waiting.

Inga regarded her anxiously as Faro climbed into the gig. She looked worse than he did, as if all the life had been drained out of her, and there were no words for any of them as Inga drove swiftly back along the shore.

When they reached Scarthbreck, Faro had observed the change in Baubie. She looked small and pale, and with an arm supporting her, he said, 'No, Inga. Don't stop for me. Let's get her home first.'

At Spanish Cove, Inga bustled Baubie inside while Faro went across to join the group gathered by a couple of carriages.

Stavely was there with a man being carried on a stretcher.

Amos Flett.

'Yes, he's alive, lost a lot of blood,' Stavely said. 'But he's young and strong enough to hang, if he doesn't turn Queen's evidence against the others.'

'Who shot him?' Faro asked.

Stavely nodded towards the police carriage where Emil sat statue-straight alongside the

Claydons. All three handcuffed while Mr West issued instructions to the policemen in charge. 'Got to get this lot behind bars. We got Latour too. Attempted murder among other things. Yes, he shot Flett when they decided he knew too much.'

'There's your smugglers, Faro. Been after them for a while now. And thanks to West's lookout and his homing pigeons we got them red-handed, and Latour as well. There's a French ship offshore there, waiting to take them to Marseilles.'

'The artefacts, too?'

He shook his head. 'All in good time. We're waiting to find out.'

And taking in Faro's bedraggled state, 'You look like the next casualty. Better get into some dry clothes.'

They didn't have long to wait. While Faro had been wrestling with angels in the unlikely shapes of grey seals, back in Scarthbreck, Beau, in one of his boisterous chases, skidded across the floor and knocked down a couple of Emil's pictures.

In a panic Mary Faro rescued them and heard something rattling inside. Removing the torn backing, a shower of gold coins rolled across the floor. The missing doubloons, treasure trove from the wreck of the *El Rosario*, waiting to be loaded on the French ship arriving in Spanish Cove that evening.

Regarding Latour's arrest, Mary said sadly, 'Never thought much of his paintings. I mean, not nearly as good as those prints in our parlour,' she added, referring to the Millais reproductions. 'I never really believed I would go to Paris, that was too good to be true.'

Faro put an arm around her and kissed her.

'You are too good to be true sometimes, Ma. Always trusting folk, taking them at face value.'

As they sat down at the table, she sighed. 'Emil seemed a nice enough fellow, if a bit flashy, and I felt guilty, thinking what if he asked me to marry him? I'd never be able to care about him that way. There could never be another man like your dear pa.' Smiling, she leant over and kissed him. 'Except you, Jeremy. You get more like him every day.'

And, Jeremy thought, what a reputation to live up to.

Stavely arrived looking pleased with himself. West, the retired botanist, was a government agent who had had the smugglers under surveillance for some time, his homing pigeons a fast and efficient means of communications with the Orkney Constabulary.

'You can't expect to win every time, Faro,' Stavely crowed. 'The lads in Kirkwall have to have some of the glory. Can't deny them that.'

So saying, he darted a resentful look in Beau's direction, wishing he could say the same about being upstaged by the mongrel pup who had accidentally discovered the smugglers' secret hiding place.

On the day of his departure for Edinburgh, Faro realised that Jimmy Traill would get his sensational story, an abridged version. The most sensational part of it would remain Faro's secret: how Inga had rescued him from drowning and Baubie had used her selkie power over the seals.

There was one final moment, a last word shared between himself and Baubie, a final mystery that had lacked a solution.

As he thanked her yet again, she said, 'This is for your ears only, Jeremy. We may never meet again, but you wanted to know what became of Sibella Scarth.'

He took her mittened hands and held them. 'I know. I think I have always known since that very first meeting.'

She smiled, leant across and kissed his cheek. 'Aye, and you're a grandson to be proud of. But this must be our secret, remember.'

'But why?' Even as he said the words, Faro remembered Mary Faro and the conversation he had overheard between his parents so long ago.

'There are some things, like selkies, that ordinary folk, even the best of families living in small communities, are not able to cope with. Selkie blood, let's just leave it at that.'

Faro smiled. 'Never. Something to be proud of, and what goes with it.'

Before he left he had a final visit from Stavely.

'How did you find out about Josh Flett?' Faro asked. 'I seem to remember you didn't believe a word of my theory.'

Stavely smiled wryly. 'It seemed too far-fetched but it set me thinking, and the more I thought . . . Then a chance meeting with the local doctor over a pint in the Lamb & Flag. Just back from holiday, he was astonished to find the patient he had left on his deathbed had made a miraculous recovery. Naturally he went to visit him and see for himself, but Amos turned him away. Josh, he said, refused to see him.

'I also heard that various other folk, intrigued by this miracle, had caught glimpses of this new Josh who always took avoiding action.'

He paused and said, 'Suddenly your absurd theory began to make sense. Too many coincidences.'

As he turned to leave, Faro said, 'Before you go, Sergeant, there's another one for you.

Remember Thora, the seal king's bride? Here's what really happened.'

Stavely listened this time. At the end, Faro said, 'I solved that mystery, but I'm afraid it's left you another corpse to unearth.'

If you enjoyed *The Seal King Murders*,
read on to find out about Inspector Faro's recent case . . .

❦

To discover more great fiction and to
place an order visit our website at
www.allisonandbusby.com
or call us on
020 7580 1080

MURDER IN PARADISE

The year is 1860 and Inspector Faro has been transported back to one of the darkest moments of his career – the chase of the notorious Macheath across the Scottish border to the Kent countryside. Whilst there, Faro meets an old school friend, Erland Flett, who is working alongside the artist William Morris and the Pre-Raphaelites whose unconventional lifestyle is a startling revelation.

Erland is about to marry a beautiful but mysterious young lady, Lena Hamilton. Faro recognises her as the famous Madeleine Smith, accused of murdering her lover, but never convicted. Now Faro realises that he must apprehend Macheath and save his friend from certain death at the hands of the ruthless Miss Smith . . . and time is running out.